DOG BLESS YOU

A GOLDEN RETRIEVER MYSTERY

BY NEIL S. PLAKCY

My beloved Samwise accompanied me on my amazing journey to publication, whether he was curled up protectively behind my computer chair or exuberantly tugging me down the street on our long walks together. I miss him every day.

Brody came into our lives a few months after Sam left, a bundle of adorable golden retriever puppy energy wrapped in soft white fur. He has staked his claim to our hearts and begun to put his own paw prints on my books.

I wouldn't be where I am today without Marc's love and support. A big sloppy golden thank you to Miriam Auerbach, Mike Jastrzebski, Christine Jackson, Christine Kling and especially Sharon Potts, for their help in bringing this book together. Puppy kisses to Jackie Conrad, DVM, for veterinary advice, to Brian Sullivan for help with Christian relics, and to Ramona DeFelice Long for excellent editorial advice. As usual, any mistakes in this book are my own errors and no one else's.

1 – Roof and Kibble

"Rochester!" I said, skidding to a stop in the kitchen just before I stepped into a big pile of dog vomit.

My goofy golden retriever was sprawled on the tile a few feet beyond the mess, a sad expression on his usually cheerful face. "Why did you have to do this today, dog? I don't have time to mess around."

Normally in the mornings Rochester was a bundle of energy, ready to go for a long walk, then ride to work with me and spend the day sleeping in a sunny place in my office at Eastern College. He looked up at me with wide, apologetic eyes, and I reached down to pet the soft fur on the top of his head. "I'm sorry, puppy. I know you didn't get sick on purpose."

I stepped around the liquid mess, unrolled a few paper towels, and got to work cleaning up. Rochester was a friendly, happy dog but he had a tendency to snoop into everything and put a lot of crap in his mouth that didn't belong there or in his digestive tract. When I finished I gave him an anti-diarrheal pill inside a piece of cheese. He gobbled the cheese and spit the pill out, then grinned at me.

"Fine, we'll do it old school." I pried open his jaw and dropped the pill into his mouth, massaging his throat until he swallowed. I watched him carefully to make sure he didn't upchuck the pill, and when I was satisfied I hooked up his leash.

He scrambled to his feet and tugged me toward the front door, then down the driveway. It was a warm morning in mid-July, bright sunshine sparkling on the dew-soaked lawns, and the temperature promised to climb into the eighties. We'd had a lot of summer rain, and I had to drag Rochester past puddles of standing water and avoid a couple of lawns that were more mud than grass.

We lived in a townhouse community called River Bend, a mile north of the center of the small Bucks County, Pennsylvania town of Stewart's Crossing, where I had grown up. It was built as the Soviet Union was collapsing, and all the streets bore names of Eastern European cities.

We walked down our street, Sarajevo Court, Rochester sniffing and peeing and me observing the neighborhood. The Camerons' springer spaniel was whimpering in their gated courtyard, and one corner of the covering Bob Freehl kept over his vintage Porsche had come loose in the wind. Air conditioners hummed and in the distance I heard the whistle of a train.

I looked at my watch. Still plenty of time to get to work before my appointment with my boss, Mike MacCormac, the director of the college's fund-raising campaign. I didn't know what it was about; summer is a slow time in academia, and I was surprised over the weekend when he texted me with a request for a nine o'clock meeting. Had I done something wrong? Alienated a donor or a reporter? Forgotten about a deadline?

I was still obsessing as we rounded a curve in the street and I saw Phil and Marie Keely's son Owen sitting on the low stone wall in front of their townhouse, smoking a cigarette. The Keelys were both in their sixties; Phil had the kind of flushed face I associated with habitual drinkers, and Marie had suffered a stroke that required her to use a walker. Owen had moved in with them about a month before.

"Morning, Owen," I said as Rochester stopped to sniff the base of an oak tree in front of the house.

"Good morning, sir." I found it weird that Owen was so formal, when I was probably only about fifteen years older than he was. I figured it was some vestige of the military.

He had close-cropped dark blond hair and a thin mustache in the same color. His upper arms were covered in colorful tattoos, and he wore sleeveless T-shirts to show them off. He was in his late twenties, the youngest of three kids, and I wondered what chain of events had brought him back to his parents' house.

"Hey, boy," he said, getting up and approaching Rochester. "How's the puppy?"

Rochester backed away from him. "It's okay, boy," Owen said quietly. He held his hand out palm up for Rochester to sniff, but my dog wasn't interested.

"Sorry," I said. "He's not feeling so good this morning."

Owen shrugged. "Not a problem. I had a dog over in Afghanistan just about his color, though more like a lab mix."

"A military dog?"

He shook his head. "Just a mutt that attached itself to my unit. But he always liked me best." He smiled. "He's still back there, my buddy says. Hanging around, scrounging food, looking for a belly rub now and then."

Rochester tugged me forward. "Have a good day," I said.

Owen took a drag on his cigarette and sat back down on the wall. Ahead of us, an old Thunderbird with big patches of primer cruised slowly down the street. The driver passed us, then beeped his horn.

I turned around to see Owen stub out his cigarette in the driveway and then get into the T-bird, which accelerated away.

Most people in River Bend are friendly. I knew the dogs Rochester played with by name, as well as some of their affiliated humans. Kids played ball in the street and ran in and out of their friends' houses. It was a lot like the suburban neighborhood a few miles away where I had grown up.

But that morning was the first time I'd had a conversation with Owen Keely. I guessed it was hard for him, coming back from the war, living with his parents again. I wished Rochester had been nicer to him.

Half a block later, the dog let loose a stinky stream of diarrhea. "I guess you really don't feel well, boy," I said, leaning down to pat his head. "We'll go see Dr. Horz and get you fixed up." I struggled to pick up what I could in a plastic bag, and hoped that a rain shower would wash the rest away.

I hadn't always been a dog lover. Rochester and I first met soon after my next-door neighbor, Caroline Kelly, had adopted him. When Caroline was murdered a few months later, I took the big goof in for a couple of days, leading to a permanent love affair.

Back at the house, I wiped his butt and placed an emergency call to the vet's. Then I laid towels on the passenger seat of my elderly BMW sedan and loaded the dog in. Usually Rochester loves riding with me, sitting up on his haunches and sticking his head out the window. But that July morning he curled up on the seat with his head resting on my lap.

I put another towel between his head and my leg, and drove as quickly as I could to the vet's. The Beemer was one of the last vestiges of my old life; I had bought it new when I was a successful executive in Silicon Valley, and a friend had kept it for me while I was a guest of the California state prison system for a relatively minor computer hacking offense. By the time I got out, I was nearly broke and couldn't afford to buy anything else. It had survived the drive across country, though it had developed a rattle under the hood which needed a mechanic's attention.

We walked into the vet's waiting room, which smelled like wet dog and disinfectant. "Steve Levitan with Rochester," I said to the receptionist, and then we found ourselves a spot across from a yippy Yorkie and a baleful basset. One of the morning shows was playing on the TV in the corner, a young blonde with her frowny face on, talking about the poor state of the economy.

The Yorkie across from us launched into paroxysms of barking at the entrance of a skinny, demonic-looking Papillon, whose pointy ears stuck out of its head like antennae. I rubbed my sweet dog under the chin. "You feeling any better, boy?" I asked.

Rochester looked at me and I thought he smiled. Then he dry-heaved as Elysia, the vet tech, approached.

"Somebody's not feeling well, huh?" she asked, kneeling down to the dog's level. She was a round-faced older woman with an Italian accent, and usually Rochester loved to see her, but he put his head down instead of licking her face. "Poor baby. We'll get you into a room so Dr. Horz can see you."

I stood up and took Rochester's leash, and we followed Elysia inside to the floor-mounted scale, which looked more like a treadmill to me. I tried to get Rochester to step up on it but he planted his big paws on the tile floor and wouldn't move.

"Go on, you big goof." I pushed against his hindquarters and he looked at me woefully. But he wouldn't move, no matter how I tugged. Was he remembering a bad experience there? The vet and her techs had always been so good to him. Or was he just being difficult?

I lifted his front paws onto the scale, and reluctantly he stepped forward. "Eighty pounds," Elysia said approvingly. "Good boy." Then she led us to the first examining room, the one with illustrated posters of canine digestive and respiratory systems.

"I know, you don't like this," Elysia said, squatting on the floor next to Rochester, who had sprawled out on his stomach. "But I need your temperature."

She lifted his tail and inserted the thermometer. I sat on the floor next to Rochester and scratched behind his ears, and told him what a good boy he was. Then I held his head as Elysia retrieved a stool sample. Not for the first time, I was glad my parents had pushed me to go to college so I could get a job that didn't involve investigating dog poop.

Oh, wait. I got up close and personal with it every day—for free.

Elysia left us in the room. Rochester rolled on his side and snoozed. I paced around the room, trying to figure out what Mike wanted to talk to me about. Eastern College was my alma mater, "a very good small college," nestled in the countryside halfway between Philadelphia and New York, focused on teaching and making students feel unique. The campus was in Leighville, a half hour north of Stewart's Crossing.

It had been a hectic couple of months. I lucked into the job in January, after spending a semester as an adjunct instructor in the English department. I had been immediately plunged into the launch of the college's capital campaign in the winter, then kept busy with graduation festivities. But as the semester ended, it was hard to keep the publicity momentum going when many of the faculty left town.

I looked at my watch and realized I wasn't going to be able to make my nine o'clock meeting. I hoped Mike wasn't too angry with me; I knew he had a busy schedule and a short temper and wouldn't like postponing the appointment.

I pulled out my cell phone to call him as Dr. Horz came in. "Sorry to keep you waiting," she said. "But we're busy this morning. We've got a St. Bernard in the back whelping her twelfth puppy." She was a small, slim woman with prematurely gray hair. I slipped my phone back in my pocket as she knelt down next to Rochester and said, "Good morning to you, handsome. What's the matter?"

He looked up at her with the kind of doggy adoration he usually reserved for me. She gave him a thorough physical, and then Elysia brought in the results of the stool sample. "No evidence of bacterial infection," Dr. Horz said, after she glanced at them. "Probably just ate something outdoors that didn't agree with him. I'll have Elysia come in with some pills to calm his tummy down, and if he's not a hundred percent in a couple of days, bring him back."

As we were waiting, my phone buzzed with the five-minute reminder of my meeting. "Shit," I said, looking down.

I dialed Mike and was relieved when he answered right away.

"Sorry, puppy emergency," I said. "Rochester ate something that disagreed with him and I had to bring him to the vet. Can I push back our meeting an hour?"

Mike was a dog lover himself, with a pair of Rottweilers. "My boys do that once or twice a year. Rochester will be right as rain in no time."

"That's what the vet said. I'm waiting for some pills now."

"I've got to head out to meet with a prospect," Mike said. "I was hoping to give you this news face to face, but Babson wants to talk to you at eleven, and I don't want you to go in there unprepared."

That made me nervous. John William Babson was the college president, and the ultimate micro-manager. He had his finger in everything that went on, from faculty hiring to the choice of new outdoor trash receptacles. I met with him whenever he had a brilliant idea he wanted to pass along to me. But the meetings were always scheduled by his secretary, not by Mike. He hesitated and my bad feeling intensified.

"Babson's happy with all the publicity you got for the campaign launch. But now that we're moving along, he wants to consolidate all public relations activities."

I'd worked cooperatively with the News Bureau, which tracked the College's media exposure and provided journalists with access to faculty experts. Ruta del Camion, a recent Eastern graduate who was the department's sole employee, was struggling to keep up with those activities. I had used my background in database development to reorganize our digital alumni records, and my writing skills to develop stories about faculty research and student achievements, which I passed on to reporters.

I'd always known my job was going to be a temporary one, but I'd thought I would have at least another few months of full-time work before I was back on the job market. I was still following up on a couple of stories about graduating seniors with stellar accomplishments, and developing a series focused on incoming freshmen with quirky backgrounds.

"I'm sorry, Steve," Mike said. "I wish I could keep you on, because there's a lot more that you could contribute. But once Babson gets his mind set there's no changing it."

Crap. I thought that Babson liked me and would keep me around. I said, "I appreciate the opportunity you gave me. Do you know how long—"

He interrupted me. "Sorry, I've got a call on the other line. We'll talk again this afternoon after I get back."

The cell phone went dead against my ear. Crap and double crap. I was losing my job. And that was going to screw up my life twelve ways to Tuesday.

Since returning to Stewart's Crossing from California, I had begun to rebuild my life—adopting Rochester, worming my way into the Eastern administration, even meeting a woman I had begun to care about a lot. But I had little financial cushion; between paying restitution to California for my crimes, and my basic household expenses, I was skating on the financial edge.

My life was coming back together. But would one loss lead to another, and another, the way I'd lost my wife, my job and my freedom in the past?

When Elysia came back with Rochester's pills and a copy of the bland diet Dr. Horz had promised, she found me sitting on the floor with my dog's head in my lap as I stroked his soft, golden fur. I didn't know what I was going to do without a job, but I knew that whatever happened to me I was determined to take care of him.

2 – Opportunity Knocks

Once we were finished at the vet's, I drove Rochester to the campus with the windows up and the air conditioner on. He sat on his haunches next to me, already looking better. I hoped I'd be able to bounce back as quickly as he had.

Two years before, I'd had a very different life in Silicon Valley. My wife was a successful software marketing executive and I had a job writing instruction manuals and developing web-based training, which involved a bit of programming and a lot of Internet expertise. We owned a big house in the suburbs and we were trying to have a baby.

Mary had suffered a miscarriage a year before, and then went on a spending spree with our credit cards as a form of retail therapy. I picked up as many freelance writing assignments as I could to pay off the resulting charges. By the time she got pregnant for the second time I'd wiped out all the debt and felt like I could breathe.

Then she miscarried again. I had developed some basic skills as a computer hacker through my tech jobs, and I got the idea to hack into the three major credit bureaus and block Mary's credit cards. I thought I was looking out for both of us.

I got caught, and though I hadn't done any real damage, the credit bureaus wanted to make an example of me, and I was sentenced to two years. While I was in prison Mary divorced me and my father died, leaving me the townhouse in Stewart's Crossing, only about a mile from the ranch-style house where I'd grown up. After a year, the state's rules on prison overcrowding offered me the opportunity to swap my last year inside for two years' parole, and I took the deal.

My mother had passed away soon after Mary and I moved to California, so by the time I was released from the California Men's Colony in San Luis Obispo, I was an orphan, with no wife, no job, and no family other than a bunch of cousins. I petitioned the parole board in California for permission to return to Stewart's Crossing, and once it was granted I was assigned Santiago Santos as my parole officer. He was an amateur boxer with a sociology degree, and through a series of unannounced home visits he kept track of everything I was doing to rebuild my life.

My parole was due to end in September, and I had been looking forward to regaining my freedom. But Santos was determined to ensure I wouldn't be tempted to do anything that might send me back to prison. He worried that if I didn't have a solid income I'd be tempted to return to hacking – this time for profit. Suppose he saw this job loss as a setback he needed to monitor further? And if he did, would he be able to convince a judge to extend my parole?

I had some advantages I hadn't had when I first returned to town. I had reconnected with an old high school acquaintance who became my best friend. I met my neighbors and got to know a lot of employees at Eastern. And I met Liliana Weinstock. At forty-five, it was silly to think of Lili as my girlfriend, but the English language hasn't caught up to twenty-first century mating practices yet.

But how long would that network hang together if I was unemployed and running low on money? Clouds gathered overhead as we drove up to Leighville along the River Road, and by the time we reached the college the sky was gray and gloomy. I had to park at the outer edge of the parking lot and then hustle Rochester out of the car before it began to pour.

He was still moving slowly as I shepherded him past the deep pools of water at the edge of the parking lot and the marshy patches of lawn between there and Fields Hall, the 19th-century gothic mansion that had been converted to college offices. We passed a young female student reading on one of the wrought-iron benches, seemingly oblivious to the coming storm. Her T-shirt read "Girls Just Want to Have Funds."

Boys, too, I thought. My first-floor office was small, tucked away in a corner of the building that had once been part of the formal dining room, but it had French doors looking out at the garden, and I left Rochester there with a chew bone and a plea not to get sick on anything. I was worried that Dr. Horz hadn't been able to diagnose him more specifically and I hated having to leave him alone, even for what I was sure would be a very quick exit interview with President Babson. At least when I finished with that I could clean out my office and then take Rochester home.

Fields Hall was a warren of small offices carved out of larger rooms, and I had to navigate past a copier in the middle of the narrow hallway to get to the small alcove where Babson's secretary sat.

She waved me into his office, where the great man was finishing a phone call. He was tall and rawboned, an urbane, well-dressed John Wayne. But instead of being taciturn he bubbled over with enthusiasm, no matter what the subject or his knowledge of it. He had deep green eyes and dark curly hair that he styled with the kind of greasy kid stuff I had abandoned when I reached puberty.

"Steve, come on in," he said, waving me to a spindle-backed chair embellished with the Eastern College logo, across from his desk.

I sat down and he said, "You grew up in this area. Ever heard of Friar Lake?"

That threw me for a loop. I was expecting some kind of termination speech, to end with me and Rochester being escorted out of the building by security guards. Sure, Eastern had a human resources department, but Babson was such a micro-manager I was sure he liked to handle hiring and firing himself.

My brain was a jumble. "It sounds familiar, but I can't quite place it."

"About a hundred years ago, the Benedictine Order built a monastery on about twenty acres of land a mile inland from the Delaware River. The building overlooks a lake, and down by the water's edge they built a cabin for the use of mendicant friars. Eventually the local people started calling the area Friar Lake."

"Mendicant friars?" Those weren't covered in my dozen years in Sunday School at Har Sinai Temple in Trenton, or in the three years of weekday afternoons I spent studying Hebrew in preparation for my bar mitzvah.

"Both monks and friars are men devoted to religious service," Babson said. "The difference is that monks live in cloisters, while friars perform service to the sick and needy out in the community. When friars get old and sick themselves, they need a place to go. The Benedictines hosted them in a cottage down by the lake."

I still wasn't sure where this was all going. I wasn't a friar; I wasn't even Christian. Was he trying to say that these monks and friars ran some kind of halfway house? I appreciated the thought, but even though I was a convicted felon on parole, I could still manage for myself.

Babson was still talking. "The monastery closed about two years ago, and the remaining monks and friars moved to another one in western Pennsylvania. I guess even the church has to cut costs where it can."

My impatience got the best of me. I was worried about Rochester back in my office, and about my own need to get started on a search for a new job. "This is interesting, but..."

"Of course. I'll cut to the chase. Eastern is buying the property from the Benedictine Order, and I want to develop it as a conference center where our faculty can teach executive education courses."

"And?" I was still confused, and getting irritated.

"And I want you to run it. Didn't Mike tell you?"

So I wasn't out of a job, just getting transferred? That was amazing. My head was filled with a jumble of relief and confusion. "All Mike told me was that the News Bureau was taking over the responsibility for press relations for the campaign, and I was out of a job."

Babson frowned. "I'm sorry, Steve. I thought he would have mentioned it, but I guess he didn't want to steal my thunder. I just signed the paperwork transfer on Friday, and I talked to Mike on Saturday about giving you the job. He said he was sorry to lose you but he was certain you'd do a bang-up job."

I was glad Mike and Babson were so certain. I knew nothing about executive education or running a conference center. But I would do whatever I had to in order to keep body and soul together – mine and Rochester's.

Babson pushed a report encased in a plastic folder across the desk to me. "This is the feasibility study I commissioned. Start thinking about the kinds of programs we could offer up at Friar Lake. Talk to the faculty, see what ideas they have. We need to put on programs that adults and corporate learners can use—and that they'll pay for."

Put together a whole continuing education program while setting up a brand-new conference facility. That was John Babson for you. It was a lot to process at once.

"When you've had a chance to get your feet wet, set up a meeting and we'll go over your ideas. Oh, and you'll want to talk to Elaine in HR about your new status. You might as well stay in your office for the time being, at least until Physical Plant starts the renovation work at the abbey. You'll want to be out there by then."

I picked up the report. "Why me?" I asked. "I don't know anything about construction or running a conference center, or developing programs."

He leaned forward. "What is it that we brag our students really learn here at Eastern?" he asked.

The twists in this conversation were as confusing as some of the back roads leading from the Delaware into the countryside, but I struggled to keep up. "We teach our students how to learn," I said, and I felt like I was reciting something from a brochure I might have written. "How to read and assimilate information, how to communicate what they've learned, and how to use those skills to survive and prosper in the work world."

"Absolutely. I chose you for this position because you know Eastern College and what we stand for – not only as a graduate but as a member of our adjunct faculty. And between the campaign launch and your help with Joe Dagorian's murder, I've seen how well you can multi-task."

I thought Babson would be finished, but he was in a reflective mood. For the next ten minutes or so, he lectured me on Eastern's history and his plans for its future. I couldn't pay much attention because my brain was so muddled.

I dimly understood that I was being given a great opportunity. This was a permanent position—which in academia often means for the rest of your working life. That was a big relief—I'd gone from unemployed to long-term employed in the span of a few minutes. But it was frightening at the same time. In addition to my lack of background, this was a huge project with high visibility. Why hadn't I heard about it before?

I realized that I had – there had been a line item at the last Board of Trustees meeting about the property. But I'd been so busy with my own job I'd paid it little notice.

"I'm proud of you, Steve," Babson said, and I snapped back to attention. "You've made some bad decisions in the past, but you've paid the price, and you've managed to bounce back. I have every confidence in you."

I realized that what Babson was telling me was that he knew I'd been in prison—and despite that, he believed in me. I gulped, stood up and shook his hand. "Thank you for the opportunity, and for believing in me." I held up the report in its plastic folder. "I'm looking forward to reading this and getting up to speed."

As I turned to walk out, he already had the phone in his hand, ready to move on. I needed to do that, too-- but I was in a daze. It wasn't a surprise that John Babson knew I'd been in prison; he knew almost everything that went on at Eastern, from the leaky faucet in the women's room at Blair Hall to the birthdays of each of the members of the Board of Trustees. He could switch easily from a conversation about college investments to one about a student's lack of progress in a math class.

But he had never mentioned it, and I was embarrassed that he had felt the need to bring it up in our meeting. It did make his faith in me that much more dramatic. I wasn't just an alumnus with a skill set that happened to fit in at the college. I was a project, like the female sophomore who wanted to spend the summer in Tanzania teaching personal hygiene to young girls. Babson had championed her cause, introducing her to wealthy sponsors and even helping her fine-tune her project proposal.

There were dozens more like her—students who wanted to create individualized majors, faculty members with innovative teaching techniques that needed funding, athletes who wanted to compete internationally. If Babson believed in you, he put himself behind you and pushed.

He had also been known to take strong action when disappointed. Students transferred, staff members terminated, faculty members encouraged to pursue their careers elsewhere. It was up to me to take the pressure and prove to him – and myself—that I could succeed.

3 – Trust

Rochester didn't get up when I opened the door to my office, and I hurried to see if he was all right. His nose was warm, but he sat up, and when I hooked his leash he got to all fours and followed me outside.

The rain had ended and the clouds overhead were moving away as I led him around the gray-black stone bulk of Fields Hall to the Cafette, an on-campus sandwich shop in an old carriage house. It was a worn, homey-looking place, decorated with Eastern pennants and faded T-shirts, with old wooden picnic tables and benches. Rochester stopped beside a trash can and lifted his leg to pee, his nostrils quivering as he did so.

I looped his leash around the leg of an Adirondack chair painted in Eastern's colors of light blue and white and went inside. The kitchen took up most of the back of the room, while the front was cluttered with small tables and uncomfortable metal chairs. Off to the left was an inglenook, almost a separate room, with a fireplace in the center and overstuffed chairs around it. In the colder months the staff kept a fire going, and it was a favorite place for students to curl up and study. In the summer, the multi-paned windows at the far end were kept cranked open and a warm breeze floated through.

I ordered a strawberry-banana smoothie and a pair of chocolate croissants, then went back out to Rochester. A cluster of undergrads filled one of the nearby picnic tables, each of them busily texting on their phones. A couple of other chairs were occupied by individual students, some reading textbooks, others intent on their iPads or laptops. A white butterfly swooped around the oak branches above my head.

I settled down in the oversized chair and began to read. Babson's plan included courses that might last anywhere from three hours to three weeks, taught by our regular faculty. A professor of accounting might offer an update on tax law, while a professor of folklore could host a residential program during the summer on Pennsylvania Dutch handicrafts.

"I guess you college types don't work much during the summer, huh?"

I looked up to see Rick Stemper standing beside my chair. The only indication that he was a detective was the Stewart's Crossing Police Department logo on the breast of his white polo shirt—and the fact that his shirttail was out, covering the holstered gun attached to his belt.

"I'm working," I said, holding up the report. "What are you doing up here?"

Rochester jumped up to greet him, and Rick ruffled the big dog's furry neck. He had a tall clear plastic glass of lemonade in his hand, and he pulled another Adirondack chair over to face mine. He reached over and took one of the croissants.

"You're a bad man," Rick said. "You know I'm trying to watch my waistline."

"And you've got it right out there where you can see it," I said.

"Asshole." At least he said it with a smile. And I was kidding him, of course. Rick was almost as lean as he'd been when we were at Pennsbury High together. We hadn't been friends then—just acquaintances and occasional classmates. But after I returned to Stewart's Crossing we bonded over our divorces, and the bond between us had been solidified when he adopted Rascal from the local shelter. The Australian shepherd had become Rochester's best friend.

"How's the Rascal?" I asked, picking up the other croissant before Rick could grab it.

"Wild as ever. Yesterday he tried to herd Mrs. Kim's schnauzers."

Mrs. Kim was Rick's elderly Korean neighbor; she was a sucker for rescued schnauzers and usually had at least three or four in the house.

"How'd that work out?"

"One of them nipped him on the nose, and he came whimpering back to me."

"So what brings you up here? Digging up hidden secrets of faculty members?"

"Nah. Looking into a series of robberies in Stewart's Crossing, and turns out there have been similar ones up here. Tony Rinaldi and I met this morning to compare notes. Thought I'd get something cold before heading back downriver."

I had met Tony, Rick's counterpart in Leighville, a year before, when the investigation of Caroline's murder led to Eastern College. "But the towns don't share a border, do they?"

Rick shook his head. "No, Washington's Crossing is in between, along with a big chunk of unincorporated Bucks County. But in each case, the robbers are targeting single-family houses on oversized lots."

"Like Crossing Estates?" When Rick and I were kids, the hills above Stewart's Crossing had been lined with endless fields of corn and U-pick strawberry farms. But in the early eighties, a couple of larger farms had been developed into a sprawling landscape of mini-mansions.

"Exactly," Rick said. "Every house either has no burglar alarm, or had it shut off at the time of the break-in. No dogs to make noise either." He pointed at Rochester, who looked up at him in hopes of a piece of croissant. "Homeowners drive luxury cars. Each house has sliding glass doors with cheap locks and no pry-bar keeping them in place."

"Doesn't breaking the glass make noise?"

He shook his head. "These crooks don't break the glass, they pick the sliding door lock. Then they have access to the whole house."

"Any leads?"

"Not a one. They don't disturb much in the house, for a day or two the homeowner doesn't even realize he's been burgled. The thieves are careful not to leave fingerprints, and they've only been taking small high-value items like watches, jewelry and collectibles."

Rochester lifted his head up as if he'd been listening. The sunlight glinted off his fine, wiry whiskers, which sprouted from his eyebrows as well as his muzzle. "Nothing showing up in pawn shops?" I asked.

Rick held up a hand to me. "I know, your Hardy Boy senses are all twitchy. But I don't need any of your computer mojo – or your dog's crazy coincidental discoveries. It looks like they're pawning outside the area—maybe Philly or New York. Tony and I are upping patrols in the targeted areas, and I'm going to put out an advisory memo to the at-risk neighborhoods."

Rick might crack wise about me being one of the Hardy Boys, but the truth was that Rochester had a nose for crime, and I had computer research skills well beyond the capabilities of the Stewart's Crossing police force.

"I had a scare this morning," I said, after taking a gulp of my smoothie. "I thought I was getting canned."

"And you weren't?"

"Nope. Just getting reassigned. You ever hear of a place called Friar Lake?"

"The Abbey of our Lady of the Waters?" Rick said. "Sure. We went out there on a CYO trip once."

"I never knew you were Catholic," I said.

"St. Ignatius all the way," he said. "I was even an altar boy. No cracks about diddling priests, please."

St. Ignatius was the big Catholic church in Yardley, and I'd known a bunch of kids from Stewart's Crossing who had belonged to the Catholic Youth Organization there. "Seriously?" I asked. "I never pictured you as the religious type."

"I did it for the basketball," he said. "We had a great coach and a strong team."

I digested that piece of information. It's funny how you can know somebody for years—I'd known Rick as far back as junior high, been a close friend for more than a year—and still learn new things.

"What makes a nice Jewish boy like you interested in Friar Lake?"

"The monks and friars have moved on, and Eastern is buying the property. President Babson wants to create a conference center out there, and he wants me to run it."

"Full-time gig?"

"Yup."

He raised his palm and we high-fived. "Santos will be happy." Rick worked out at the same gym as my parole officer, and I knew they had talked about me once or twice. "Steady job, something to keep you busy."

"I'm still figuring it out. My boss told me my job with the capital campaign was being phased out, and I thought I was SOL. I was freaking out for an hour or two, until Babson gave me the news." I picked up my smoothie. "He pretty much came right out and said he knew about my criminal record. Which makes it kind of surprising he's willing to trust me."

"Didn't you have to disclose it when you first applied there?"

"Yeah, but that was just an adjunct job. The chair of the English department was my professor when I was in school, and I was embarrassed to tell him. When I filled out the application for the part-time job I checked the box that I'd been convicted of a felony, and I wrote a few sentences of explanation. But I doubt he ever saw that form—it was just a personnel thing."

"What about when you switched to the full-time job?"

"When Mike MacCormac offered me the job, I told him that I was on parole for a computer offense back in California, and he waved his hand like it made no difference to him. Since I was already on the college payroll by then, the only forms I had to fill out were to transfer from part-time to full-time status."

"How do you think Babson knew, then?"

"He knows everything that goes on at that campus. He must never sleep."

"Better keep your nose clean then," Rick said. "You screw up, you won't just have me and Santos to deal with. You'll have President Nose-in-your-Business, too."

"Yeah, thanks. Just what I need right now – a little extra pressure." Of course there was also my own internal desire to snoop around in computer databases where I didn't belong. I had justified my activities over the last year because I was trying to find evidence to identify some very bad people. But I knew I had a compulsion and it was tough to resist.

We sipped our drinks, and Rochester snoozed by my feet.

"So," Rick said after a minute or two, "I had a date on Saturday night."

"Stop the presses," I said. Rick was a serial dater; I hadn't known him to get involved in a relationship since his ex-wife left him for a fireman a couple of years before.

"Not a first date," he said. "It was like our third or fourth."

"Anybody I know?"

He nodded. "You met her once. Paula Madden."

"The crazy shoe lady who's obsessed with her little dachshund?"

"Hey."

"Sorry. I meant to say, that attractive blonde who runs the shoe store at the mall? The one with the adorable little dog?"

"You don't have to lay it on that thick." Rick slurped some more lemonade. "The dog is kind of a problem. She takes him everywhere."

Lili and I had met Paula when we were investigating the death of the woman who had bred her doxy, Lush. Since then I knew Lili had been back to Paula's store a few times to buy shoes.

"So?" I asked. "You like dogs."

"Yeah, but I don't carry Rascal around with me in a little shoulder bag. Or feed him from my plate at dinner. Or call him my little cuddly-wuddly."

"Hey, I don't know what you do with him when no one else is around. But I can't see you carrying him." Rascal was as big as Rochester, which put him in the 70-80 pound range. "But you must like her, if you've gone out with her a couple of times."

"She's lots of fun, when she's not obsessing about the dog," he said. "You wouldn't know it to look at her, but she's not a girly girl at all. She loves football and country-western line dancing."

"Don't tell me she dances with the dog," I said.

"Thank god, no. She says country music makes him drowsy, so she leaves him in her bag and he sleeps."

"You know what happens when you play a country song backwards," I said.

"You get your truck back, your dog back and your girl back," he said, standing up. "I know all the same jokes you do."

My phone buzzed again. Great. I was due in yet another meeting – something called the College Connection. I couldn't remember what it was but I was due in the auditorium in Granger Hall, which housed communications and performing arts.

I rousted Rochester from his slumber. He still didn't look one hundred percent, but I hoped if he slept the afternoon away he'd be better by dinner time. I gave him some fresh water when we got back to my office, and after he drank he slumped to the floor and rolled on his side. "Take a nap, boy," I said, as if he needed prodding to do that. I hoped he wouldn't make a mess. And who knows, maybe while I was gone he'd come up with a slate of courses that would make Friar Lake a huge success.

Right. Rochester was a smart dog—too smart to get caught up in human problems.

4 – Connections

I had to scramble to make it across campus to Granger Hall, and with the sun back out the air was hot and heavy. As I walked and sweated I grumbled about the proliferation of meetings in academic environments. At least in the corporate world, there were deadlines and profit projections to meet; in academia, meetings seemed to spawn more meetings, with little progress. I hadn't bothered to investigate the meeting request from President Babson—attendance wasn't optional at meetings he called anyway. I clicked "attend" in the right box on the email and sent in the response, then forgot all about it.

As I approached Granger Hall, I ran into Jackie Conrad from the biology department. I'd gone to her for help earlier in the spring about a kind of poison that had been used in the murder of a dog breeder, and enjoyed her company. "You know anything about this meeting?" I asked, as I held open the big glass door for her.

She was a tall, broad-shouldered blonde, a former veterinarian who taught anatomy and physiology classes at Eastern. She was wearing her white lab coat, which I figured meant she'd just come from a lab.

"You didn't read the attachment?" she asked.

"There was an attachment? To what, the meeting request?"

"Yup. It was about some non-profit that exposes inner-city teenagers to college life. Our beloved president signed Eastern up to participate this summer. We're getting our first group at the beginning of next week."

We ran into a few other faculty members and all of us trooped into the auditorium together. I was surprised there were only about thirty people in the room, a mix that leaned heavily toward administrators. Jackie was one of about a dozen professors there—the other couple hundred must have been on summer break, or too savvy to click "accept" on an unknown meeting request.

Babson was up on the stage next to a video screen, talking to a tech from the IT department who had a laptop open in front of him.

Jackie opened her shoulder bag and held up a small stuffed animal that looked like a plush gray crab with a starfish attached on a long, nobby cord. Rochester would destroy it in about sixty seconds.

"I recognize that," I said. "It's a brain cell."

She held it up to her head like an earring and wiggled it so the starfish part bobbed up and down. "We can all use a few extra brain cells during the summer term, don't you think?"

"You bet. How come you're not taking some time off?"

"Two teenaged kids who need college educations. Sometimes I think they could use a few extra brain cells, too." She looked over at me. "How are things in the fund-raising department?"

"The capital campaign's moving along. But then, so am I." I told her about the move to Friar Lake.

"Sounds impressive," she said.

"Scary is more like it. I didn't apply for the job—just got moved over there like a chess piece on a board."

Babson stepped up to the microphone and introduced a video supplied by the group coming to Eastern, the College Connection. It began with a couple of menacing inner-city shots—burned out buildings, graffiti, trashed cars and discarded needles. Then the scene shifted to a bucolic college campus, much like Eastern's. A group of teenagers, mostly African-American and Hispanic, stepped off a bus as if they were entering a foreign country. Over the next few minutes, we watched them reading, sitting in classes, playing pick-up volleyball games and exploring farms and forests.

By the end of the video, these kids, who had started out looking like gang-bangers, had been transformed into contemporary college students. It was a pat video, yet it had an undeniable power.

"Did we somehow sign up to participate in this project?" I whispered to Jackie.

"If you responded to the meeting request, you did."

I slumped back in the plush armchair. I was always complaining about people who didn't read emails, who blindly hit "reply to all" and committed other electronic sins. And here I was, as guilty as the rest of them.

Babson stepped up to the podium after the video finished. He cued the geek in the orchestra pit to begin showing a series of PowerPoint slides, as he sketched out what the group of CC kids would experience at Eastern. They were going to read the first book in the *Hunger Games* trilogy, and watch the movie. Then they would meet in small seminars with faculty members to discuss issues in that professor's discipline.

"Professor Conrad has already volunteered to lead a discussion on genetic modification," Babson said, pointing toward Jackie. I immediately sat up in my seat next to her, not wanting Babson to see me slouch. "Professor Shelton will teach a seminar on the totalitarian regimes of the past and present."

He looked out at the rest of us. "I hope you will all consider how you can connect your own disciplines to the material in the novels. I'm pleased that so many of our administrators have volunteered to lead sections. Many of you have graduate degrees, and I look forward to seeing what you can contribute."

The rest of the program would include social events, explorations of the area around Leighville, and a series of college-themed movies, including *Love Story, Legally Blonde, Wonder Boys* and *A Beautiful Mind*.

"Babson could have picked *Animal House*," I whispered to Jackie.

"I think these kids will be wild enough without the incentive."

Babson let us go a few minutes later, with the promise of many emails to follow.

"What am I supposed to talk about?" I asked Jackie as we walked out. "I haven't read the book or seen the movie. And I have this whole other project to work on."

"You teach English, don't you? As an adjunct?"

"I have. I don't know if I will be in the fall." I doubted I'd have the time to teach even one section as I was trying to set up Friar Lake.

"It's a book, Steve. Surely you can find something to talk about."

I should have been excited about the College Connection; it was an interesting experiment, a chance to engage with students other than the traditional ones at Eastern, and maybe have a real impact on a teenager's life. But I was overwhelmed—first the assignment to Friar Lake, and now this. And I realized I hadn't told Lili about my new job yet. I knew she'd be happy for me, even though it meant I'd be relocating away from the campus and we'd lose the opportunity for casual get-togethers.

When I checked my mail slot at Fields Hall, I found a copy of *The Hunger Games* there. Even though I loved to read, the idea of having a book assigned didn't sit well with me. "Great, homework," I said, picking it up. I started to wonder why people would go to academic seminars at a place like Friar Lake—who wanted assigned reading as a grown-up?

When I got back to my office Rochester was sprawled across the tongue-and-groove oak floor, sleeping. I tiptoed to my desk and went back to the report on Friar Lake.

The more I read, the more scared I got. The property needed a lot of work to make it suitable for the kind of continuing education classes Babson wanted to offer. The large open yard between the religious and secular portions of the complex would be landscaped for relaxation, with sculptures and cozy areas for one-on-one meetings or small outdoor classes when the weather was fine.

I didn't know a thing about construction. My father used to joke that I didn't know which end of the screwdriver you hammer the nails with. I had always preferred to read or watch TV or play kickball and "Mother, May I?" in the street with my friends instead of hanging around in his basement workshop learning about the intricacies of table saws and drill presses. When he did coax me into helping him it was always for simple jobs, like sorting nails or sanding rough wood.

Rochester woke up, looked at me, and groaned.

"Oh, no, you're not going to hurl again, are you?" I jumped up and opened the French doors that led to the garden outside my office. He made a deep belching noise and opened his mouth wide, but nothing came out. Then he yawned and went back to sleep.

I closed the doors, shutting out the hot air that was already flooding in, and went back to my desk. I was still reading the report when Mike knocked on my door frame. A former college wrestler, he was thick-set and muscular, with dark hair and a heavy five o'clock shadow.

"You spoke to Babson?" he asked.

"Yup. "

Mike walked over and scratched Rochester behind his ears, then sat down across from me.

"You could have told me Babson had a new job for me," I said. "I thought I was getting canned."

"You know how he gets if someone steals his thunder. What's the job?"

I sketched the plan out for him. "It's huge. I've been reading the feasibility study he commissioned and I still don't have a handle on it. He wants me to move out there once the renovation work starts. Can I keep this office until then?"

"Nobody else needs this office for now. And you'll have to figure out a transition plan to shift your work away, and that'll take you a while."

I nodded. "I'll set up a meeting with Ruta del Camion at the News Bureau and start passing over my files and bringing her up to speed on my work in progress."

Mike stood up. "Let me know if you need anything." He leaned over to shake my hand. "Congratulations and good luck."

"Thanks."

I was glad I could keep my office for a while, because I wasn't eager to relocate off campus. I had started feeling comfortable here—I knew where I could walk Rochester, where all the good lunches were down in Leighville, and I liked being able to meet Lili for coffee in the middle of the day. I made a note to check how far Friar Lake was from the campus. Would I be able to move back and forth easily?

Rochester groaned again, and rolled over. It was already past lunch time, and the morning's smoothie and croissant felt like ancient history. I didn't want to leave him alone again, but I needed something to eat and a cup of coffee, and I wanted to talk to Lili.

I dialed her office number. "Hey, sweetie, I need a huge favor," I said. I explained about Rochester's illness. "Can you pick up some lunch for us and bring it over here? I don't want to leave him here for too long. And I have some news to share. Good, I think."

"I've been jonesing for a roast beef hoagie from Demetrio's," she said, mentioning a sandwich shop in Leighville famous among undergraduates for its low prices and large portions.

"You fly, I'll buy," I said. "Make it two, and let's split a bottle of Black Cherry Wishniak." That was my favorite soda, a Philadelphia invention that Demetrio's stocked in tall glass bottles.

"You got it. I'll be at your office in a half hour or so."

Lili and I had developed a nice groove, where she knew without being told the way I liked my sandwich—on a long white submarine roll, with lettuce, tomato and Russian dressing, with a small bag of salt and vinegar potato chips.

I roused Rochester and took him outside. Then back in my office I poured fresh water into his bowl and gave him a rawhide to chew. He looked expectantly at the jar of treats on my desk, but I shook my head. "Not til your stomach calms down, bud," I said.

I sat on the floor next to him and rubbed his belly, and he stretched, his front legs raised above his head, his back ones almost vertical. The skin of his belly was taut, covered with a layer of fine golden hair. "Things are changing, boy," I said, stroking the soft hair of his head and neck. "Daddy's got a new job. I don't know anything about it, and I'm feeling kind of scared. So I'm depending on you to be here for me, all right? You've got to feel better and keep on giving me all your puppy love."

When I was younger, I had a sense of entitlement that came from growing up in a stable home where I was praised and encouraged. My parents told me I could do anything I set my mind to, so whenever I had a setback I had the sense that things would work out fine in the end.

Going to prison had changed that mindset. At forty-five, I wondered how many fresh starts I had left in me, and I'd seen what happened to men who had been hit with one too many body blows. I no longer had my parents as a fallback, and I worried that if I got sick, or laid off, or suffered some other defeat, I might not be able to bounce back.

I leaned down and buried my head in Rochester's flank, mumbling "puppy love" again and again.

5 – Slipping and Sliding

Rochester belched again, then yawned and went back to sleep, and I returned to the report. When Lili walked in, the big dog jumped up and threw himself at her as if there was nothing wrong with him. I was just as glad to see her as he was, and I stood up to kiss her, with the dog trying to nuzzle his way between us.

She pulled away and handed me the paper bag with our lunch, then turned to the dog. "What's the matter, boy? You not feeling well?" she asked, chucking him under the chin. "You look fine."

She wore a scoop-necked black sundress and matching ballet flats. Her exuberant auburn curls streamed around her face, and her upper body was deeply tanned.

"Don't believe that angelic look," I said, as I spread our lunch out on my desk. "He might hurl again at any minute."

"Gee, that really boosts my appetite."

Rochester jumped up and put his paws on the desk, and she hauled him down with a firm hand on his collar, then pulled a chair up across from me. "So what did you want to talk about?" she asked, beginning to unroll the paper around her sub.

"I met with Babson this morning. He wants me to take on a new job, and he's going to shift responsibility for press relations for the campaign to the News Bureau," I said.

She picked up the sub. "What are you going to be doing"

In between taking bites of my own sub, and draughts of black cherry soda, I explained to her about Friar Lake. "What do you think?" I asked when I finished.

"Are you sure it's the right move for you?" she asked. "Since you got out of prison you've been like a pinball, bouncing around. Tech writing, adjunct teaching, then public relations. Now this. Have you ever even been on an executive education course?"

It was hard not to sound defensive, but Lili was right, and she was just voicing the fears I had myself. "My boss sent a couple of us to a two-day seminar to learn HTML, back when nobody knew what it was," I said. "But we met in an office building and went home at the end of the day."

"I think Babson is trying to make this seem a lot easier than it's going to be," Lili said, sitting back in her chair. "Not that you can't handle it—I know you, you're smart and you work hard when you need to. But I think you need to take a day or two and think this through before you jump blindly into it."

"But if I don't take the job, then I'm unemployed again, scrambling to piece together a living from freelance work and adjunct teaching. At my age, with my background, I'm not going to get too many opportunities."

"Slow down," Lili said, reaching out for my hand. "I'm not saying you should turn the job down, and even if you did I doubt you'd be out on the street. Just slow down and look at all your options."

I took a deep breath. "You're right. I don't even know where this place is yet."

"Then let's check." She nodded toward my computer, and I turned the monitor so she could see it. I pulled up Google Maps and searched for the property's address, on Birch Road. There was no indication of it on the map view; I had to switch to the satellite view to figure out where along the road the buildings were.

Leighville sat on a bluff overlooking the Delaware, halfway between Stewart's Crossing to the south and Easton to the north. The college's buildings occupied most of the hilltop, while the town was spread on the flat plain between hill and river. Friar Lake was about five miles north of campus, along a country road that passed behind the town and then dipped down toward the Delaware. It was about a mile inland from the river.

I zoomed the computer's display and saw the abbey proper, laid out as I'd seen in the plans. A two-lane road curved from the hilltop church down to the lakefront where a suburban-style ranch house hugged one shore. The roadway continued to the street through a stand of trees.

"That must be where the mendicant friars lived," I said, pointing.

"I didn't think mendicants ever got this far out of the city," she said.

"You know what they are?"

"Of course. Didn't you?"

I shook my head. "I'm Jewish. What do I know from friars, mendicant or otherwise?"

"I'm as Jewish as you are. Just better educated, I guess."

Rochester was sitting on his haunches so peacefully that I rewarded him with a piece of fatty roast beef. Better his cholesterol than mine. "I got my degree from Eastern College," I said. "That should tell you something."

"Back when I was doing photojournalism, I did a lot of inner-city shoots," she said. "I ran across friars in a bunch of different places, living among the poor, providing education and medical services."

"When they get too old to mendicate, or whatever the verb form is, they retire to abbeys, according to Babson's report. The monks lived in the dormitory on top of the hill, next to the church, while the friars needed more modern quarters, all on one floor."

"Where are the monks and friars now?"

"They relocated to an abbey in western Pennsylvania after the property was sold."

She looked at her watch. "I'm done with class for the day. Want to drive out and look at the place?" Though she didn't have to, she was teaching one class during the summer session, because that cut one course from her load during the regular term, which gave her more time for her own photography.

"Sure, as long as Rochester's up to it."

The big goof heard his name, raised his head, and nodded it once, his metal collar and rabies tag jangling.

"Let me go back to my office and close up for the day," Lili said. "I'll meet you in the employee parking lot in fifteen."

I took Rochester on a circuitous route behind Fields Hall, hoping that if he had anything inside he needed to evacuate he could do it outdoors rather than in my car. But all he did was sniff a lot and pee a couple of times.

Lili was standing by my car as we approached. She had a digital SLR camera slung around her neck and a cargo vest over her sundress. I knew that the pockets contained extra lenses, filters, and a rubber lens hood.

She had pulled her curls into a ponytail and exchanged the ballet flats for a pair of duck boots—a smart move, given how marshy the college property had become after the week of heavy rains. Who knew how bad it would be out at Friar Lake, especially if the property had been abandoned for a while.

We hopped into the Beemer and headed out. "I didn't tell you before," I said, as I navigated my way through the campus to the road that would lead us down to Friar Lake. "But I got roped into this College Connection thing. Have you heard about it?"

"I was in the meeting, Steve." She leaned against the door and looked at me. "I slipped in late, and I waved to you as we were walking out. But you were busy talking to Jackie Conrad and you didn't see me."

"She lent me a brain cell for the meeting." Before I could explain, though, we reached the bottom of the hill, where the swale on both sides of the road was underwater, and I had to focus on driving. The Beemer's rattle startled a couple of mallards who lifted gracefully and winged away.

I drove carefully, staying to the center of the country road as much as possible. "I don't need the extra aggravation of this College Connection thing," I said. "I wish there was a way I could duck out of it, but I'm sure Babson will be on me all the time about Friar Lake and he'll definitely notice if I drop out."

"You'll have to come up with something that doesn't take a lot of effort on your part," she said. "We can brainstorm once you read the book."

"Yeah, my homework," I grumbled.

She elbowed me. "You sound just like a student."

"Don't get me wrong, I love to read," I said. "I just hate having my books chosen for me. I had enough of that getting my master's degree. I remember after I graduated walking into a bookstore and realizing that I could pick any book I wanted and have plenty of time to read it."

The land along the road was flat and the water table high. A hedgerow of mature oak, maple and sassafras framed the farms we passed. It looked like the kind of place Peter Rabbit would live, and as I drove I longed for the easy days of childhood when all I had to worry about was when my library books were due.

We came to the turnoff for Friar Lake and I pulled to a halt at the access road. It was blocked by a rope tied around a pair of leafy green maples. A sign that read "Private Property No Trespassing" hung from it.

I stepped gingerly out of the car. The ground underneath my feet was spongy, but the gravel road seemed in pretty good shape.

"Not much of a deterrent," I said, as I undid the simple half-hitch knot on one end of the rope and dropped it to the ground. I returned to the car, kicking the dirt off my soles before I got back in.

The road wound through a stand of trees and then branched in two. The right fork led to a low-slung ranch house, and beyond it the sparkling waters of Friar Lake, with a couple of ducks paddling near the shore. To our left, the road climbed up the hill to the monastery. "Might as well start down here," I said, turning right. I pulled up in the gravel lot in front of the ranch and we piled out.

Rochester immediately took off for a tree at one side of the house and lifted his leg when he reached it. Lili and I began to walk carefully around the exterior of the building where the friars had lived. She'd been smart to switch to boots; I was still wearing my deck shoes, which had a good sole but were already getting mucked up.

I recalled from the report that the building had been acquired by the monastery in the 1970s to serve as housing for the friars. It looked like it had once been a standard suburban ranch, with a clapboard extension on the right, a series of windows implying that the bedrooms were down there. On the left was what looked like a large workroom or assembly room, and then a double-wide garage.

I looked around for Rochester. "Where is that dog?" I didn't see him, but I could hear him. It sounded like he was digging. "Oh, no. Rochester! Don't you eat anything!"

I took off running around the side of the house, my shoes desperate for purchase on the slippery wet grass. Rochester was a few hundred yards away, down near the water's edge, digging at something.

"He's going to eat some dead thing and then throw up again, I just know it," I called back to Lili, who was following me at a more careful pace.

I slid on a muddy patch and lost my balance. But I was able to windmill my arms and catch myself. "Rochester!" I yelled. "Bad dog. Stop that right now!"

He ignored me. Not a surprise. I stepped more carefully toward him, my deck shoes covered in mud and squelching as I walked. "You're in big trouble, buster!"

I finally got close enough to grab hold of his collar and pull him back. Looking down, I saw what he'd been digging up.

A decomposed human hand, palm up, attached to partially skeletonized arm which continued down into the ground.

6 – Deerstalker Hat

Lili was right behind me. Neither of us screamed or shrieked, but I caught my breath and heard Lili do the same thing. We'd both been around dead bodies before. Lili had been a globe-trotting photojournalist, and I'd already followed Rochester's nose for death a couple of times. But each one still represented a human being who had lived once, and now lived no longer. It was a sobering thought. I reached for Lili's hand and squeezed.

I bent down and tugged at Rochester's collar, and he reluctantly turned away from his new discovery.

The ground beneath our feet was mucky, and Lili stepped carefully forward and then leaned close to the body. "It's been here about three months," she said, after taking a look. "You can tell by the level of decomposition."

"How do you know that?" I asked, still holding tight to the dog's collar.

"I've seen a lot of bodies," she said. "In war people tend to bury their dead by hand, in shallow graves. The body starts to dry out after a couple of weeks as maggots eat the flesh. When all that's left is tendons and ligaments, like we have here, the beetles take over."

"That is truly creepy," I said. "I mean, that you know that kind of thing."

She shrugged. "Bodies often rise up like this if they aren't buried deep enough, especially when we get rains like we've had lately." She looked at me curiously. "You're enjoying this, aren't you? Are you some kind of death magnet?"

"Not at all. I just happen to run across bodies." Not that I enjoyed seeing them; the first one I discovered was that of Rochester's former owner, my neighbor Caroline. Since then—well, it wasn't something I wanted to dwell on. But I did have a kind of insatiable curiosity that drove me to snoop into places I didn't belong. That's how I had discovered my ability to hack into websites – which led, in the end, to my incarceration.

"And this could be perfectly innocent," I said. "The Benedictines were in a hurry to move to Western Pennsylvania, and they didn't take the time to bury this guy properly."

She shook her head. "Don't be sarcastic. I don't think he's a friar. If the Benedictines had buried friars back here, this body would have been in a coffin, and there would be a headstone or a marker."

"Well, it could be he or she died naturally and the family or whoever couldn't afford a funeral. They might have thought this was sacred ground, because of the abbey nearby. The property's been deserted for the last few months, so anybody could have gotten in here and left the body."

"It doesn't matter right now how the body got here, Steve. Even if this person died naturally, it's not right that he or she was dumped out here. The police need to figure out who this was and what happened. And you don't need to have any part of that. Let's get out of this mud and call 911."

We turned and trudged back up to the house where the friars had lived. I had left Rochester's leash in the car, so I was forced to walk like a hunchback with one hand around his collar. Mud was seeping into my shoes, and I'd lost my interest in exploring the property.

"Why don't I call Rick Stemper directly?" I said. "I don't think this is his jurisdiction, but he'll know what we should do." And because I had helped him in the past, he might let me snoop around in the investigation, I thought, but I didn't say that to Lili.

"Fine. Whoever. Just make the call. I'll keep the dog busy."

She took Rochester's leash and walked off as I dialed Rick's cell. My hands were shaking; I guess seeing the dead body did bother me. But I tried to keep my tone light when Rick answered.

"Hey, Steve, what's up?"

"I've got a little problem and I need your advice."

"Please tell me this isn't a criminal problem. Rochester isn't snooping around somewhere, is he?"

"I'm afraid he has been. And he found a body."

There was a silence on Rick's end. Finally he said, "A human body?"

"Yeah. At least, I'm assuming there's a body attached. Right now there's only a hand sticking up from the dirt. Kind of like some creepy horror movie."

I heard a slight quaver in my voice and resolved to steel myself. It was just a body, after all. And a stranger. There was probably an innocent explanation why his hand had risen up from the grave for Rochester to find.

"Does it look fresh?" he asked.

"Not really. A lot of the flesh is gone. Lili says it looks about three months old."

"I'm not even going to ask you how your girlfriend knows that," he said. "Where exactly is this body? Or this hand."

"At Friar Lake. The monastery I was telling you about. Lili and I took Rochester out here to look around. Before we could get far he started digging and going nuts."

Rick sounded like he was thinking out loud. "If the dog found a hand, then that means the body wasn't in a coffin," he said. "That's not a good sign." He took a deep breath. "Here's what you do, Steve. Don't touch anything. Call 911. And then call Tony Rinaldi. The Leighville PD covers that area."

I still had Tony's cell number stored in my phone from the last time Rochester had found a body, on the Eastern campus. "Will do."

"And Steve? Try and stay out of this one. Even a cat only has nine lives."

"Yeah, yeah," I said, keeping it light. But I knew that there was no way my curiosity was going to let me ignore a dead body dumped at my feet.

Since there was no imminent emergency, I decided to call Tony Rinaldi first, rather than 911. "Hey, it's Steve Levitan," I said when he answered. "Does your jurisdiction cover Friar Lake?"

"That's unincorporated Bucks County, but we respond," he said. "What's up?"

"Rochester dug up a body. Or at least a hand that looks like it's still attached to a body."

"You let your dog disturb a crime scene?"

"Hey, we had no idea it was any kind of scene," I said. "We were walking out behind the house by the lake, and after all the rain lately it looks like a lot of the dirt covering a grave was washed away. I pulled Rochester away as soon as I saw what he was digging around. I called Rick Stemper, and he told me to call 911 and then call you. But this isn't exactly an emergency, is it? So I just called you."

"I'll be there in a half hour. Don't go anywhere."

"Do we need to stay here with the body? Or can we go up the hill and look at the monastery?"

"Is the scene secure?" he asked.

"There's nobody else here," I said. "And we're pretty far off the road."

"Just stay in the area, all right?" he said.

"Will do." I hung up, then took my shoes and socks off and wiped my feet reasonably clean. I finished up as Lili and my dog returned.

"What did Rick say?" Lili asked.

"He told me to call Tony Rinaldi. Tony's going to come out here and take a look. I told him we'd wait up at the monastery."

I kept a couple of old rags and a roll of paper towels in the trunk of the BMW for Rochester emergencies, and I managed to do a quick clean up of his paws, then lay the towels on the back seat. Rochester scrambled in the back while Lili slipped into the front seat next to me.

"You do realize that this body is no business of yours," she said, as we drove about a half-mile up the curving, tree-lined road. It was late afternoon, but the sun was still strong, dappling the roadway and dancing between the leaves of the ancient oaks and maples.

"What do you mean?"

"I mean you have no reason to nose around in Tony's investigation."

I knew enough about women not to argue, even though I felt that my new job managing Friar Lake certainly gave me the impetus to look into who the body belonged to and how it had ended up there. So I just smiled and pointed out the patches of daisies and black-eyed-Susans, and even a stand of raspberry canes beginning to come into fruit.

"It's really a pretty property," I said, trying to change the subject.

Lili wasn't believing me. "Uh-huh," she said, staring out the passenger window.

I pulled into a cleared space of gravel in front of the chapel. "Rochester's staying in the car this time," I said. "I don't need any more unfortunate discoveries today."

We both hopped out quickly, closing the doors behind us before Rochester could weasel his way out. I was still barefoot, and the gravel was sharp against my tender soles. The front door of the chapel was locked, which was a good sign. We walked along a concrete path around the corner and through an arched passage into a broad yard that I recognized from the plans. Roses had been trained up the sides of the chapel, and in the silence we could hear the buzz of bees and the chirp of crickets.

"I'm feeling a bit creeped out," Lili said, rubbing her bare shoulders. "Too many memories of life in war zones coming back. I want to walk around a bit on my own."

I knew that when Lili was faced with troubling situations, she preferred to approach them through the lens of her camera. I guess we all have our coping mechanisms.

"Try not to get yourself in any more trouble while I'm gone." To soften the words, she leaned over and kissed my cheek.

She walked back out of the yard, and I began checking the door locks. I found a side entrance into the chapel with a broken lock, and pushed the door in.

The room was cavernous, three stories tall with an arched roof, and lined with hard wooden pews. The light coming through the stained glass windows threw jeweled squares over the solid wood floor. It was spookily quiet except for a low scratching sound.

I stood on the scuffed wooden floor, and realized I'd have to familiarize myself with church architecture pretty quickly.

Through my bare soles I could feel the way thousands of footsteps had smoothed the way before me. I rarely go into churches, except ones that have become historical sites, and I felt like an interloper. I hoped that the souls of all the dead monks and friars who had passed through the place weren't going to get cranky over Eastern's plans to secularize the place.

To my right I could see where the two wings branched off, and the rounded space at the far end. The long-gone crucifix left a ghostly shadow on the wall above the dais. That reminded me of the dead body down by the lake. Who was it? If Lili was right about how long the body had been in the ground, that meant the Benedictines had already decamped for western Pennsylvania by the time it was buried.

To the outsider, Bucks County looked like an idyllic place. In the spring, dogwoods and magnolias blossomed, and in the summer bright red strawberries glistened in the U-pick fields and acres of farmland swayed with corn stalks. The fall brought a blaze of color as the leaves changed, and in the winter the landscape was cloaked with a white blanket.

Revolutionary War landmarks dotted the river towns, children rode their bikes along the narrow sidewalks, and McMansions on immaculately groomed acre lots housed wealthy commuters. But pockets of poverty hid around the curves of country roads, and Rick had told me stories of domestic violence and drug abuse in the midst of the suburbs.

I knew enough not to generalize about felons—after all, I was one myself. But even out here in the countryside, people were willing to commit murder to achieve their goals. Whether the body down by the lake belonged to an innocent victim or a hardened criminal, it was still a reminder that danger could lurk around any corner.

I shivered and walked forward. The dais was raised about two feet above the floor, and a beach-ball sized hole loomed in the vertical support wall. The scratching noises were louder, and I worried that animals nested under there. I'd have to hire an exterminator to come in and clear the place out. Great. More displaced souls to haunt the space.

I decided against having a close encounter with any home-protecting wildlife, and returned to the open yard, where I spotted Lili down on her right knee, focusing on the outline of the chapel against the sky. I didn't want to disturb her, so I walked behind the chapel to a grove of old-growth maples and pines. A doe grazing in the sunshine raised her head, looked at me, and then took off through the woods.

Friar Lake was turning out to be a lot wilder than I'd expected. I walked back to the dormitory building, where I noticed a broken window. I looked through it to a narrow monastic cell. The Benedictines hadn't left any furniture behind, so the only thing in the room was a closet with an open door. It was going to take a lot of imagination and hard work to make this place into a comfortable retreat. All the emptiness continued to spook me and I turned back to where I'd seen Lili.

She was still there, aiming her camera at the stark outline of the wrought-iron spire against the bright blue sky. She snapped a final shot and stood up as my cell rang.

"Hey, Tony. We're up at the abbey. We'll meet you back down at the lakefront."

I felt silly as I walked beside Lili to the car, tiptoeing over the gravel to avoid cutting my feet. Rochester greeted us as if we'd abandoned him, and I had to push back against his snout to keep him in the rear seat.

As I pulled up next to Tony's unmarked sedan, I got a good look at him. He hadn't changed much in the months since we'd last met; he was still tall and dark-haired, in his late forties. He had light-green eyes, which were arresting in combination with his brush-cut dark hair. They gave him a look of intensity that I was sure suspects found unsettling.

Lili and I hopped out of the car, once again leaving Rochester behind. He barked out his resentment as I introduced Lili.

"Pleased to meet you," Tony said, shaking her hand. Then he looked to me. "Where's the body?"

"Around by the lake," I said. Lili and I led him through the muck, around the corner of the house. I'd have to wipe down my bare feet again, but at least the grass was soft and spongy. I pointed. "It's pretty mucky out there. Be careful."

Tony looked down at his black dress shoes, and I think that's the first time he realized that I was barefoot.

"Crap," he said. "I usually keep a pair of boots in my trunk but the sole started separating so I had Tanya take them to the shoemaker's to be restitched."

I'd heard about Tony's wife when he investigated a murder at Eastern during the winter, but I had never met her. I knew she was a nurse, and that he had a young son. But we'd never become friends, the way I had with Rick.

Tony frowned as he bent down and took off his shoes and socks, then rolled the legs of his black dress pants up to the knee. He looked so comical I had to struggle not to laugh. His top half didn't match the bottom at all—a perfectly pressed dress shirt, with a red and blue striped tie held in place by a diamond clip, contrasted with the little-boy look of rolled cuffs and bare feet. He walked through the muck, and I could hear it squishing under his feet.

He pulled a small digital camera from his pocket and took a number of photos, as Lili and I stood in the background and watched him work. When he'd covered all the angles, he put the camera back in his pocket and withdrew a pair of bright blue rubber gloves. He slipped them on and crouched down next to the upturned hand, which reminded me more and more of something from a low-budget horror movie.

Tony gingerly scraped away dirt covering the skeletonized arm, digging deeper the farther back he went. When he reached the shoulder, he gave up and stood. He peeled the gloves off as he walked back to us.

"I get a bad a feeling about this," he said. "Looks like a body dump to me. How long did you say the property was abandoned?"

"The Benedictines moved out about three months ago," I said.

"Finding an unidentified grave on a property where there's a regular cemetery is suspicious enough for me to order an exhumation," he said. "I'm going to have to isolate this area and then make the arrangements with the ME's office. This is going to be a big headache, you know that?"

"Sorry," I said. "Can't you just call the Benedictines and see if anyone in the order knows who it is?"

"I'll do that, but I'm willing to bet they know nothing about it. Give me a hand with the crime scene tape?" he asked. "As long as you're here and your feet are already mucky."

"Sure."

While he walked back to his car to get the tape, I turned to Lili. "So much for our pleasant little excursion out into the countryside."

"Better to find this body now, than later, when you've got some kind of conference going on the property," Lili said. "And better for whoever that is in the ground, too."

A chill ran up my spine. "You're right." I took her hand and squeezed. "I'm glad you were here with me."

"For a mild-mannered college administrator you lead a very interesting life," Lili said. "When I gave up photojournalism to come teach at Eastern I worried I might get bored out here in the boondocks. Then I met you." She smiled. "You definitely keep things interesting."

Tony returned with a roll of yellow tape and a couple of wooden stakes. I helped him secure a perimeter around the location of the grave. "You guys can go now," he said. "I'll be here for a while longer."

"Let me know if I can help you with anything else," I said.

Lili and I returned to the car, where I cleaned my feet off once more. As we backed down the driveway I saw Tony leaning against his sedan, talking on his cell phone.

Rochester lay down on the back seat and pouted, annoyed to have been left out of the fun, as I drove barefoot back to Stewart's Crossing. "There's most likely a body there, don't you think?" I asked. "I mean, more than just the hand and the arm."

"Most likely," Lili said.

"I wonder if Tony will be able to match the remains to any missing persons report. Those have got to be computerized, right?"

"Steve. You're not going to start hacking into police databases checking for missing people, are you? You're not a cop and if you do anything like that you're going to get into big trouble."

"I know. I'm just curious, is all. I mean, we don't even know if the person is male or female yet, how old, or any of that stuff."

I turned to look at her. "What if that's not the only body there? Suppose a serial killer has been burying his victims back there?"

"Stop. You're getting downright gruesome."

I concentrated on driving back to River Bend, though I felt like I was pouting just as much as Rochester was.

The first thing I did when we got there was wash my feet and put on clean shoes and socks. Then Lili fixed us dinner while I took Rochester for a long walk. He peed a lot but nothing else came out, and I was grateful for that. When we got back I found that Lili had boiled up some chicken for Rochester, and added white rice. "This'll help settle his stomach," she said. "And I made enough so you'll have it for a few days."

"How did you know that?" I asked. "You've never had a dog."

"I've been around the world, Steve," she said, as she drained a big pot of pasta for us. "I picked up a few tricks along the way."

"I've noticed." I stepped up behind her and kissed the nape of her neck.

She pushed back at me playfully, and we both laughed.

7 – The Strange One in the Bunch

That evening, Lili and I relaxed on my king-sized bed together, both of us preparing for working with the College Connection by reading *The Hunger Games*. By the time Rochester was bumping his head against me for his pre-bedtime walk, my mind was buzzing with ideas for a seminar with the CC kids.

"This book is cool," I said. I closed it and pushed Rochester away so I could find my shoes. "I love the whole dystopian theme. I could get them talking about how this kind of thing could happen."

"Says the man who didn't even want to read the book to start with."

"Just because someone was making me read it," I said. I wondered about that. Was it that I was so far removed from being a student? Or did I just not like people telling me what I could and couldn't do? Was that a remnant of life behind bars, or had I always been that way?

"Remember, these kids are coming from the inner city," Lili said, sitting up. "They've probably got a good idea of what life is like already for these characters. You don't want to talk down to them. Try and let them lead the conversation."

"This won't be my first time at the rodeo," I said. "I do know how to teach."

"I'm not saying you don't. Just that these kids are different from the ones you teach at Eastern. They're younger, they're probably more jaded, and they see difficult things all the time."

"Oh, you mean like finding dead bodies?" I said. "Creepy hands rising up from unmarked graves?"

I turned my hand over in a mimicry of the one we'd found at Friar Lake.

"That's just tragic," she said. "Get the dog's leash so we can get moving."

We walked Rochester together, and I was glad to have Lili there for company. Despite my joking, I had been unsettled by that disembodied hand in the muck at Friar Lake, and didn't want to worry about every stray noise in the dark.

After Rochester had left all his doggy messages, Lili and I went back up to the bedroom, where we put the books aside and enjoyed each other's company before we went to sleep.

The next morning, Rochester gobbled more of Lili's chicken and rice, and I continued to give him the medication the vet had prescribed. I wasn't taking any chances on a repeat performance. We played out the same routine – I hid the pill in a chunk of peanut butter, which he ate, then he licked my finger clean. Then he spit the pill out, and I had to drop it down his throat. You'd think one of us would learn.

I liked the fact that Lili had begun leaving a few clothing and toiletry items at my house. It made our relationship seem that much more solid, and when she stayed over she was able to get ready for work with me and we could ride up to Eastern together.

As I pulled into a parking space behind Fields Hall, Lili said, "Remember, I'm going into Philly this afternoon to see my friend's gallery show, and then dinner with some people. I'll call you when I get home."

"Have fun." We kissed and then got out of the car.

"Remember what I said about thinking this job offer through," Lili said. "Don't just jump at it because John Babson says so. You have skills and you have options."

"I wish I had your confidence in my abilities," I said. "But don't worry, I'll think."

As I walked Rochester to my office, I thought about what Lili had said. Did she really have faith in me – or did she just have her own vision of the person I could be? That was the case with Mary, for sure. It took me a long time to understand that when we met, she saw me as a ball of clay she could mold into her idea of the perfect husband. When I resisted her efforts – to get an MBA like my friend Tor or to seek a promotion at work—she got angry. Part of the reason why our marriage failed was because I couldn't conform to the man Mary wanted me to be.

I didn't want to recreate that pattern with Lili. I needed her to see me as who I was, warts and all. While Rochester sniffed around the base of a pine tree, I wondered if what I saw was the real Liliana Weinstock. Because we shared a Jewish background, she was familiar to me in many ways; but because she had been born in Cuba, and grown up in a Latin-influenced household in the US, she was also exotic. That blend was fascinating to me.

She'd been married twice and divorced both times, and had pursued a career in photojournalism around the world before choosing to become an academic. Sometimes her intellect awed me; she had a PhD, took amazing photos and then manipulated them into awe-inspiring art through her computer skills. I had relied on my intelligence and skill with words and computers to slide through life and had overcome the brief interruption provided by the California penal system to resume my lifelong pattern by falling into my jobs at Eastern.

It seemed Lili had deliberately made herself into the person she was, while I had simply taken what came to me. In her view, at least, I was continuing in that same pattern by accepting the job at Friar Lake. Could she accept that I was that kind of guy— or would she give up on me the way Mary had?

Those were troubling questions so early in the morning. I was glad that I had a meeting scheduled with Joe Capodilupo, the director of physical plant for Eastern, so I could avoid considering them. I left Rochester snoozing in my office when I walked over to meet with Joe.

His department was headquartered in a converted carriage house at the back of the Eastern campus, near the road that led down to Friar Lake. The quaint stone and shingle exterior was a contrast to the bland efficiency of the inside. To the left, beyond a receptionist's desk, was a series of cubicles and one big office. Tall metal storage cabinets lined the other wall. From the ones with open doors, I could see they were used to store some of the equipment that kept the campus humming.

There were nearly twenty buildings at Eastern, from the original stone ones like Fields Hall and the carriage house to the 1960s-era dormitories like Birthday House and the brand new, pill-bottle-shaped Granger Hall, donated by a pharmaceutical magnate, which housed the visual and performing arts. Every building had its own maintenance issues, and Joe supervised a team of engineers, plumbers, handymen and groundskeepers. It was a function of the college that students took for granted—until a toilet leaked, a cockroach was spotted or a boiler failed on a cold winter day.

Joe was a gruff, heavyset guy with white hair and a white beard, and he looked like he'd have been at home with the Benedictines if you slapped one of those black robes on him. He had already been involved in hiring the architect to do the drawings I'd seen, and had a contractor ready to get started as soon as the permits were approved. He was going to handle the actual renovation process.

We stood beside a broad plan table in his office and Joe began to go over the large-sized version of the drawings I'd seen in Babson's report. "The whole property's going to need to be rewired," he said. "Right now it's a firetrap, with frayed wiring, places the squirrels have chewed through, missing outlet covers. We have to bring the place up to code with sprinklers, fire alarms, emergency exits, and handicap access. And the kitchen needs to come out. The appliances there come from the year dot."

I laughed. "My dad used to use that expression."

He turned to a color-coded schedule hung on the wall next to the plan desk.

"Once we have the permits, we start with demolition. We'll knock out anything that isn't going to stay, move on to structural reinforcement, then MEP-- mechanical, electrical and plumbing. After that we slap on the drywall, spackle and sand, install the light fixtures and all the other little crap. Then we paint and carpet and bring in the furniture. We're aiming to open right after graduation next May."

"That's almost a year. What am I supposed to do while all that work is going on?"

"Oh, there'll be plenty for you," he said. "I'm only handling the physical renovation to the building. You're going to have to get a designer to source all the furnishings and décor."

My brain was reeling as I walked back to Fields Hall. It was almost lunchtime, so when I got back to my office I took Rochester out for a walk downhill to where the lunch trucks clustered along Main Street. I got a double-patty bacon cheeseburger and fries, ignoring the potential for cholesterol overload, and sat down on the side of a concrete planter to eat, Rochester on his haunches next to me.

I pulled out the extra burger and fed it to him between my own bites, trying to pull my head together. My dad had never been the type to complain, but I knew there had been situations where he'd been transferred from one department to another. My mom had a cancer scare when I was a little kid—that surely must have freaked him out.

There must have been times when he worried that he wasn't doing the right thing, or doing a good enough job. He'd never betrayed that insecurity to me, but that was what men of his generation did. They just got on with the task at hand. Could I do the same thing myself?

I liked working at Eastern, and I really liked the security of having a regular paycheck. Babson had shown faith in me, and I had learned since my return from prison that not everyone would – and that I needed to repay that faith. So I was going to take the job he offered at Friar Lake, even if I worried that I couldn't handle it.

I finished my lunch and walked Rochester back to my office, then called Elaine in HR. "President Babson told me to let you know he's reassigning me."

"Hold on, I think I saw an email about that."

She typed, and then groaned, which wasn't a good sign. "You're going to be the first employee of a new cost center," she said. "We don't even have the job posted yet. I just got the forms from the president's office this morning. But that's typical. You'll have to wait until the job is posted, and then fill out an application. As soon as I have it in the system, I'll email you. He's indicated that the position is open until filled—so if you apply right away, then we can railroad through the paperwork and close the position. If you wait too long and we get a raft of applicants, we'll have to go through a formal interview and hiring procedure."

"I thought this was just an internal transfer," I said.

"Well, it is, and it isn't. Because the position is new we have to jump through some extra hoops, and ensure that we're abiding by all the relevant hiring laws."

When I hung up from Elaine, I was more confused than ever. Did I really have this job? Babson ran Eastern as his private fiefdom, moving people around at will. But I knew Elaine had to make sure all the right procedures were followed.

What if the pool was opened to all candidates, and someone more qualified applied? That wouldn't be hard, since I had none of the skills the position was going to require. And if I had to fill out a whole new set of forms, that would involve disclosing once again that I had a felony conviction on my record. Suppose Elaine or someone else in HR raised a fuss, and Babson decided I wasn't worth the trouble? I'd be back on the street.

8 – Design Sense

I struggled to push those doubts aside and focus on the task at hand. If there was a chance I had to fight for the job, I was going to do my best to entrench myself. I began by making a list of everything I had to do. Coordinate with Joe. Hire a designer to source all the interior finishes. Develop programming. Create a publicity campaign for the center. Write an operating budget. Hire support staff.

I also needed to tell President Babson about the body that we had found out at Friar Lake but I wanted to wait until we had more information. If the body could be connected to the monks, then it was nothing to do with Eastern. Though at that point I couldn't figure out how the college could be connected to the dead body at all.

I began to sketch out a timeline and realized that I needed to find an interior designer. I didn't know anyone like that. But then I remembered Mark Figueroa, an antique dealer in Stewart's Crossing. I often ran into him at The Chocolate Ear café in the center of town, and at some point he'd told me his college degree was in visual merchandising, and that he'd worked as an interior designer in New York before opening his store. Maybe he could help me out, or at least direct me to someone who could.

I stood up. "We're cutting out early today, Rochester," I said. I grabbed his leash, and he hopped up from his place by the French doors. It was a sunny hot day, and summer-school students crowded the lawns and pathways, tanning and throwing Frisbees. Most of the girls wore bikini tops and short shorts, while the boys wore Eastern T-shirts and football shirts and board shorts that hung down from their waists.

I tried to remember what it had been like to be so young and carefree, to know that I had my parents to fall back on in case of emergency. Then Rochester squatted next to an ivied wall and let out a stream of diarrhea.

"Yuck. Guess feeding you that burger at lunch wasn't a good idea."

I had nothing with me to clean up after him, and I wouldn't have been able to get much of the liquid gunk up anyway, so I just tugged him away and kept my head down, hoping no one had noticed. When we got back to the BMW I used a baby wipe to clean Rochester's butt.

When he was all minty fresh, I put the windows down and we cruised slowly down the River Road, in and out of the shade of weeping willows and stately maples. Butterflies flew in lazy circles among the daisies and black-eyed Susans by the river's edge. Just like the summers of my childhood. The big difference was that I was the dad now, responsible for myself and my furry son. And once again, I wished I had my father there to ask his advice—about Friar Lake, about Rochester, even about my relationship with Lili.

Decorating wasn't one of my strengths. My townhouse looked pretty much the way it had when I inherited it, with bits and pieces of the furniture I'd grown up with. I remembered when my parents bought the oil painting of red and yellow sunflowers that hung over the sofa, at a charity auction at our synagogue. The two wing chairs flanking the sofa had belonged to my grandparents, and my mother had them reupholstered when she inherited them. My father had rewired the antique torchiere lamp in the corner.

The worries I had about my ability to handle the new job were jumbled together with Lili's comments and memories of my father. He was an engineer and a home handyman, comfortable tossing around all those terms Joe had been using. I was a clumsy kid, and my dad didn't like me hanging around his basement workshop too much; he was afraid I'd impale myself on a drill, or cut off some body part with one of his sharp saws. I never did, but I banged myself up in a dozen other ways.

After my mom died, while I was living in California with Mary, my father sold our family house and moved to River Bend. He needed to downsize, he told me then. "Too much crap in the house," I remembered him saying. He asked if I wanted anything, and I told him that my memories were enough.

Now, I wondered what had happened to all his tools. Throughout my childhood my mom, dad and I spent Sunday afternoons at the flea market in Lambertville. My mother collected Lenox china, Boehm porcelain birds, and a host of other knickknacks. I looked through boxes of books, often paperbacks with the covers ripped off that retailed for a dime or a quarter.

My father always had an eye out for tools. He'd walk up to a flea market table full of wrenches, screwdrivers, pliers and other ordinary stuff, and pick out the strange one in the bunch. He'd hold it up and ask the guy behind the table, "What does this do?"

Usually the owner would say something like, "Damned if I know."

"How much do you want for it?" my dad would ask. If the price was right, he'd buy it and add it to his collection. Any time something broke around the house, or I needed my bike adjusted or a toy fixed, my dad had the tool and the skill to handle the repair.

I didn't talk to him much about my criminal case, and I don't think he ever quite understood what the state of California was punishing me for doing. While I was in prison I shut down every emotion, focused only on living day to day, and when the warden notified me that my father had died I don't think I cried at all.

I didn't realize how much I missed my father until I returned to Stewart's Crossing, into the house full of memories. I kept wanting to ask his advice, to watch him fix something. I hunted through the artifacts in the garage, looking for old home movies, hoping I could hear his voice. But he was gone for good.

When we got home, I put a fresh bowl of water in Rochester's crate and tossed in a couple of chew toys. "Come on, boy, time to go into your house," I said, standing by the open door of the crate. "Come here."

Rochester was a pretty well-behaved dog. But he was still only two years old and he had his wild moments, and though he slept in my bedroom at night, and had the run of the house while I was around, I was afraid that if I left him in the house on his own, I'd come home to mayhem and destruction.

He was sprawled on the floor about ten feet from me, his head resting on the tile. "Come on, Rochester, let's go." He ignored me. I walked over and grabbed a handful of fur and flesh between his shoulders—where I'd been told his mother would have gotten hold of him as a pup. He resisted, splaying his paws on the tile floor.

"I'm only going to be gone a little while," I said.

He looked up at me with his big brown eyes, as if to promise he'd be good on his own. "Will you be a good boy?" He thumped his tail a couple of times, and I gave in. "All right. But if you make a mess you're in big trouble."

He rolled on his side and yawned, and I walked out to my car.

My hometown is still compact, with a single traffic light at the corner of Main and Ferry Streets, and a cluster of one- and two-story buildings that date back to the colonial era, when the Stewart family ran a ferry service across the Delaware. I grew up in a suburban neighborhood about a mile south of downtown, and I used to ride my bike into town after school to buy candy at the five and dime, to check books out of the gingerbread Victorian library by the lake, or sit on the banks of the lazy, slow-moving canal and daydream about places that canal could take me, if I only had a mule and a barge.

River Antiques occupied a restored barn that had once served as a way station for mules traveling on the canal, which ran from Easton down to Bristol. It had been a feed store when I was a kid and the countryside around Stewart's Crossing was still peppered with farms. Mark had bought it a few years before, after his grandmother died and left him a houseful of antique furniture and a business opportunity.

I parked at a spot on Ferry Street a block away and walked up to the store. The bell over the door jangled as I walked in, and the door from the back opened. I was surprised that it wasn't Mark Figueroa who appeared, but Owen Keely, my neighbor's son. He was tanned and fit and something about his ramrod-straight posture seemed out of place when surrounded by doilies and delicate statuettes. He wore cargo shorts, sneakers, and a T-shirt that read "Don't Bro Me if You Don't Know Me."

For a moment I worried that I'd interrupted him in the middle of a robbery, but then I stopped myself. "Hi, Owen. I didn't know you worked here."

"Just part time. It's been hard to find something regular."

I nodded. "Yeah, I've been reading about how tough it is for vets to find work after they get out. It's a real shame."

"Especially vets who get screwed up in the service," he said. He leaned on the counter. "I got hooked on crystal meth in the Army, and they kicked me out for it. Went to the VA for a while trying to get rehab but they're swamped. My parents ended up sending me to a private place to get cleaned up." He shrugged. "But people, you know? They just look at the dishonorable discharge and the drugs and stuff, and they don't want to take the chance. There's plenty of vets who don't have my troubles who still can't find jobs."

I didn't know what to say. I felt bad for Owen, but I had no advice to offer, no place I could send him for a job.

"You came to see Mark?" he asked. "He's in the back. He'll be right out."

We both stood there. "So, you're interested in antiques?" I asked.

He shrugged. "Mark's been really good about offering me an opportunity. So I'm learning."

The back door opened again and Mark stepped out. He was overly tall and scarecrow-skinny, a few years younger than Rick and I, with a shock of black hair that stuck out from his forehead. He appeared gangly, but he was deceptively strong, and I'd seen him handle expensive antiques with exceeding care.

"Hey, Steve," he said. "How did your girlfriend like the Regaud photo you bought her?" I'd been in his store a few months before and bought a framed photo of a couple on a rainy Paris street, by a lesser-known French photojournalist.

"She loved it. Turns out Regaud is one of her favorites. You have any others?"

He shook his head. "But they turn up now and then. If I see one I'll keep you in mind."

"I'm going to take off for Mrs. Christiansen's," Owen said. "Striker and I loaded the sofa in the van."

"Thanks, Owen. Call me if you run into any problems."

He nodded and walked out the front door, leaving the bell jangling.

"New employee?" I asked Mark.

"Business is good. With the housing market in the toilet, people are staying put and redecorating. I finally broke down and hired some help. And he's got a friend who can help with the heavy lifting, too, another vet. Lives in North Jersey but comes down this way to hang out with Owen."

"His parents live down the street from me," I said.

"Marie Keely is a good customer," Mark said. "She asked me if I knew anybody who could hire her son and I figured I'd do her a good deed. He's a good guy at heart. Just been through some trouble."

"What's his story?"

"He's a vet. Came home from Afghanistan with a drug problem. His parents sold their house in Crossing Estates to pay for his rehab. Had to downsize and move to River Bend."

Mark's store was a hodgepodge of fifties furniture, rusty farm signs and antique china. Framed posters shared wall space with watercolors of local scenes. I turned to watch Owen back the van out of the driveway, and nearly knocked over a china statue of an Irish setter, and that reminded me of Rochester, home alone and getting into who knew what kind of trouble.

Mark reached over and picked up an ornate figurine of a ballerina on pointe, and rubbed his sleeve on it to wipe away some dust. "What can I do for you?" he asked.

"I have something I want to talk to you about," I said. "If you have a couple minutes?"

"Sure."

I told him about the college's acquisition of the Friar Lake property, and Babson's plans, leaving out the bit about finding a dead body there. "I'm going to need some help with design stuff. You do that kind of thing?"

"I haven't done anything like that for a while, and like I said, the shop is very busy right now."

"Come on, Mark, you're the only person I know who could help me out." I had Joe Capodilupo handling the construction; I really needed someone like Mark to take point on the interior decorating, and if Mark couldn't help me I'd be up a creek.

He pursed his lips together. "What's your timetable?"

"Right now I need some general guidance—I'm pretty lost when it comes to decorating. If you could come out to the property in the next week or two, take a look, and point me in the right direction, I'd really appreciate it."

"From what you've said, this is a big project."

I nodded. "You bet. But most of the interior work is going to happen during the winter. And I'll bet your business slows down when the tourists disappear, right?"

"All right, you've worn me down," he said, smiling. "I'll come out and take a look. I can't commit to anything more than that right now."

"Very cool." We made a plan for him to meet me at Friar Lake on Monday, when the shop was closed. I felt like I owed him something for agreeing to meet with me, so I scanned the shop for something to buy – maybe for Lili? I spotted a collection of antique hair combs in a display case and walked over there. "How much is that one?" I asked, pointing at a fan-shaped comb sprinkled with rhinestones.

Mark grimaced. "You don't want that. It's hideous. If your girlfriend likes Regaud, she'd probably like this one better." He pointed to one in the shape of an Oriental arch. "1920s Art Deco, midnight blue enamel on a sterling silver base. I can let you have it for twenty-five."

"Sold."

I drove back to River Bend, very pleased with the way the afternoon had worked out. Mark hadn't committed to everything I needed, but I had a hook in him, and I thought that once he saw Friar Lake he'd be intrigued by the challenge. And I had a little gift for Lili for the next time I did something dumb. All in all, a very productive time.

When I got home there was a generic sedan parked in my driveway. It belonged to my parole officer, Santiago Santos. He sat in the front seat, his dark-haired head bent over his tablet computer.

9 – A Black Glove

I assumed that Santos's habit of showing up unexpectedly was part of his job; if one of his parolees was misbehaving, a drop-in might catch the ex-criminal in the act. In my case, maybe he hoped to find me sitting at my kitchen table hacking into some database. Fortunately for me, the laptop was completely clean.

Santos was intent on whatever he was doing with the tablet in front of him. Was he looking up my records? Did he have something he was planning to confront me with?

I smiled weakly and waved as I walked past him, and said, "Have to let the dog out. Be with you in a minute." He just nodded.

Rochester was barking like mad and jumping up on his hind legs when I walked in. I hurried to drop Lili's gift on the kitchen table and grab his leash, and then took him out for a quick pee. I kept looking nervously back at Santos's car, worrying about what he might have to say. His visits always set my nerves on edge; I didn't like having my faults examined, and I resented the power he had over me. I'd be delighted when my parole was up at long last and I never had to see him again.

I picked up the evening paper from the driveway and walked back in the house. After I dropped it on the kitchen counter, I looked down at the floor and noticed that Rochester had dug one of my black wool winter gloves out of my closet, and begun gnawing on the fingers. "Bad dog!" I said. "No! No chewing!"

Santos was right behind me. He was about five-seven and stocky, maybe ten years younger than I was. "You're not taking him to work with you anymore?"

I put the frayed glove down on the table beside the comb for Lili. "I had to run an errand in Stewart's Crossing," I said. "Antique shop. Not a place for Rochester."

Santos bent down to scratched behind the big dog's right ear. "How's the boy?" Rochester opened his mouth in a doggie grin and woofed once.

"I know, it's a dog's life," Santos said to him. Then he looked up at me. "How've you been, Steve?"

"All right. Changes going on at work, though."

"We can talk over coffee," he said, and began nosing around in my living room. His ability to snoop in my affairs irritated me. I always had a momentary spike in adrenaline, worrying that I might have carelessly left something around that might incriminate me. But I took a deep breath. I hadn't done anything illegal for a long time and there was nothing he could catch me on. At least, I didn't think so.

Part of our ritual was drinking coffee as we talked over my trials and tribulations, so I walked into the kitchen, pulled forward my cappuccino maker and filled the reservoir with water. Santos was Puerto Rican by birth, and he favored strong espresso in a demitasse cup. I took mine with foamed milk, chocolate syrup and whipped cream. I thought the way we took our coffee said something about our respective world views: his was strong and undiluted, and mine was complicated and needed explanation and sweetening.

I retrieved the bag of ground coffee from the freezer and poured some into the filter basket. I slotted it into the machine and flipped the switch. I opened the container of chicken and rice Lili had made for Rochester and poured some into his bowl.

I thought about how best to present my new job to Santos as he retrieved my laptop from the living room and joined me in the kitchen. Rochester began wolfing down his chow and Santos popped the computer open and turned it on.

"I just got a promotion at Eastern," I said, sitting across from him. "I'm excited, and the new job has real long-term potential."

Santos had installed tracking software on my personal laptop so he could check my activity every visit. He looked up from his log-in. "Great. Not something in computers, I hope."

Even though I knew it shouldn't, his remark rankled. I was a grown man and perfectly able to distinguish between appropriate and inappropriate computer use, though sometimes I didn't follow my own best instincts, and I hated the way he kept flinging my past in my face.

"No more than normal," I said, determined to stay calm. "I'm going to be running a conference center for the college." As I explained to him about Friar Lake, and how Eastern had come to acquire it, he ran the tracking software.

"Doesn't sound like there will be much for you to do before the place opens, though," he said, when I finished. "My *abuela* used to say *cuando el diablo no tiene qué hacer, con el rabo mata moscas.*"

Rochester looked up from his food bowl.

"The devil finds work for idle hands to do," Santos translated.

"My dad used to say that idle hands are the devil's workbench," I said. There was my dad again, popping into my mind. "But there won't be any danger of that. My workbench will be pretty busy. I have to coordinate all the furniture and decorations, and work with the faculty to organize a series of course offerings, so we can launch our programming as soon as the place is ready."

The cappuccino machine began to drip and I got up to fix our beverages. When I was in high school, my parents had taken a tour of Italy, and my mom had brought home a set of demitasse cups. I pulled out one of those cups and poured some of the thick coffee in for Santos. I carried it over to him with a couple of packets of raw sugar, then returned to the counter to assemble my drink.

When I left the California state penal system, I moved in with a bachelor friend in Silicon Valley for a couple of weeks. He had a friend who managed a coffee shop, and I applied for work there as a barista. Unfortunately my criminal record prevented me from getting a job where I'd handle cash. Even though I was a white-collar criminal whose only offense was breaking and entering into computer systems, I couldn't be trusted to work a register.

I did like making coffee, though. The ritual was comforting, and so was the drink, once I had the coffee stirred up with cocoa powder and raspberry syrup. The mug was nearly overflowing by the time I topped it off with whipped cream and chocolate sprinkles.

"How's everything else going?" Santos asked when I returned to the table. He often reminded me that a strong support system was important in keeping his parolees out of trouble, and he worried that I had no close family in the area.

"Still friendly with Rick, still dating Lili." I held up the package with the comb. "Just bought her a present today."

Santos knew Rick Stemper professionally, and he often said he was glad that my best friend was a cop. "Very good," he said. "You know I like the structure of owning a dog. And your girlfriend's a very sharp cookie. But I've worked with you for nearly two years now, Steve, and I don't think I've seen much of an adjustment in your attitude during that time."

He picked up the dainty coffee cup and sipped. "I want you to succeed. Not just while you're under my supervision, but after your parole is up. You've never really copped to the fact that what you did was wrong. Not just against the law, but wrong."

I wanted to argue, but it was true. I still believed that by hacking into those databases, I had been doing what I thought was right for Mary and for our marriage. Yeah, I knew that the law said something else.

"And until you get that idea in here," he said, tapping his head, "you're still in danger of winding up back where you don't want to be. In prison."

He swigged the last of his espresso and shut down my laptop. "Congratulations on the new job," he said. "Just don't screw up your life by letting your ego get ahead of your brains."

"Got it," I said.

I wasn't a real rebellious kid, but I hated it when my parents made blanket statements like that. If they said "don't," it made me want to "do." Especially when it was something my friends were doing. My dad used to say, "If your friends jumped off the Brooklyn Bridge would you want to do that, too?"

I was always tempted to say yes, considering that it wasn't all that easy for a teenager to get to Brooklyn from Stewart's Crossing, so it was a pretty unlikely possibility.

I restrained my smart mouth, though. Santos picked up his tablet, gave Rochester a goodbye scratch, and walked back out to his car.

I locked the front door and turned back to the kitchen, where I spotted my frayed glove. "What's up with the glove, puppy?" I asked him. "It's July. Where did you even get this?"

I truly believed that Rochester had an instinct for crime-solving. Whenever he did something out of the ordinary, I had to stop and wonder if he was trying to send me a message. But a winter glove? What could that mean?

Wait. He had discovered a hand out at Friar Lake. Was he trying to tell me that the body it was attached to had been there since winter? But the Benedictines had still been at the abbey then, and Lili's impression was that the body had been left there in springtime.

"What is it, boy? If the glove doesn't fit, you must acquit? Oh, wait, that's from the O.J. Simpson case. You weren't even born then."

I slipped my hand into the glove and held it, palm up the way the hand had come out of the ground.

Rochester came over to nuzzle me, and licked the leather palm of the glove. It was lighter than the rest of the glove, and for some reason reminded me of the way a black person's palm was often lighter than the surrounding skin.

"Is that it, Rochester? Are you trying to tell me that the hand you found came from a black person?"

He tossed his head up and down a couple of times, which could have meant anything from yes to no to I want to play. He jumped up and put his front paws on the kitchen counter, pushing the newspaper to the floor.

I picked it up, and sat down with it at the kitchen table. I flipped through quickly, until I got to the police blotter column in the local section. A body had been found at the former Abbey of our Lady of the Waters. Leighville police were investigating.

So much for keeping the news of the body from President Babson. I'd have to make an appointment with him the next day to tell him what I knew.

My phone rang as I was thinking about how to phrase that bit of information. I thought the call might be from Santos, having forgotten something—but instead it was Rick Stemper. "Hey, Frank Hardy," he said. "You and your dog want to go for a ride?"

"Sure, brother Joe," I said. "Where are we going?"

"I'll tell you when I get there. Be ready in five minutes." He hung up before I could ask him if he'd heard anything from Tony Rinaldi about the identity of the body at Friar Lake. But I'd certainly ask him when I saw him.

10 – Cruising the Estates

I hooked Rochester onto his leash, and we were sitting on the grass in front of the house when Rick pulled up in his truck. Rascal jumped up and rested his black and white paws on the side rail, and he and Rochester barked at each other.

I unhooked the tailgate, and Rochester jumped up into the truck bed and began tussling with his friend. I secured the gate, then climbed into the front seat next to Rick.

"So?" I asked. "Where are we going?"

"Crossing Estates. I downloaded a list of every address from the property appraiser's website. We're going to look for any houses that look like they fit the pattern for these burglars. Then I can write up a warning to go out from the chief along with some instructions on how to improve their safety."

"Why are you taking me along?"

"I need somebody to write down the information and all the uniformed cops are busy."

I flipped down the visor to avoid the glare of the setting sun. "How come you're not in a squad car if you're on department business?"

"I'm trying not to be too conspicuous," he said. "Just in case the bad guys are out doing the same thing."

"Cool," I said. "I just finished a session with my good buddy Santiago Santos."

"How's that going?"

"I'm getting tired of this constant supervision. It's been almost two years—my parole is up in the fall. By now Santos should have seen that I don't need a nanny."

"You haven't exactly been abiding by the terms of your parole," he said as we pulled out of River Bend and he turned inland. He held up a hand. "I know, I've enabled you a couple of times, asking you to snoop around for me, or ignoring where some of your information has come from."

That was true. Rick was a cop, but a pragmatic one, and he'd accepted information from me in the past that helped bring bad guys to justice, even though I was sure he knew that I didn't get the data legally.

"I'm not kidding myself, and you shouldn't either," Rick said. "You agreed to the terms of your parole when you left prison. You've been able to hide some stuff from Santos in the past, and I haven't said anything to him. But he's no dope. He knows. He also knows he has to catch you doing something to violate you, which is why you're still free."

"You think he does?"

Rick shook his head. "Here's your real problem, Steve. Not your interest in online snooping. This idea that you're the only smart guy in the room. Which is most assuredly not true."

I wanted to protest, but what Rick said was pretty true. There was a steady stream of traffic and our stop-and-go progress irritated me further. I just wanted us to go. Somewhere. I didn't care where.

"I'm not a moron either," I said, thought I knew I was sounding defensive. "I want to take control of my life again, and I don't want to report in to anyone. I told him about the new job at Friar Lake, and all he wanted to do was lecture me."

I shifted in my seat. "Anyway, not to change the subject or anything, but have you spoken to Tony Rinaldi lately? Hear anything from him about the body Rochester found up at Friar Lake?"

He shook his head. "Nope. But it was probably one of the monks."

"I don't think so. Lili thought the body looked to be about three months old, and the monks were gone before that. And you've told me yourself that there are criminals all over the county—grow houses and meth labs and chop shops. He was probably some kind of crook, and his body was dumped there because the property was abandoned."

"Steve, Steve. You're getting yourself worked up over something that's none of your business."

"Since Rochester found the body, I feel some kind of responsibility to find out who it is, and what happened to him or her. If it's murder, then whoever did it deserves to be brought to justice."

"And you don't see the irony in that?"

"I did the crime, and I did the time. That doesn't make me believe in justice any less. And besides, I admit – I'm curious. There's nothing wrong with that."

"Besides the fact that curiosity killed the cat?"

"Yeah, but satisfaction brought him back."

He shook his head, slowed and signaled for the left turn that would take us into Crossing Estates. Two curving fieldstone walls sheltered the entrance to the community.

"A group of residents are starting a petition to close off the property and put up guard gates," Rick said, while we waited for traffic to clear.

Crossing Estates had been built before the mania for gated communities had reached Bucks County. Though there were thick hedges alongside the road, anyone could drive right in.

"That's a big project," I said.

"Yeah. There's already a community association, but it's very loose, and membership isn't mandatory. The pro-gate folks have to push through a zoning change and have the county assess the homeowners for the expense. Going to take some time."

We turned into the main drive. Huge homes with fieldstone exteriors and broad driveways sat on half-acre lots. Landscaping varied from house to house, though it looked like each had come with a maple or an oak in the front yard. Some homes sported flowerbeds, others thick patches of pachysandra around the tree bases. But almost every lawn was lovingly tended, probably by a maintenance company.

"I remember when this was all farmland," I said. "That must be why there are so few older trees here."

"Me too. I remember coming home from State College after I hadn't been out this way in a while. Drove up with my dad, and I was shocked to see all these houses going up." He pulled up just inside the stone entrance and grabbed a clipboard from the back. "Each of the four different models has the same sliding doors at the back -- part of the original design. So each house is a potential target. The trick is to start narrowing down the list."

"How are we going to do that?"

He showed me the form he'd prepared. "We check off these criteria for each house. Do they have an alarm company sign out front? Are there luxury cars in the driveway? As the sun sets we'll be able to tell if someone can see inside the house."

He pointed to the first house ahead of us. "1200 Conway," he said. "See the little sign for ADT? That's one of the big alarm companies. So we check that off on our list."

"Skateboard and bike dumped on the front lawn," I said. "So they have kids, which means the house is less likely to be empty, right?"

"Good call. All the families that have been hit so far either have no kids, older teens, or kids in college."

We checked all the houses on Conway, and then turned onto DeKalb. Number 1500 was a strong prospect—no alarm sign, Mercedes in the driveway and uncurtained windows on the dining room. A glowing chandelier illuminated a china cabinet full of knickknacks, and beyond it, in the living room, we saw a big-screen TV.

I took the notes as we cruised along the curving streets. I was surprised at how many of the houses looked vulnerable. My mother grew up in Trenton, my father in Newark, and they were alert to all kinds of dangers. From a young age I had been taught not to talk to strangers, to accept candy or to get into cars. I noticed the way my mother held her purse close to her body, the way my father seemed extra alert in dark parking lots.

We had a Sunday subscription to the *New York Daily News*, which dedicated its center spread to the crime of the week. I gobbled up the details of knife-wielding robbers, kidnappers, murderers and child molesters. When it was time for me to go to Hebrew School in Trenton, my mother arranged a carpool for me. I remember asking, "How will I know it's safe to get in the car? What if someone kidnaps me?"

"If they steal you by day, they'll bring you back by night," my father said from behind the screen of the evening paper.

"No one's going to kidnap you, Steve," my mother said.

"But last week in the newspaper—"

"Enough," my mother interrupted. "Finish your dinner. I worked all day and I want to get out of the kitchen."

I might have grown up a bit paranoid, but when I finally moved to New York myself, I was already street-savvy, despite having grown up in the 'burbs.

My neighbors in Crossing Estates didn't seem to have that same awareness that crime lurked around every corner. My parents were never burgled, mugged or carjacked, and I don't believe they ever saw a dead body outside of a funeral home. What had happened to me? Was I over-concerned, or were the people in these big houses clueless?

It began to get dark as we approached the intersection of Mifflin and Lincoln, having finished about half the properties on the list. Rick asked, "You know what all these streets have in common?"

"They're all paved?"

"Numb nuts. They're all named for Revolutionary War generals."

"How do you know that?"

He shrugged. "I liked US history in college. Recognized a couple of the names, and so I looked them up."

"Want to teach a class at Eastern? You could connect the American Revolution to *The Hunger Games.*"

"I'll pass," he said. "I have enough to do keeping track of real life."

The dogs started barking in the back of the truck as a white van approached us on the cross street, moving very slowly. As it got closer I recognized it.

"That's Mark Figueroa's van. He hired this son of one of my neighbors to work for him." I leaned forward. "That's strange. He left Mark's store at about three. Wonder why he's still out here this late."

"You'd be surprised how late deliveries come out here," Rick said. "People work all day, and then when they get stuff it needs to be assembled."

"All Owen said before he left Mark's was that he was delivering a sofa," I said, as he drove through the intersection.

"Hold on. Owen? Owen Keely?"

"Yeah, his parents live down the street from me."

Rick turned into a driveway, then backed out and returned the way we'd come. "Owen's a person of interest at the moment," he said. "You remember where he was making his delivery?"

I thought. "I wasn't paying much attention. Sorry."

"No worries." Rick pulled up against the curb and we watched Mark's van move slowly down Conway Street.

"What's going on?" I asked. "Why are you interested in Owen?"

"He's been strange since he got back from Afghanistan," Rick said. "We've had to escort him out of The Drunken Hessian a couple of times because he got loud with the bartender."

The Hessian was one of the oldest bars in Bucks County, in the middle of downtown Stewart's Crossing. Rick and I had spent many hours there together since my return.

"I thought at first he might have lost his license for a DUI," I said. "Because I only see him riding a bicycle."

"Can't be that, or he wouldn't be driving the van. He's probably just too broke to afford a car." Rick stayed at the stop sign and we watched the van continue down Conway.

The van turned right, and Rick eased through the stop sign and followed. As we did, the van exited Crossing Estates, heading out Ferry Road towards town. "I'll have to give Mark a call tomorrow," Rick said. "For now, we should get back to our original plan. We still have Phillips, Schuyler, St. Clair and Spencer to check."

As it got darker it was harder to identify the houses with alarm signs, but easier to see inside. There were an awful lot of plasma TVs, game systems and small electronics in Crossing Estates.

"You want McDonalds before I take you home?" Rick asked. "My treat."

"Thanks for the offer, big spender," I said. "But Rochester's still got an upset stomach, so he's getting boiled chicken and rice for dinner, and if I ate a hamburger in front of him without giving him some he'd never forgive me."

Rick dropped me and Rochester off at home, and I boiled up some fresh chicken and rice, which I mixed in with some of his regular chow. I heated up a TV dinner for myself. We ate together in the kitchen, and then I took him out for his evening walk.

A car was cruising slowly down Sarajevo Court, and my first reaction was to think someone was scoping out houses for burglary. Was that because of my cruise through Crossing Estates with Rick earlier? Or just because of the way my parents had raised me?

The car sped up after it passed us and disappeared around a corner. As Rochester sniffed and peed, I thought about crime and wondered if I could find any information on line about crime in Bucks County. Maybe I could discover something that would help Rick with the spate of robberies he was investigating. Or maybe by figuring out where the crime was around Friar Lake, I could give Tony Rinaldi a clue to the identity of the dead body that had been buried out there.

My heart rate accelerated as I thought about it, and I tugged on Rochester's leash to get him moving back toward home. I felt that same surge of adrenaline I got whenever I contemplated doing snooping online. It was probably what Rick's burglars felt when they found a house to break into, that sweet sense of breaking society's bounds.

I hurried Rochester along. I was probably over-thinking things, as I usually did. From what I'd read in the years since my own incarceration, most criminals did what they did not because they were inherently bad people. They stole, dealt drugs and committed murder because they didn't see other options.

My behavior, I thought, as I unlocked the front door and ushered Rochester inside, was more akin to an addiction. Goosebumps rose on my skin and my pulse accelerated when I thought about hacking. And like many addicts, I thought I could control my behavior and keep myself out of trouble.

In that way, I guessed, I wasn't much different from Mary, the way she used retail therapy to ease her psychic pain over the loss of our unborn children. And probably like Owen Keely, too, who I presumed was using chemicals to wipe out bad memories of the war in Afghanistan.

I got the stepladder from the garage and carried it to the upstairs hallway, where I set it up just under the hatch that led to the attic. I climbed up and popped the lid. There wasn't much up there—a single light bulb, a lot of pink insulation and my next-door-neighbor Caroline's laptop.

I had found the laptop in her house while I was investigating her murder. Santiago Santos didn't know it existed, and if he ever found it I was sure it would be enough to revoke my parole, because I'd installed a suite of hacking tools on it which I kept up to date by visiting certain underground forums I wasn't supposed to know about.

My fingers tingled as they always did when I was getting ready for a stint of cybersnooping. I wasn't sure what I was looking for but I rationalized that anything I did wouldn't be bad because I was on the side of the angels, just trying to help the police.

I considered myself a very moral person, and I only broke the law when I felt it was justified in pursuit of a greater good.

It's a slippery slope, I know.

And sure, I could have left all that investigation to Rick and Tony. They had the badges and the legal access. But where was the fun in that?

11 – Police Blotter

Rochester followed me downstairs, where I opened the laptop up on the kitchen table. While it booted up, I closed the vertical blinds that faced out into the courtyard. No need to announce what I was doing to anyone who happened to drop by.

When I sat back down, Rochester came up to me with a rope in his mouth. "I can't play right now, boy," I said. "Daddy has work to do."

Looking for inspiration, I logged in to a couple of hacker databases. The addresses were always changing; you really had to keep up in order to stay current with all the available tools and places to find them. "Think your neighbors are growing pot in their house but aren't sharing with you?" read one message. "Use this tool to track power consumption in your area. Unusually large spikes in usage = neighbors up to no good!"

Somebody running a grow house near Friar Lake would be a good candidate for dumping a body at the abandoned property. Maybe our victim had been a nosy neighbor, or a power company inspector, or one of the conspirators.

Rochester abandoned the rope and put his paws on my thigh. I had to push him away as I downloaded the tool and followed the instructions to configure it for the area around Friar Lake.

He gave up on play and fetched one of his bones, and began chewing noisily right beside me as I waited while my computer's tentacles searched the net for an open port I could use to launch my hack. You never want to run a hack that can be traced back to your own IP address – your unique connection to the Internet. You want to find somebody who hasn't secured their own gateway so you can drop in and mask your activities with their address.

It's getting harder to do, because it seems everybody has some kind of firewall on their computer to keep out folks like me. But eventually my snooper found an unsecured gateway I could use.

Rochester seemed determined to distract me. He made so much noise with the bone I had to take it away from him, and then he slurped up some water from his bowl and tried to dry his mouth on my khakis.

But nothing the dog could do would keep me from hacking once I set my mind to it. I pushed him away, and he gave up and padded upstairs. Once he was gone, I focused on directing the hacking software to look at the electric company that covered our area.

It was slow, tedious work, but it was the kind of thing I could do with only one part of my brain, leaving the rest free to conjecture other approaches. By the time the software popped up a message that read "downloading consumption data," I'd already come up with another idea.

I found a legitimate website that tracked criminal activity by zip code and plugged in several for areas surrounding Friar Lake. I found two guys who had been arrested for running a chop shop a few miles down the country road that led north from the property. A chop shop is a garage that takes apart stolen cars in order to sell the parts. They had only been arrested a few weeks before, so they'd probably have been in business during the time the victim was killed.

To avoid any connection to Caroline's laptop, I logged into the web interface for my personal email, and sent the information I had found to Tony Rinaldi, with a suggestion that the dead man might be connected to the chop shop. I made sure to include the link to the website where I'd found the information.

Maybe it was overkill – but my paranoia kicked in again. I knew that having the extra laptop in my possession could be enough to violate my parole. Add in the hacking software, and I'd be back in prison before you could say Travelocity. So I was determined to be like Caesar's wife, avoiding even the appearance of impropriety.

By then the power results had been downloaded, and I disconnected the hacking software, the connection to the open port, and the sniffers from my – or Caroline's – laptop. My fingers were clammy, and I felt an empty spot at the back of my throat. By then, my feelings of paranoia had been trumped by reality. If I could be traced to any of the hacks I'd committed, I'd face another trial and another sentence.

Why did I keep doing it? I couldn't answer that question, and I did my best to ignore it. In one compartment of my brain I rationalized my activities; after all, I was trying to solve a crime, to bring justice to the world. In another part I made excuses – there was some chemical lacking in my brain that made me crave this kind of stimulation. It wasn't my fault at all – just a biological defect. I shut down any other options before they could form.

I opened the spreadsheet file that had been created through the hack into the power company. At first, I was baffled – how was I going to figure anything out? Then I noticed a button that laid the data over a map, with color-coded results.

The hotter the red color, the more power that was being consumed in that area. I zeroed in on a property that backed on Tohickon Creek. The map view showed a single suburban house there, but the power use was bright red. I did some cross-referencing and discovered that the consumption still wasn't high enough to flag the property.

I was still suspicious, so I went to Google maps and zoomed in on the property. A large boathouse stood on stilts over the creek behind the house. Thermal imaging for the area showed that boathouse was bright red, too—meaning there was a lot of heat being generated there.

I was pretty sure there were generators back there, and they were being used to mask some of the power consumption, keeping it below the electric company's radar. Maybe the farmers had even figured out how to harness some of the water from the creek.

It was getting late, and Rochester was antsy for his bedtime walk. I already had Tony Rinaldi's official email address, but I thought it was better to camouflage my tracks whenever I could. So I checked the website for the Leighville Police Department and found an address ordinary citizens could use to ask questions or report crimes.

I logged into an email account I had set up years before with an anonymous remailer. I knew that the remailer computer would strip away the (fake) name and address I had used to set up the account, and replace it with a dummy address. If Tony, or whoever got the message at the Leighville PD, wanted to reply to me, he could, because the remailer would forward the message to me. But no one could connect the email to me.

I wrote a note pretending to be a neighbor of the property, and bundled up the power consumption data for the house by the creek. I attached it to the message. Just in case the police computer wouldn't allow the attachment of files to emails, I summarized the information in a couple of sentences. Then I clicked "send."

By then, I was exhausted. The initial adrenaline surge had run through my body, and the mental focus I had put into hacking, and then reading the power consumption results, had wiped me out. It was too late to check in with Lili, and I didn't have the energy to speak to her either.

I forced myself to stand up, stretch, and put away Caroline's laptop. Then I went downstairs for Rochester's leash. He followed me eagerly, scampering around as I tried to hook him up. I gave up and collapsed on the couch, which convinced him to calm down enough to let me clip on the leash. He dragged me out the front door and down the street.

The skies were overcast and there was no one else out on Sarajevo Court that late. I let Rochester drag me along until he was ready to go home, and once back in the house, I stripped down and fell into bed. I was asleep almost immediately.

The next morning Rochester hopped up onto the bottom of my bed and sat on his haunches, staring at me as I roused. When he saw that I was awake, he pounced. I ducked my head beneath the comforter but he wasn't fooled. He sniffed around, pawing at me, until I emerged. Then he lavished me with puppy kisses. It was our regular morning love fest, and I wrestled him down onto his back so I could rub his belly.

He flailed his legs around like a dying cockroach and turned his head to face me. I marveled once again how his nose was like a baboon's, black and moist, and the way the black of his muzzle faded into golden so quickly. I had slept off my energy drain of the night before, so I hopped up, pulled on a tank top and a pair of shorts, stepped into my Crocs, and wrangled Rochester onto his leash. I was pleased that he seemed to be feeling better.

We walked through the center of River Bend, past the twin lakes. As we were circling back home, Owen Keely's mother Marie approached us on her three-wheeled bicycle.

She was a slim blonde in her early sixties, but she'd had a stroke a year before and was still recovering. She'd gotten the bike, with one front wheel and two in back, for exercise, and now she often rode around, waving and smiling at everyone. She had a big basket in the back of the bike, with a bumper sticker that read "I Brake for Yard Sales."

"Such a beautiful dog," she said, pulling up beside us. She reached her hand out to him, and he bounded up to her. I remembered his reluctance to sniff her son and wondered about that. Did he have some drug-addict scent that Rochester had reacted to?

"How are you this morning?" I asked her.

"I'm here for another day," she said cheerfully.

What a contrast she was to her son, I thought. Owen must take after her husband; Phil had never been that friendly, either. He was a retired Marine, and Corps logos and stickers decorated his SUV and his garage. He often wore Marine T-shirts, and even had a license plate frame on his car that read *Semper Fi*. Seeing it always tempted me to look for one that read *Semper Fido*.

"I saw Owen at River Antiques yesterday," I said. "How's he settling in?"

She sighed. "You don't have children, do you, Steve?"

I shook my head. "Didn't work out that way."

She scratched Rochester behind his ears, and he opened his mouth in a big doggy grin. "Owen was such a sunny child, but the Army changed all that. When he came back he was like a different boy. And then of course we found out about the drugs. It's been a real battle. But that Mark Figueroa is such a nice boy. I think he'll be a good influence on Owen."

"I hope so too," I said.

She put her feet back on the pedals and waved a cheerful goodbye. "Have a lovely day!" She continued past, wobbling a bit from side to side. Rochester tried to chase her but I reined him in.

Rochester and I made our way home, and then I drove up to the Eastern campus, with the big goof riding shotgun and his head out the window. He seemed to have recovered, but I was going to keep on mixing the chicken and rice with his food for a day or two and make sure that he finished all the pills Dr. Horz had prescribed.

I spent the morning cleaning up my files, deciding what I could trash and what I ought to send over to Ruta del Camion at the News Bureau. My only big projects were a couple of fund-raising events over the next few weeks, and I put together a report with everything I'd done, including all my press contacts.

Using the college's online email and calendar program, I scheduled a meeting with Ruta, so I could explain what I was giving her. Most of my materials were digital, and I zipped them up and then emailed the lot to Ruta. The paper files went into a cardboard box, which I'd carry over when I met with her.

Within a couple of minutes after I'd sent the meeting request, Ruta called me. "Hey Steve," she said. "I just got a weird call from a reporter. He said that he understood a dead body had been found on Eastern property. I told him I had no idea what he was talking about. You hear anything?"

"Not on the campus," I said. "Out at Friar Lake. Do you know about Babson's plans for a conference center out there?"

"Just the outline. You know about this body?"

"I found it," I said. "Or to be more specific, my dog did." I explained to her what I knew. "I don't know if the police have identified the body yet."

"So it's a big no comment from us," Ruta said. "If you hear anything, will you let me know?"

"Sure thing, Ruta." When I hung up, I looked back at my computer. What was I supposed to do for the next year? I'd already met with Joe Capodilupo and with Mark Figueroa. The missing piece seemed to be the kind of programming I would be running out at Friar Lake.

Babson had given me a free hand in developing the slate, but I was sure he'd have a lot of input as I began to come up with program ideas. I figured the first thing I could do was remind myself what kind of research and scholarship we had going on at Eastern, so I could investigate building programs based on that.

I had a boss once who said that he liked to practice MBWA – management by walking around. He'd stroll past our cubicles, checking in on us, getting involved in conversations and decisions. It might have worked for him; I preferred to practice MBWR – management by walking Rochester.

"Want to go for a walk, puppy?" I asked.

He jumped up and nodded his head in agreement. Or maybe he nodded because he liked going for walks.

We went down the hill behind Fields Hall, where Rochester could romp among the pine trees and be admired by fawning students. I liked the slower pace of the campus during the summer. Most students were only taking one or two classes, and there were a lot of pick-up Frisbee games on the lawns that Rochester could join. Girls sunbathed in skimpy bikinis while boys pretended to read in the shade. There was always the faint sound of music coming from somewhere.

Though I looked for inspiration everywhere, I couldn't find any. I returned to my office, feeling glum, but perked up as soon as I walked into my office and saw Lili at my computer, typing like a fiend. "Hey, sweetie. What's up?"

"Give me a minute to finish this email and then I'll tell you all about it."

With Lili monopolizing my desk and computer I wasn't sure what to do. So I opened the glass jar full of tiny imitation T-bone steaks and Rochester's head popped up like a puppet on a string. I figured he was feeling well enough to manage a treat or two. I sat down on the floor next to him, fed him the treat, and scratched behind his ears.

As I watched Lili type, I felt a bit grumpy. She could do anything online she wanted, without worrying about a parole officer lurking in the bushes, and I couldn't. But then my inner adult piped up and reminded me how I'd gotten myself in trouble, and that it was my own fault I had those restrictions.

"Sorry," Lili said, turning toward me. "I wanted to come right over and tell you but you weren't here and I figured I might as well send some emails and get things rolling."

"Are you speaking English? Because I'm not following."

"I thought President Babson spoke to you."

"You mean Monday? About Friar Lake? But what does that have to do with you?"

"You didn't talk to him this morning?"

"No."

She pushed a couple of stray tendrils of auburn hair away from her face. "He called this morning and asked me to come over to his office. I had no idea what he wanted, but you know him, he's always full of surprises. He told me he wants me to put together a coffee-table book about the history of the Friar Lake property. He thinks he can sell copies to alumni as a fund-raiser."

"Why you?"

"The pictures, of course. He asked if I'd be willing to not only take current shots, but dig into some archives and pull out older ones as well. I'm interested in the process of restoring old photographs anyway, and how we can apply new technologies to the process. You know that article I've been working on."

I nodded. Lili was a good writer, but sometimes her prose got too academic and convoluted, and she brought things to me for clarification.

"Where are you going to fit this in?" I asked as I stood up. Lili was already running the fine arts department, teaching, taking photos of her own, working with the College Connection kids, and working on academic articles. I didn't want her getting so busy that she'd squeeze me and Rochester out.

"The fall schedule is already set, and the department only has a half-dozen courses running in the summer term. Matilda could run that department without me."

Matilda was her secretary, a formidable Filipina who shared Imelda Marcos's taste in shoes—though on a much lower budget.

"Babson offered me another release time for the fall to work on this. Teaching my seminar for The College Connection will only take a few hours. And we'll get the benefit of working together."

I was still having trouble following her logic. "How's that?"

"You'll have to write the text for the book, of course. Babson was clear about that. This is my project, but he knows what a great writer you are."

I could just imagine Babson laying on the blather. I knew a lot of couples whose relationships had fallen apart when they spent too much time together, and I was afraid of what Lili would think when she saw how little I knew about construction and running a conference center, but I didn't want to say anything and spoil her excitement.

"Just think, we'll be able to spend the rest of the summer together." She came over to me, and stepped up on her toes to kiss me. At five-ten she's tall for a woman, but still a couple of inches shorter than I am. Her lips tasted like strawberries. "Won't that be fun?"

"Yeah, fun," I said.

"We'll have to do some research." She sat back down at my computer. "I've already done some quick searching for archival information on Benedictine properties. We may even be able to squeeze in a road trip."

"I'll look forward to it."

"You hear anything more about that poor man whose body we found?" Lili asked. "Was he a monk or a friar?"

"No idea. Haven't heard anything from Rick or from Tony Rinaldi."

"I hope they're able to get him reburied quickly. That's so sad, the way his body was rising up out of his grave."

"Sad, or symbolic," I said. "Even more so if it was Easter." I opened my mouth wide. "But this is Eastern College. What if we witnessed the start of the second coming?"

"Go back to work, goofball." She kissed me goodbye and she left.

Her mention of the dead body reminded me of the email I'd sent anonymously to the Leighville Police Department the night before. I was curious to know if he'd learned anything more about the body's identity, and if the information I found had been helpful. But calling him up to ask would defeat the purpose of the anonymous address, and open a whole new set of problems for me. Instead I tamped down my curiosity and tried to focus on programming for Friar Lake.

I couldn't focus, though. I kept thinking about the dead guy. Could I casually call Tony? It had been two days, after all. Would he have the autopsy results? I picked up the phone to call him, then put it down again. If the information I'd found had been useful, he'd probably be too busy arresting people to talk to me.

I picked up Rochester's leash and he jumped up from the floor. Maybe some fresh air would lead to fresh ideas. As we walked around the back of Fields Hall, I remembered my previous work career, as a technical writer and web developer. What would have drawn me back to Eastern for some kind of executive learning course?

As a tech writer, I had to know the basics of how everything worked at the company, because I had to write the instruction manuals. I'd taken a workshop on inventory management (a big snooze) and one on logistics and transportation (an even bigger snooze.) I'd also been sent for seminars to learn new software as we incorporated it.

There was no way we could compete with the big business schools, though. Our faculty didn't have the depth or breadth or real world experience. I decided that I needed some input from someone on the faculty. The problem was that even though I'd been back at Eastern for a little over a year, I didn't know that many professors.

The only professor I felt completely comfortable with was Lucas Roosevelt. He was one of my favorites when I was an undergraduate, and when I returned to Eastern I was stunned to realize he was only about five years older than I was, and had become the department chair.

Lucas (he was always quick to point out that he was not related to <u>those</u> Roosevelts, as his family name had been Rostnikov prior to arriving on Ellis Island) was willing to give me a chance as an adjunct, and we had shared shots of Cuban rum smuggled in from Canada for him by a grateful student to celebrate. I called his office in Blair Hall and found that he was free. Well, that would give me a start.

12 – Tug of War

Rochester was sleeping on his back, his rear paws extended and stretching the skin of his belly so taut he reminded me of a skinned rabbit hung up to dry outside a hillbilly's house. I snuck out without waking him.

Eastern's campus, usually so busy, was dreaming sleepily in the summer heat. A pair of girls had spread a beach towel on the sunny lawn in front of Fields Hall. Wearing bikinis and oversized sunglasses, they were both reading—one a big art history textbook, the other a paperback edition of *The Great Gatsby*.

A cluster of students lounged on the grass beneath a towering maple, each of them intently reading—a mix of textbooks, novels, a Kindle, and a couple of iPads. I remembered my own days as an undergrad. I'd relaxed under that same tree with my own friends, and an assortment of books – all paper, of course—for classes from English literature to introduction to economic theory.

There were more students reading on the stone steps of Blair Hall, which housed the English department. It had undergone an unfortunate makeover in the sixties, and a lot of the character you could see in old photographs had been stripped out—the wood moldings, the stone finials—and replaced with fluorescent lights and linoleum floors.

Candice ("Don't call me Candy") Kane, the English department secretary, was away from her desk, though I could see that the spider plants she cultivated were still going strong. Lucas's door was open, and I stuck my head in.

"My dear boy, how good to see you!" Lucas boomed. He was a tall, lanky man, with somewhat of a resemblance to Abraham Lincoln in his rail-splitter days, though with no beard or stovepipe hat.

Because I was a former student, I was always going to be a boy to him, despite how close we were in age. "Have a minute?" I asked. "I need to do some brainstorming."

"My brain is always available," he said, motioning me to a seat across from him. "Doesn't get enough of a workout these days, but can't complain. What can I help you with?"

I sketched out the broad outline of the Friar Lake project. "I was walking outside, and I passed a whole group of students lounging on the lawn reading. About half were holding physical books and the other half e-readers or tablet computers."

Lucas shook his head. "I can barely remember those days, when I had the whole summer off to read."

"That's what I was thinking," I said. "And I remembered my senior seminars, a half dozen or so of us sitting around talking about books. One of those was with you."

I vividly remembered Lucas in front of our seminar group. He could recite whole passages of the middle English of Geoffrey Chaucer, quote from T.S. Eliot's "The Wasteland," declaim sonnets and gesture to Shakespearean dialogue. He made those works come alive in front of us, while challenging us to analyze, think, paraphrase and examine.

"I thought we could recreate the seminar experience," I continued. "Small groups of alumni and other intellectually curious adults, focused on a single topic, over a long weekend."

Like many of the friends and classmates I kept in touch with, I missed the intellectual stimulus of the academic environment, and I regretted the gaps in my education. There were whole disciplines I'd never studied, from sociology to astrophysics, and hundreds of authors and books I wanted to read but lacked the time or the motivation.

I knew accountants who belonged to book groups, doctors who collected art, business people who loved to travel. If I could replicate the Eastern experience in a few intense days, I thought I might have a chance at succeeding.

"What do you think, Lucas?" I asked. "Is it possible to create that same feeling students have?"

"If we can't, then we don't deserve to be called professors," he said. "Suppose we took some of the content of one of those seminars and narrowed it down? Instead of a whole semester on modern American novels, we focused on one author— Hemingway, for example."

I nodded. "But they can't spend the whole weekend reading. We'd have to mix things up. We could have them read *The Sun Also Rises* before they arrive. Then we could show that Woody Allen movie, *Midnight in Paris*. And add some videos of the running of the bulls in Pamplona. Throw in some Spanish wine and tapas."

"I think we're on to something here," he agreed. "We talk about Hemingway's notion of masculinity, provide some examples of how he prefigured some of the more modern writers like Raymond Carver. Very doable in a long weekend."

"I'd sign up myself," I said. "Can I put some ideas together and then bring them back to you? You could help me find the right faculty."

"I'd be delighted. Count me in for the Hemingway seminar."

I stood up. "Thanks, Lucas. I feel like I have a direction now."

When I got back to my office, Tony Rinaldi was sitting on the floor playing tug-of-war with Rochester. I was a bit disconcerted to see him. There was no way he could have tracked that email back to me, but he could be guessing. Guesses, though, were not enough to violate my parole.

"Don't get up on my account," I said, as I walked in.

Tony looked embarrassed. He stood anyway, brushing some of Rochester's long golden hairs from his black slacks.

"What can I do for you?" I sat down behind my desk, and he sat across from me.

"Got a little problem."

"I don't like the sound of that." I expected him to mention the anonymous emails but he had something different in mind.

"Neither does the chief of police. Turns out that guy whose body you found? The ME figured out that he was African-American. Called the Benedictines, and discovered they had no black monks or friars living out there."

"I thought he was black," I said. "Or at least Rochester did."

"How did he know? He have a different bark depending on the race of the victim?"

"He got a black winter glove from my bedroom and started chewing it," I said. "You know, black glove, black hand."

Tony raised his eyebrows. "You have some crazy ideas about that dog, Steve." He paused. "Anyway, because of the position of the hand that was still underground—it was underneath him, so it was protected by his clothes – there was enough skin that the ME could pull off some prints."

"Find a match?"

"Yup. His name is DeAndre Dawson and he has a criminal record that would stretch from here all the way back to New York City, where he was last known to reside."

"Then how did he end up dead at Friar Lake?" I asked.

"That's what I need your help to figure out."

"What can I do? I told you I just got this job two days ago. I don't know anything about the property."

"Right now DeAndre is residing at the medical examiner's office, lined up for his turn on the autopsy table. That'll tell me what the cause of death was. But while I'm waiting for those results, I want to figure out what DeAndre was doing down here." He leaned back in his chair. "I made a couple of calls to New York, and spoke to his parole officer. He said that DeAndre used to hang out at a drop-in center on the Lower East Side called The Brotherhood Center."

"And?"

"And the center's run by a couple of Franciscan friars."

"Any connection to Friar Lake?"

"I don't know as yet." He took a deep breath. "I hate to drag a civilian into a murder case, but we're stretched thin in our department as it is, and I have nothing to base a warrant on, and places like that have an innate distrust of the cops."

I was surprised. Tony Rinaldi was actually going to ask me for help? That was a big turnaround in his attitude.

"You have a way of getting people to talk to you." He held up his hand. "I know you say it's all the dog. But you've been able to find out information from people who wouldn't talk to the police in the past. I was hoping I could convince you to go up there and talk to people. You're from the college, you discovered the body, you just want to talk to people, satisfy your curiosity." He grinned. "You have a lot of that."

I was curious, but I was reluctant, too. When I was a kid, my mother had cousins in Brooklyn, and every now and then when we'd go visit them we'd stop on the Lower East Side to pick up authentic New York bagels or pastrami or other Jewish delicacies that were hard to come by in the wilds of suburban (read goyish) Pennsylvania.

Then Tor and I had lived on the Lower East Side years before, right after we both graduated from Columbia, and it had been a pretty marginal neighborhood. I felt I was lucky never to have been mugged or burgled. After years in the suburbs, was I too soft to face tough areas? I had no desire to revisit the Bowery or Needle Park. I had enough panic in my life as it was.

"I don't know, Tony. Tough neighborhoods are out of my wheelhouse."

"Please? Take the dog if you want. He'll protect you." He smiled again. "Talk to the monks, see if there's any connection to Friar Lake. If they have any idea what DeAndre was doing down here."

Rochester got up from his place by the French doors and came over to me.

"See, the dog wants you to go," Tony said.

"When do you need this information?"

"Depends. How soon do you think you could get up to New York?"

"I'll have to check with President Babson. If he's willing to give me some time to look into this for you, I could probably go up there tomorrow."

"That would be great. I'll email you the details I have about the drop-in center." He reached over and scratched behind Rochester's ears. "You see what you can do to help out, boy."

Rochester woofed in agreement.

"Any other irons in the fire?" I asked casually.

"I looked into that email you sent," he said, and for a moment I forgot that I'd sent two messages – one legit and one cloaked. "About the chop shops."

"Yeah?"

"Went out there this morning. The place was completely shut down. Doesn't mean there isn't a connection, but it'll take some time to track where those guys went."

"It was a try," I said.

He nodded, then looked at me. "You know anything about grow houses?"

My heart skipped a beat but I stayed cool. "What do you mean?"

"Somebody sent us an anonymous tip about a potential grow house out on Tinicum Creek," he said. "I passed it on to the state police, and they made a big bust out there this morning."

"Wow."

He stood up. "Yeah. Gave me some good cred with the state guys. And always nice to knock a couple of crooks out of town. Wish I could thank whoever sent in the tip, but like I said, it was anonymous."

"Probably a neighbor," I said. "Or a rival."

"You never know with anonymous tips," he said. "Let me know if you go up to New York and what you find out."

"I will."

I checked with Babson's secretary. He was in a meeting, she said; she could squeeze me in to see him at four. I sent an email to Ruta del Camion, telling her that the dead body at Friar Lake had been identified, but there was still no indication of a connection to Eastern.

Then I did some basic Googling on DeAndre Dawson. Nothing that Santiago Santos would object to—just checking public records to find the dates of his incarceration. I was well aware that such information was readily available online; I'd found my own records online as soon as I had access to a computer after leaving the California penal system.

I began with the New York state criminal records system. Everyone who had ever been in the system since the 1970s was listed there, except youthful offenders (who were governed by different statutes) and a few other categories.

DeAndre's record began with his name, sex, race and birth date. Since he was born in March 1990, he had celebrated his twenty-second birthday a few days before his death.

He had been arrested and convicted in New York County of two class D felonies, assault and attempted robbery. I knew that assault meant committing physical harm to another person, and that robbery meant taking money or goods from another person using force. He had served two years at Sing Sing and then been paroled in early January.

I figured Tony already had this information, but it was useful for me if I was going to New York to talk to people about him. I kept surfing around, looking for information on DeAndre. There wasn't much. I found a few addresses and phone numbers, all on the Lower East Side, with no indication as to which was the most recent. I wrote them all down, on the off chance that talking to someone at one of those locations might turn up a clue.

At four I walked down to Babson's office. I had been rehearsing what I wanted to tell him; I didn't want the dead body to be a big deal, but I needed some time to help Tony. As soon as he waved me into his office I jumped in. "Do you remember Sergeant Rinaldi from the Leighville Police? He was up here a lot this winter after Joe Dagorian was murdered."

"Of course. Very sad time." He eyed me appraisingly. "Nothing happened here on campus, I hope."

"Not here. Out at Friar Lake. A dead body was discovered out there on Monday."

I deliberately used the passive voice so I didn't have to state that I was the one – accompanied by my dog – who had found the body.

"That's terrible," he said. "Why did he come to you, and not directly to me?"

"Probably didn't want to bother you." I thought I might need to embroider a bit, to distract Babson from his usual curiosity and need to micro-manage everything, but I wanted to be careful not to say anything that wasn't true. I recapped the situation quickly, and then said, "Sergeant Rinaldi spoke to the Benedictines, and he discovered that they had sold the property to Eastern. Since he and I worked together quite a lot during the winter, he thought I'd be a good place to start asking questions."

"Has he discovered who it is? One of the monks or friars? Not a student, I hope."

"A drug addict from New York named DeAndre Dawson. Apparently he was there after the monks had already left, so Sergeant Rinaldi wondered if he had a connection to the College."

"Check with Dot Sneiss. She can look at our student records."

"I will. He also asked if I can help him do some research. I thought it would be a good chance for me to stay involved, and maybe deflect any bad publicity that might come up. I know how important this project is to you."

"Good idea. I've always thought you had excellent instincts," Babson said. "But I want you to keep me in the loop, all right? If there's any way this could disturb our plans, I need to know as soon as possible."

"Will do."

I walked back to my office, pleased at the way I had been able to massage the situation. That was PR, after all. Putting the right spin on any news.

I called Tony and let him know that I was going to New York the next day. "The guy in charge of The Brotherhood Center is Brother Macarius," he said. "I'll give him a call and let him know you're coming up."

"I thought you wanted me to talk to people instead of sending a cop."

"I want this Brother to know what's going on. You don't have to tell anybody else you're working for me. Be honest with people but don't be specific."

I hung up and went online to see what I could find about The Brotherhood Center. It had a single webpage, with lots of color and pithy sayings. It served a diverse population of homeless men and women, veterans, and recovering drug addicts. A soup kitchen offered a hot lunch seven days a week and a counselor was available to talk and help navigate bureaucracy.

That was about all I could find from a casual search. I looked at the clock, and it was close enough to five that I thought I could call it a day.

I called Lili to check about dinner. She was too caught up in researching Friar Lake, she said. I told her I was going to New York the next day, thinking she might want to come along—but she told me she was too busy, though she wished she could.

That night, I kept thinking about DeAndre Dawson. There had to be something online that could give me an idea of who he was. Was he a New York native? Where had he gone to school?

Online restrictions are so pesky when it comes to kids, though. I understood the need to keep information away from predators—but I wasn't looking for some kid to molest. I was interested in what kind of childhood had led DeAndre Dawson to end up dead at Friar Lake.

I retrieved Caroline's laptop once again. I ran the anonymizer software that protected my identity online, and then started to surf. The New York City Public Schools website was very well-secured, but I managed to sneak in and check out DeAndre's records. He had attended P.S. 110, Florence Nightingale School, on Delancey Street, until fifth grade. I couldn't find any record of discipline problems.

He transferred to Middle School 131 on Hester Street, and that's when the problems started. He was often tardy or badly behaved, and he was regularly suspended. He finished eighth grade there, and then went on to Emma Lazarus High School on Hester Street.

I stopped for a minute to reminisce, because so many of these names were evocative of my own childhood. I studied Emma Lazarus in both public school—where we had to memorize her inscription on the Statue of Liberty—and Sunday School, where she was hailed as one of the earliest American Jewish heroines. I had fond memories of the area when I was a kid, and even a couple from when Tor and I lived there.

But Memory Lane was a detour, and I refocused on DeAndre. He had dropped out of high school after ninth grade. Was that because he was already in juvenile hall? Or had he gotten tired of the discipline and routine?

I went back to public records for his birth date and found that the only parent listed on his birth certificate was his mother, Rashida Dawson. I did a quick search on her and found that she had died of a drug overdose in 2004.

Well, that explained DeAndre's dropping out of school. I almost hoped he had been in juvenile detention for a while; at least then he would have had a relatively safe place to sleep and three meals a day.

I was sure that DeAndre had a juvenile court record so that database was my next step. But it was a lot harder to hack into those records. I thought I'd gotten in, after an hour of trying, when suddenly a big red X popped up on my screen with the words ILLEGAL ACCESS. I shuddered and my hands jumped off the keyboard. I quickly closed the browser and all the windows I had open, and shut the laptop off.

It took a couple of minutes for my pulse rate to get back to normal. It was interesting that it was easier to break into the school system and learn about innocent (or mostly innocent) kids than it was to learn about their criminal counterparts.

By then it was almost eleven o'clock, and time for Rochester's last walk of the day. I stood up from the computer and stretched; my back ached from leaning over it without stop for so long. Rochester jumped up and began his demented kangaroo routine, and I hooked up his leash and took him out. The last thing I did before bed was wipe Caroline's laptop clean, except for the hacking software, and climb back up to the attic to hide it away.

13 – Brother Macarius

I don't usually drive into New York; it's easy to head over to Trenton and catch the train, and I can read or otherwise multi-task. The train would have been a good time to keep reading *The Hunger Games*—I really wanted to finish all three books before I started putting together a seminar program.

But Tony had specifically asked me to take Rochester, so the next morning I bundled him into the car. He seemed to have recovered completely from whatever had been bothering him, and he stuck his head out the window as I drove up the River Road to the industrial town of Easton, where we hopped onto the I-78 for a straight shot across Jersey.

Rochester didn't like the Holland Tunnel. Too claustrophobic for him, I guess. He pulled back from the window as we drove and settled his head on my lap and I petted his fur with one hand. Once we were back above ground, though, he scrambled back to the window, absorbing all the smells and sights and sounds of Canal Street, the Bowery and Houston Street.

He had never been to the city before, and he was excited. A couple of times I worried that he might try and jump out the window to track down a hot dog cart or the smell of dim sum wafting through the open door of a Chinese restaurant.

I lucked into a street parking space a few blocks from The Brotherhood Center. I put Rochester's leash on and let him out, and he went right to the single spindly plane tree and lifted his leg. I could imagine he was proclaiming, "Rochester is here!" Or else he just had to pee after the long trip.

We walked together down the sidewalk, skirting bags of trash and open metal doors that led to basements. Rochester nosed his way down, sniffing everything, and I had to rein him in a few times.

The Brotherhood Center was an unassuming storefront sandwiched between a launderette and a locksmith. The glass windows were protected by roll-up grills, and had been painted with Christian symbols and inspirational quotes. "If it's meant to be, it's up to me," read one that I particularly agreed with.

The door was open, so I walked in, tugging Rochester along. A strapping black guy with a shaved head was sitting behind a desk, and I asked, "Okay if I bring the dog in? He'll behave."

"Everyone's welcome here," he said, standing up. "I'm Brother Macarius."

He wasn't what I'd expected of a religious brother; he looked like he'd be more at home in a wrestling ring if he wasn't wearing a plain brown robe with a cowl neck, full sleeves and a hood on the back. When he stood I saw he had a single white cord wrapped around his waist in lieu of a belt.

I introduced myself. "Tony Rinaldi suggested you might be able to help me learn some more about DeAndre Dawson."

He shook his head. "DeAndre was a difficult case. Come, sit in the back with me. We'll have some tea and we'll talk. I may even have a biscuit there for your friend."

"This is Rochester."

Macarius bent down and scratched behind Rochester's ears, and he smiled a doggy grin. As they got to know each other I looked around.

On one side, an earnest-looking young guy behind a scarred desk was counseling a middle-aged woman wearing layers of grimy T-shirts and sweaters and skirts over a pair of worn sweatpants. Across from them, three young black men clustered around a TV set and a game system. I could hear the gunshots and panicked screams from the soundtrack.

The walls were decorated with the same mix of Christian material and inspirational posters. A crucifix was centered on the back wall. I recognized images of Saint Sebastian, pierced with arrows; the Virgin Mary; and the Pieta.

"Interesting name, Macarius," I said, as he led me to a cozy room at the back, furnished with a couple of oversized sofas and a squat black machine that dispensed hot or cold water. "Was he a saint?"

"I took the name when I became a friar," he said. "Saint Macarius was a smuggler who turned monastic. Seemed to fit me. I did five years in Attica for possession with intent to sell."

"I did a year in California for computer fraud," I said. "Didn't make me into a monk, but it did change me." I sat on one of the sofas and Rochester settled on the floor beside me.

"Time inside does that," he said, as he pulled two mugs out of a cupboard. "Sometimes for good, sometimes for bad." He turned to me. "Green tea or oolong?"

"Oolong. No sugar or milk."

"Wise man. Take care of your body and it will take care of you."

He stuck each mug in turn under the spigot, and curls of steam arose. While the tea steeped he rummaged in the cabinet again and came up with a dog biscuit. Rochester jumped up, grabbed it from him, and then returned to chew on it next to me.

Macarius pulled the tea bags out of the mugs and handed me the one with the darker liquid. I lifted it to my nose and smelled the rich tea.

"You're not a policeman," Macarius said, sitting across from me. "So why are you doing the investigating?"

I shrugged. "I'm not quite sure myself. Rochester and I have helped Tony out before, and he seems to think people are more willing to talk when there's a dog around."

Macarius nodded. "I'm glad someone is looking into what happened to DeAndre. All too often we accept the deaths of young black males as part of our culture. As if their violent deaths are foretold at their birth, simply because of their skin color."

"Tell me about DeAndre," I said.

"What do you want to know? What he was arrested for? Where he served his time?"

I shook my head. "Tony can find all that out from official channels." I paused, thinking about what I wanted to say. "The college where I work recently bought this property from the Benedictines. We call it Friar Lake. I was assigned to manage it, and Rochester and my girlfriend and I were out there walking around when he discovered DeAndre's body."

"Where on the property?" he asked. "One of the friars who works here is elderly, and I've driven him out there to recuperate a few times from illnesses."

"A few hundred yards from the house down by the lake," I said. "Someone had buried him in a shallow grave down by the lake front. We had a lot of rain recently, and DeAndre's hand had come up out of the earth."

The ends of Macarius's mouth turned down, either in sadness or in anger – I couldn't tell which. I remembered that he had known DeAndre, and I was sure that the news of the young man's death had hit him harder than it had those of us in Stewart's Crossing who didn't know him.

"But that area is nowhere near the cemetery on the grounds," he said. "Why was he down there?"

"I have no idea. We thought that the body belonged to one of the monks. We had the same question about why his body wasn't in the cemetery. I called the police to report the body, and Tony is the one who tracked down DeAndre's identity."

Macarius sipped his tea, and I did the same. I thought about DeAndre Dawson, who had spent time in this place, probably happily – maybe playing that video game out front, or talking to the monks. I felt closer to him there, somehow, than I had in the presence of his remains.

In the quiet we could hear Rochester crunching his treat. "DeAndre was an impatient young man," Macarius said at last. "As so many are today. He wanted to be rich and successful immediately. Sadly that led him to make the wrong choices."

He sat back against the sofa. "He was born not too far away from here, and grew up in Alphabet City. Single mother, too many kids. Very common story. But DeAndre was smart and ambitious, and he was on his own after his mother died. He started working as a lookout for drug dealers when he was eight or nine. Then he moved up to dealing himself. He was in and out of juvenile hall a few times until he turned eighteen."

I had a momentary vision of a young black boy, hanging around a street corner when he should have been playing or studying. Sad. "How old was he?" I asked.

"Twenty-four, I think. When he was twenty, he got caught in a crackdown, and charged with intent to sell. Went to Attica for two years. When he came back, he started hanging around here."

"Why?"

"The Lord works in mysterious ways," Macarius said. "DeAndre was smart enough to know that he was on the wrong path, but no matter what I did I couldn't get him to see any other way. I tried to get him to finish his GED, but he couldn't focus on it."

"Was he using drugs when he was here?"

Macarius shook his head. "We have a very strict policy about that. You use, you lose. Did he smoke the occasional joint? Probably. We don't make our clients take drug tests. But if he'd been on anything stronger one of us would have noticed."

"How many of you are there?"

"Three brothers, and three lay workers," he said. "Brother Anselm doesn't do much these days. He's almost seventy, and he can barely walk. But he refused to go with the Benedictines when they left Friar Lake. He wants to continue serving as long as he can. Brother James and I carry the load." He nodded toward the front. "We have three counselors. Vivek, whom you saw out front, helps with government benefits and paperwork. Barbara works with recovering addicts. And Kefalexia comes in regularly to teach life skills workshops."

"Were any of them particularly close to DeAndre?"

"DeAndre was fondest of Brother Anselm. They used to sit and talk for hours."

"Do you know if he ever went out to Friar Lake when Brother Anselm was there?"

"I couldn't tell you. But perhaps Brother Anselm can. The three of us share an apartment on the second floor. I can take you up there, if you'd like to talk to him."

"I'd appreciate that."

He finished his tea and put the mug down on the table next to him. "Let me see if Brother Anselm is up to visitors." He stood and walked to a door at the back of the room. He unlocked it, and when he opened it I saw it led to a staircase. "Be back in a moment or two."

I sat back on the sofa and sipped more of my oolong tea. It was dark brown and the tannins were strong. I wondered what else I could find out while I was there. The connection was clear: Brother Anselm had been out at Friar Lake several times, and he had spoken to DeAndre, most likely telling him about the place. But what had drawn this street-smart young man from the city to the country?

It was almost impossible to get to Friar Lake without a car. I supposed that DeAndre could have taken the train to Trenton, where he could have caught a bus that, with transfers, might get him as far as Leighville. From there he'd have to go on foot. Or conversely he could have taken a bus to Easton from the Port Authority, and then what? Hitchhiked down the river road?

The more I thought about it, the more I knew he had to have gone there by car. But since we didn't find a car on the property, that meant he had driven there with someone else. His killer? Perhaps.

14 – Brother Anselm

I was startled when the door opened again, and Brother Macarius stuck his head out. "Brother Anselm can see you. But he's not up to coming downstairs."

"No problem." Rochester and I both stood up and followed Macarius through the door.

The stairway was narrow and dark, and Rochester balked. "Come on, boy, it's just a staircase," I said. "You climb stairs at home all the time."

Macarius waited halfway up the stairs.

"Don't be stubborn." I grabbed Rochester's collar and dragged him up the first couple of steps. Suddenly he took off, dashing ahead of me and passing Macarius too.

"I'm sorry," I said, hurrying up behind them. "He's not usually like this."

We exited the staircase to a small living room with a couple of torn armchairs and another lumpy, worn-out sofa like the one downstairs. The walls were decorated with faded posters of Italy—St. Peter's Square, the Spanish Steps, the Coliseum. A wizened old man in a similar plain brown robe sat in one of them. Rochester had already made a friend; he was sitting at attention next to Brother Anselm, with the friar's liver-spotted hand resting on Rochester's head.

"Brother Anselm, this is Steve, who's come to ask questions about DeAndre."

"And you've already met Rochester, I see." I walked across the room and reached out for the old friar's hand. That's when I realized he was blind.

I pulled my hand back awkwardly. "I'll leave you to chat," Macarius said, and walked back out to the staircase.

"You have a beautiful dog," Anselm said, as I sat in a chair across from him.

It took me a moment to realize he was talking about Rochester's inner beauty. "Yes, he's a sweetheart."

"And you two have a very strong bond. I can feel that."

"I think so, too." I hesitated, then said, "Brother Macarius said that you often spoke with DeAndre Dawson. "

"I expected his death," Anselm said. "He was too bull-headed to listen to reason, and he was too eager to make money without working for it."

"Brother Macarius had the same impression. Do you have any idea what DeAndre was doing out at Friar Lake? He wasn't interested in a vocation, was he?"

Anselm shook his head. "No, not DeAndre. He was out there searching for the reliquary that holds the thumb of Saint Roch."

"I'm sorry. I'm not following you. He was looking for a thumb?"

That was a creepy thought. Why were hands and fingers popping up all over the place?

Brother Anselm settled back into his chair. "Let me explain. You have heard of Joseph Bonaparte?"

I was starting to feel like I was in one of those dreams I used to have in college, where I showed up for class and hadn't done the reading, and had no idea what the professor was talking about. That had already happened to me once that week, when President Babson began discussing Friar Lake with me before I knew what he intended.

Was this another of those situations? Or was Brother Anselm crazy, as well as blind? The only way to find out was to follow along. I said, "I remember when I was a kid, we used to drive up along the Jersey Turnpike to visit cousins, and my father pointed out this old building up on a hill. He said that Napoleon's brother had lived there. Was that Joseph?"

As I said it, I realized that once again, my father had popped into my thoughts, and I wondered why. Fathers and sons. Brothers—of which I had none. And hands and thumbs. I shivered despite the heat in the upstairs room.

"Joseph was Napoleon's older brother, and I think sometimes the Little Corporal must have despaired of him," Anselm said. "He made Joseph King of Naples, and when that didn't work out, King of Spain. While Joseph was on the throne he systematically looted the Spanish crown jewels. When he abdicated from that position he came to the United States, specifically to New Jersey, and he sold those items to support a lavish lifestyle."

"That's certainly interesting, but I don't see—"

"Patience, my boy. When you get to be as old as I am, you relish the opportunity to tell a good story."

Rochester looked at me balefully, as if he was saddened by my bad manners. "I'm sorry. Please, go on."

"Joseph was not particularly religious, but for some reason he took a liking to the Abbey of Our Lady of the Waters. You probably didn't know that was the formal name of the place, did you?"

I nodded, then remembered Anselm was blind. "Yes, a friend who used to go there for CYO outings told me."

"Joseph visited the abbey several times to pray with the brothers. The legend says that on one visit, a shepherd dog that the abbot kept to chase away predators became friendly with Joseph, and saved him from a fall on a path through the woods. In gratitude, Joseph made a donation to the Abbey."

"This reliquary?" I asked.

"Exactly. The first time I went out to the abbey I was a younger man, recuperating from a broken hip, and I still had my sight. I became interested in the legend and researched it as best I could. "

Rochester sprawled on his side, resting his head on the threadbare carpet.

"Do you know what a reliquary is?" Anselm asked.

"I can guess. Something that holds a relic?"

"Yes. In this case it was a small box made of hammered silver, encrusted with precious gems. Most likely made by a Turkish craftsman during the reign of the Byzantine emperors, then taken to Spain by looting Crusaders."

"It holds a saint's thumb?"

"So it is believed-- Saint Roch, the patron saint of dogs, as it were. Hence the reason why Joseph chose that particular object to donate."

"I'm afraid I don't know much about saints," I said. "Was Saint Roch a particularly important one, to deserve such an object?"

"The history is unclear. But the legend surrounding him says that he was a mendicant, like those of us here, and that he was a healer in the time of the plague. When he became sick, he isolated himself in a forest hut so that he would not infect others. A dog belonging to a local noble is said to have brought bread to him, and licked his wounds, healing them. There is a statue of St. Roch in Prague, with a dog by his side. That's why he popularly became the patron saint of dogs."

I sat back against the worn fabric of the sofa to sort through everything Anselm had said. "So Joseph Bonaparte gave this jeweled box to the Benedictines. Where is it now?"

"That is the question, my boy. At least a hundred years ago, it disappeared from view. Some believe it was stolen, or sold to fund the abbey's good works. There is also speculation that the abbot hid it somewhere on the abbey grounds."

The pieces were coming together. "You told this story to DeAndre, didn't you?"

"We talked of many things. But yes, I did tell him. I'm afraid I might have mentioned that there is a black market for such items. Unscrupulous people and avaricious collectors."

"Did he come out to Friar Lake when you were there?"

"This last time, yes. Perhaps six months ago, just before the Benedictines closed the property and moved west. He joked with me that he was going to find the reliquary, and then he would sell it to one of those collectors, and use the money to help our outreach efforts here."

"An unselfish gesture."

Anselm nodded. "And quite uncharacteristic of DeAndre. That's why I referred to it as a joke."

"Did anyone else know about this reliquary?"

"DeAndre was the only one who was willing to sit and listen to the ramblings of an old man. But he may have told others. I don't know."

"Friar Lake isn't an easy place to get to," I said. "How did you get out there when you needed to recuperate?"

"The Jesuits. They have several vehicles, and Brother Macarius borrows a car from them now and then—for trips to the Super Wal-Mart and so on."

I could imagine Macarius, in his long brown robe, shopping the aisles and loading up his cart. Friars needed food, toilet paper and household cleaners like the rest of us.

"And DeAndre? When he came out to visit you? Do you know how he got there?"

"I don't believe I ever asked him. I assumed that he had come along with the Jesuits on one of their visits."

I tried to arrange a chronology in my mind. "So about six months ago, you were at Friar Lake, and DeAndre came to visit. Did you see him after that?"

Anselm nodded. "I spoke with him here in New York after I returned."

"When was that?"

"I can't say for certain. Perhaps Macarius can tell you. I know we keep records of when our clients visit."

Rochester pulled himself up on his haunches and nuzzled Anselm's hand. "You must be tired," I said. I stood up myself. "Thank you very much for your time."

"It has been a pleasure. Do you think you will find the person who killed DeAndre?"

"I'm not a police officer," I said. "That's not for me to say. But I hope there will be some justice for him."

"Justice," Brother Anselm said, nodding. "He will have justice, in the next world, even if not in this one."

I wasn't sure if that was a good thing for DeAndre, or not.

15 – Shenetta Levy

Rochester charged past me going down the stairs. When I followed him into the main part of the storefront I found Macarius talking with Vivek, the young blond man who handled paperwork. The homeless woman he had been helping was gone.

"Was Brother Anselm able to help you?" Macarius asked me, as Rochester crossed the room and curled up next to Vivek's desk.

"Yes, he was. He said DeAndre had been to see him after he returned from his recuperation at Friar Lake. Do you have any idea when that might have been?"

"I'll check," Macarius said. He walked over to his desk, and I turned to Vivek.

"Did you know DeAndre?" I asked.

"Just in passing. Most of my work is with the homeless and the poor, those who need help with government assistance."

He had an interesting accent that I couldn't quite place. "May I ask where you're from?"

"I was born in Poland, but came here when I was ten. I know, I still have some Polish in my speech."

"What brought you to work here?"

"Growing up under Communism, you gain an appreciation for bureaucracy, and how to get around it," he said. "I am studying for my master's in social work, and I was able to get an internship to work here."

"Did DeAndre ever talk to you about Friar Lake, the place where Brother Anselm went to recuperate?"

He nodded. "He asked once where it was. I didn't know, but we looked it up together. He was surprised that there was no bus or train he could take to get there."

Macarius rejoined us. "The last time DeAndre was here was May 2."

"And it's July now," I said. "Was he a regular visitor?"

Macarius shrugged. "So many of our clients come and go, whether they are hospitalized or incarcerated. It's hard to say."

"So you wouldn't have noticed that he wasn't coming around."

"No. Is there anything else we can help you with?"

I pursed my lips together and thought. I had a good guess as to why DeAndre had gone to Friar Lake. But I believed he had to have gone with someone else. The question was who?

"Can you tell me anyone else who knew DeAndre? Any friends or family?"

"He brought his girlfriend in one day for help with Medicaid," Vivek said. "Let me look in my files and see if I still have her paperwork."

He turned to his file cabinet and began sorting through folders. A buff-looking guy in his mid-thirties arrived, wearing a sleeveless muscle T that showed off the intricate tattoos along both arms. His cargo shorts revealed an artificial right leg. "Hey, Jimmy," Macarius said. "Steve here was just asking about DeAndre. You knew him, didn't you?"

"Just to say hello to," Jimmy said. He walked over to Macarius and the two of them sat down in a conversation.

Vivek wrote something on a piece of lined yellow paper. "Her name is Shenetta Levy. Here's her address. The little boy's name is Jamarcus."

I took the paper from him. The address was nearby, on Avenue D near the corner of Houston. I thanked him, and waved goodbye to Brother Macarius.

As we passed where I had parked, I added more money to the meter, and Rochester and I continued on foot, passing bodegas and loading docks and low-rise tenements. Every so often there was a sign of gentrification—an upscale coffee shop or a cell phone store. The sun was bright and reflected off the cars lining the streets.

Shenetta Levy lived in a four-story brownstone apartment building shaded by a couple of big plane trees. Four young women with toddlers sat in the shade as their children played. When Rochester and I walked up, a pair of the boys ran over to him. "Jawayne! Jamarcus! You let that dog alone!" one woman called, in a lilting Jamaican accent. She wore a pair of green scrub pants and a nurse's blouse covered with pictures of small animals.

"It's okay, he's very friendly." I looked down at the two boys, who were both about four or five. "You can pet him if you want."

One boy was much bolder than the other. He stuck his hand out, palm down, and I was pleased to see that someone had trained him how to approach a strange dog. Rochester licked his palm, and the boy giggled. Then they both began petting his head and stroking his soft golden fur. Rochester opened his mouth and yawned, and the bolder boy said, "He got big teeth."

"He sure does." I looked over at the cluster of young women. "I'm looking for Shenetta Levy," I said. "Do you know if she's around?"

"What do you want with Shenetta?" the woman in the nurse's blouse said. Her hair had been knotted in precise cornrows, with tiny blue beads at the end.

"I want to talk to her about DeAndre Dawson," I said.

"That fool," another woman said. "You turn and walk away, Mister. Shenetta don't need nothing to do with DeAndre no more." She had a New York accent, and a New York attitude to go with it.

"I'm Shenetta," the woman in the blouse said. I had gone to graduate school with a Jamaican woman named Sheryl Cohen, and she had told me all about the Spanish and Portuguese Jewish entrepreneurs who'd fled the Inquisition for the islands, which were then under Spanish rule. So that's most likely why Shenetta had a Jewish last name.

"I haven't seen DeAndre in months," she continued. "And he owes me money."

"I'm sorry, but he's—"

"Dead," the other woman interrupted. "I knew it."

"Be quiet, Laquisha," Shenetta said. She turned to me. "Is it true? DeAndre's dead?"

I nodded.

"You'd better come inside then," she said. She called her son and when she saw Jamarcus still had hold of Rochester, she said, "That dog isn't going to tear up my house, is he?"

"He's very well-behaved. I promise."

Jamarcus, Rochester and I followed Shenetta into the tiled foyer of the building, and then into a first-floor apartment. Jamarcus tugged Rochester over to a corner of the floor, and he sat down. Rochester sat with him and put his big shaggy head in the little boy's lap.

"Who are you exactly?" Shenetta asked me. She sat at a linoleum-topped table in front of the galley kitchen, and I sat across from her.

"My name is Steve Levitan, and I work for Eastern College, in Leighville, Pennsylvania. The college just bought this neighboring property from the Benedictine monks who lived there."

I took a deep breath. I could have gone into a long explanation about Tony Rinaldi, and the way that Rochester and I had helped him in the past. But instead I lowered my voice so that Jamarcus couldn't hear and said, "Rochester found him. DeAndre, I mean. Someone had buried him in a shallow grave and with all the rain, the soil above him had started to wash away."

Shenetta shook her head, and the beads in her hair made a soft, musical sound. I saw her brush away a tear from her eye. "How did he die?"

"I don't know. The police were still waiting for the autopsy results, the last I heard."

"Why aren't the police here, then?"

I didn't have a good answer for that. "The detective is a friend of mine," I said. "He asked me to come up and talk to the people at the Brotherhood Center, see what I could find out about DeAndre. They gave me your name."

I leaned forward. "I'm sorry. I should have called my friend and given him your name so you could hear directly from him."

"Was he at peace?" she asked me. "DeAndre?"

"I hope so," I said. "It's very pretty down there, right by the lake."

"Friar Lake?"

"You know about it?"

This time her beads clattered when she shook her head. "It's all that fool talked about. How there was some treasure there he was going to find, and then he was going to buy me and Jamarcus a big house out in the suburbs, have his half-brother's hand fixed and send him to college, even send some money to Merline, the little Haitian girl he got pregnant when he was sixteen."

"DeAndre had another child besides Jamarcus?"

"Not that lived. When he was sixteen he went out to the Bronx to stay with his aunt for a while. He never would tell me how he met Merline—usually he didn't like Haitians at all. Used to say they had HBO."

"Is that why he dated her—to watch cable TV?"

Shenetta looked at me like I was a fool. "HBO means Haitian Body Odor. But DeAndre must have liked her well enough. She was a skinny little thing, didn't want anybody to know she was having a baby, so she didn't eat. By the time the baby was born he was all stunted and underdeveloped. Something wrong with his heart, his lungs—you name it. Poor little thing died in the hospital."

I saw her glance tilt toward her own son, who was giggling as Rochester sniffed his hands. Poor DeAndre, to have suffered so many losses in his life – no father in place, then his mother leaving him. And to lose a son as well. No wonder he seemed to have been a magnet for trouble.

I thought I ought to ask, for Tony's sake. "What happened to Merline?"

"DeAndre wouldn't talk about her so I don't know. But as soon as I was pregnant with Jamarcus, he was after me to take my vitamins, to eat right and all that. It's because of him that I went into nursing school. He made me learn so much so I could make Jamarcus healthy."

That was nice, I thought. That DeAndre had learned from what happened to Merline and his first child, and used that to help Shenetta. She reached for a tissue and blew her nose. Jamarcus was sitting on the faded carpet, tickling Rochester under his chin. The dog was loving the attention.

"This place, Friar Lake," I said. "It's pretty hard to get to. Did DeAndre have a car?"

She laughed, though it was part sob as well. "DeAndre drive a car? How would he learn to drive, here in the middle of the city?"

"Well, he got out there somehow," I said. "He have a friend with a car? Somebody who could have driven him out there?"

Shenetta dabbed the tissue at her eyes and then blew her nose again. "He was a good man, DeAndre. I know he got himself into trouble in the past, but he was trying to turn things around. You say somebody buried him out there?"

I nodded.

"Well, that's good. Around here, a lot of boys like DeAndre end up dead, and they bodies get left by the side of the road." She blew her nose again. "At least someone cared enough to bury him."

I thought that the person who buried DeAndre wasn't trying to be respectful, but I didn't say anything. Jamarcus giggled as Rochester began licking his face. He held out his little palm, and it reminded me of DeAndre's hand, sticking up out of the dirt. I reached for a tissue myself.

"DeAndre went out there a couple of times," Shenetta said. "To that Friar Lake place. Once I know he got a ride from the Jesuits. Then he tried to get out there himself, by train and then by bus. Ended up in some little college town nearby."

"Leighville?"

"That's it. DeAndre loved that little town, those big old school buildings up on top of the hill. He said it was so pretty there, so clean and nice. He wanted to take me and Jamarcus out there. Said it would be a good place for Ka'Tar to go to college."

"Qatar, like the country?" I asked.

"Didn't know there was a country named that." She spelled it for me – Ka'Tar, with an apostrophe in the middle. "DeAndre's half-brother. Same dad, different mom. Story of life around these parts. When Ka'Tar was born with a deformed hand, his fingers fused together like a flipper, she said she was gonna give him a Klingon name, so he could be strong." She held up her hand in that Vulcan salute, the second and third fingers together, then the fourth and pinky.

"The police are going to want to talk to you about DeAndre," I said. "They're going to have a lot of questions. Is there anything I can do to help you with that?"

"I already told you everything I know. I'm going to school nights, and I work most days. I don't get much time with Jamarcus. I can't be running around to the police."

I was sure that the police would find Shenetta once I told Tony Rinaldi about her. But in case they didn't, I thought I ought to ask her as many questions as I could while I had her.

"Did DeAndre live here?"

She shook her head. "Only me and Jamarcus."

"You have an address for him?"

"Yeah. But you don't want to go over there. Bad people."

"Don't worry, I'll leave that to the police."

She sighed and reached for a pen with the name of a medical clinic on the side, and a piece of yellow lined paper that Jamarcus had scribbled something on.

"Ka'Tar's address, too, if you have it."

She nodded. She wrote down both addresses and pushed the paper over to me.

"When was the last time you saw DeAndre?" I asked.

"Mother's Day. He brought me that big old teddy bear over there." She pointed to a pink and white stuffed bear that had to be at least three feet tall, sitting on the floor in the corner of the room. "He said he knew I was going to be the best mom ever."

She began crying, and Jamarcus left Rochester and came over to her. "Don't cry, Mama," he said, tugging on her knee.

She lifted the little boy up to her lap and he snuggled against her shoulder.

"I'm very sorry for your loss," I said. I stood up, and pulled a business card from my wallet. "If there's anything I can do, please call me."

She nodded, and sniffled. I picked up Rochester's leash and we left her and her son to their grief.

16 – Blunt Force

I was tired of playing detective. I had plenty of information to bring back to Tony Rinaldi, and I couldn't bear any more sadness. Rochester and I walked back to where I had parked.

Back when I lived in New York, Tor and I used to joke that "BMW" meant "Break My Windows." But I was lucky, and my old sedan was still intact. I even had a few minutes remaining on the meter to leave as a gift for the next driver.

The access roads to the Holland Tunnel were jammed with tractor-trailers, decrepit sedans even older than mine, and a mix of luxury cars and SUVs. A pizza delivery guy on a beat-up bicycle threaded his way through the traffic.

I plugged my cell phone into the adapter that fits into the cassette tape deck (yes, the car is that old) and scanned for music. I needed something to raise my spirits and settled for the soundtrack to the movie *Welcome to Woop-Woop*. I barely remembered the movie any more, but the bouncy score never failed to cheer me up.

By the time we cleared the tunnel, I was feeling better. I paused the music to call Tony Rinaldi and pass on the names and addresses I'd collected.

"I'll type up some notes on what I heard when I get home," I said, "and email them to you."

"That would be great," he said. "I knew you'd be able to get some information out of those people. Any idea what DeAndre was doing down here?"

"Looking for a thumb," I said. "It's complicated. I'll talk to you tomorrow after you read my notes."

"Thanks, Steve. I'll catch you later."

I had spent so much time in the city that I was mired in rush hour traffic most of the way home, and it was nearly seven o'clock by the time I pulled off I-95 at the Yardley exit to head upriver to Stewart's Crossing.

I picked up the phone once more, this time to call Rick Stemper. "You have dinner yet?" I asked.

"Just got home and I'm walking the Rascal."

"How about if I pick up a pizza and bring it to your place?" I asked. "You have any beer on hand?"

"If the beer's on me, the pizza's on you."

"Deal." I hung up and placed an order from Giovanni's, in the shopping center in downtown Stewart's Crossing. Luckily Rick and I both liked the same kind—a thick crust with spicy Italian sausage crumbled and scattered over a base of homemade tomato sauce, freshly sautéed mushrooms and shredded mozzarella from an artisan cheese maker in New Hope.

The pizza was ready by the time I got there. I slid the box into the trunk to keep Rochester from attacking it, and drove to Rick's. The goofy dog jumped into the back seat and kept pawing toward the trunk.

Rick still lived in the ranch house where he'd grown up, which he'd bought from his parents when they retired to Florida. I pulled up in the driveway and let Rochester out. He peed as I was opening the trunk, then rushed to the gate into Rick's back yard. Rascal was on the other side of the gate, and they began barking at each other.

I opened the gate and let Rochester in. Rascal took off, Rochester right behind, and they raced around the yard, darting between the apple and pear trees Rick's father had planted when his son was a kid. I followed the dogs in, closing the gate behind me, then walked into Rick's kitchen through the back door.

His kitchen hadn't been changed much since the house was built in the fifties; he'd put in a new fridge, oven and dishwasher, but the Formica cabinets were original, as was the big stainless steel sink and the brown and tan patterned linoleum floor. He already had an open bottle of Sam Adams Cherry Wheat on the counter, and was pouring two bowls of chow out for the dogs.

I got myself a beer, then let the dogs back in. They both chewed noisily as Rick and I sat down at the kitchen table with the beer, the pizza and a roll of paper towels.

"Went into the city today on an errand for Tony Rinaldi," I said, between bites. I told him what I'd learned about DeAndre Dawson and his connection to Friar Lake.

"How do you keep on doing it?" I asked him eventually, when the pizza was gone and we were on our second round of beers. "Talking to people who've been victims of crimes? Today wore me out, talking to DeAndre's girlfriend."

"You want to be a Hardy Boy, you gotta take what comes with the territory," he said. "It's hard sometimes, sure. When you talk to people who are sad, you get sad, too. It's human nature." He took a swig from his bottle. "But I remind myself that I'm helping people get over that sadness, or that fear. What you did today was good. Even though you didn't know this guy, it's better for that woman to hear from someone who cares, not an anonymous New York City cop sent to notify her."

"If you say so."

He looked over at where the two dogs had settled down together to snooze. "I'll bet having Rochester around helped, too," he said. "Especially with the little boy. The dog is what he'll remember about this day."

Cleaning up was easy—we tossed the pizza box and the empty bottles in the recycling bin, and the used paper towels in the trash. "I'd better get going," I said. "I promised Tony I'd type up what I learned today while it's still fresh."

I was about to walk out when he said, "Saturday night. You and Lili want to have dinner with me and Paula?"

"The Drunken Hessian?" I asked.

"Paula may not be a girly girl, but she likes a good meal," he said. "I was thinking of Le Canal in New Hope."

"Fancy. You must really like her."

"It's one of the only nice places around that'll let her bring the dog."

"Not..." I motioned toward Rascal and Rochester.

"Absolutely not. But Lush sits in her shoulder bag. As long as she feeds him he keeps quiet."

Rick used a term for people like himself and me, who were ruled by their dogs. Puppy-whipped. Sadly, I could understand Paula Madden completely.

"Have to check with Lili," I said. "But it sounds good."

"I'll make reservations for eight," he said. "Meet you up there."

On the way home, I called Lili. She was in the middle of some research, so we didn't talk long—but I did confirm that she was okay for dinner on Saturday night with Rick and Paula.

"She told me she was dating someone new the last time I was in the store, but I didn't realize it was Rick," Lili said. She shook her head. "Paula's a trip. But her and Rick? I don't see it."

"Well, you'll see it on Saturday night."

We exchanged a few sweet nothings and then ended the call. Back home, I opened my laptop and typed up as much as I could recall of my meetings that day, regretting that I hadn't taken notes while I was talking to people. I emailed it all to Tony, then yawned. It had been a long day.

As Rochester and I walked down Sarajevo Way in our nightly before-bed ritual, I thought about my deepening relationship with Lili. I'd only known her for six months, but already I felt like she was the woman I wanted to spend the rest of my life with. We had both been burned by divorce, so we'd been taking things slowly. But at some point we'd both have to consider making changes.

Now that I had a more secure future with Eastern, I could consider moving upriver to Leighville. Or I could invite Lili to give up her apartment and move in with me in Stewart's Crossing. The townhouse was very comfortable for one human and one dog, but was there enough room to add Lili into the mix? We'd share the master bedroom, of course, and I didn't need to use the second bedroom as an office, as I had been.

With Lili around more often, perhaps I'd be less tempted to go online and snoop in places I didn't belong. That was one of those double-edged swords. Would I have to hide from her, and would that drive a wedge between us? Or would I be able to give up what I had already acknowledged was an addiction?

When we got home, I tried to read more of *The Hunger Games*, but I was beat, and instead turned on my side and went right to sleep.

The next morning I got a phone call from Elaine in HR. "The job is going to be posted this morning," she said. "If you get your application and resume in right away, I can ask President Babson if he'll sign off without a formal hiring committee. Because this was his idea, he should – but you never know with that man."

I felt a hollow place in my stomach. I knew well how capricious John William Babson could be. Suppose he changed his mind about me, or decided he wanted to hire someone with experience to run Friar Lake?

The first thing I had to do, before I could fill out the online application, was update my resume. Fortunately, I had put one together when I began working with Santiago Santos, and I had a copy of it on the jump drive I carried around with me. I pulled it up and began updating it, using all the action words and quantification I taught my students about in the tech writing class.

I was still working on it when Tony Rinaldi stopped by. As usual, he was starched and pressed, in khaki slacks and a military-style white shirt with epaulets and buttons. He wore a light sports jacket, which shifted when he sat down to reveal the gun on his belt.

"Good work yesterday," he said. "Had a couple of questions I wanted to ask you, though."

"Sure."

He had printed out the email I sent, and we went through it line by line. "His girlfriend couldn't give you names of any of his associates?"

"I didn't press her," I said. "I wasn't even sure I should be talking to her."

"But she responded to you. I'm sure she told you more than she would an ordinary cop."

"Are you going to talk to her yourself?"

He nodded. "Already called her this morning. I need to know more about who he hung out with, and who he might have told about this reliquary thing he was looking for. She wanted to see what Friar Lake looked like for herself, so the chief agreed to cover her train fare. She and the boy are coming into Trenton on Sunday morning. I'm going to pick them up and drive them out there. I hope to get her talking again."

"She's a nice girl," I said. "I think she'll give you whatever she can."

"Tried the phone number she provided for the half-brother, and it was disconnected. I've got a cop in the Bronx heading out to the location to see if he can track the kid down."

He stood up. "Thanks for the help, Steve. I appreciate it."

"Do you know how he died?" I asked.

"The ME says blunt force trauma to the back of the head. He picked out some wood fragments from the wound, and he's trying to identify them."

"There's a lot of wood at the abbey," I said. "Pews and moldings and stuff. I have to go up to Friar Lake one day next week with the guy who's going to help with the furnishings. I can look around and see if there's anything broken off."

"Good idea—but I'll take care of that."

"Okay. Sure. Let me know if I can do anything else for you."

"You can get some better locks installed up there. All it takes is a couple of teenagers looking for a place to party, and they could do some serious damage."

"Good point. I'll call the guy from facilities right now."

After he left, I phoned Joe Capodilupo and told him how I'd been able to get into the property. "I had no idea there were so many easy access points," he said. "I'll get a locksmith up there this afternoon to add some deadbolts, and I'll get a survey started on Monday morning to patch up any broken windows."

That was easy, I thought, sitting back in my chair. It was going to be nice to have people I could call on, rather than have to do everything myself.

Of course, when it came to snooping around crimes, I did tend to want to keep my hand in.

17 – Crown Jewels

I finished updating my resume, and read it out loud to be sure I hadn't made any mistakes I wasn't catching. I already had an ID and password for Eastern's computer system—but that one didn't work for the hiring site, or for the page where I could print a copy of my undergraduate transcript. And each one had its own criteria for credentials, so I couldn't use the same ones I used for work.

It was a long, tedious process, filling in the online application, stopping to find addresses of past employers, verify dates and so on.

At twelve, I took a break to meet Lili for lunch. It was in the high seventies, but under the sheltering branches of the oaks, elms and maples that dotted the campus, it was shady and pleasant. Without warning, Rochester took off after a squirrel, dragging me along behind him. The squirrel darted up the rough trunk of a maple and disappeared into its canopy of branches, which shook slightly as it darted away.

Rochester put his paws up on the tree trunk as if he was going to climb up after the little rodent. "Come on, you goofball," I said, tugging on his leash. "We're going to be late for lunch."

We met Lili at the Cafette a few minutes later. She looked beautiful and yet bohemian, as always, in a sleeveless sundress in a flowery print, with her curly hair pulled into a ponytail. Her bright yellow ballet flats echoed the sunshine of the daisies in her dress. I snagged us a picnic table in the shade, and Lili went inside to pick up salads for both of us. Rochester sprawled beside me on the cool slate, ever alert for any dropped food or offered tidbits.

I played a round of Words With Friends on my cell phone until Lili stepped outside, balancing a cafeteria tray loaded with salads, drinks and utensils. I jumped up and helped her bring everything to the table.

"What have you been working on so diligently?" I asked, as I speared a piece of chicken and some lettuce from my salad.

"You know how it is when you get online," she said. "One link leads to another and when you check the clock hours have passed." She caught my eye, then said, "Oh."

Lili knew about my intermittent history as a computer hacker, including the year I'd spent as a guest of the California penal system. She knew, too, that sometimes I couldn't resist snooping into online places I didn't belong, but she didn't know the extent of my hacking.

"I know exactly what you mean," I said. "When I was a web developer I used to spend hours not only checking things on our company's site, but researching other companies to see how they were approaching problems."

"I've been finding out all kinds of things about Friar Lake," she said, pouring a small container of dressing over her salad. I had learned that she always ordered sauces and dressings on the side, though I didn't know why—she ended up using everything provided anyway. "It was founded nearly two hundred years ago by a French Benedictine fleeing from the Reign of Terror, when his abbey in Paris was destroyed. Did you know that its real name was The Abbey of Our Lady of the Waters?"

"Rick told me. He used to play CYO basketball there."

"How was your trip to New York? Did you find out anything more about the man whose body we found?"

"Tony Rinaldi sent me to this drop-in center on the Lower East Side," I said. In between eating my salad and drinking a bottle of water, I explained about meeting Brother Macarius and Brother Anselm.

"Doesn't it sound kind of outlandish to you?" She handed a small piece of chicken down to Rochester, who wolfed it up greedily. "A hidden treasure? And what would this guy do with it, if he found it? Take it to a pawn shop?"

"I don't know if he was thinking that far ahead," I said. "He heard this story from the monk, and then took off to look for the reliquary."

"That's an assumption," Lili said. "There could be some other reason why he was at Friar Lake."

"Such as?"

"Think about it, Steve. It's an abandoned property. Remote enough that no one would stumble on it, but easy enough to get to if you know where it is. DeAndre could have been dealing drugs, or storing stolen property there. There are a whole bunch of reasons why he could have been killed, and most of them are a lot more probable than some Indiana Jones story."

We stood up to dispose of our trash. "Have they done an autopsy yet?" Lili asked.

I nodded. "Tony came by my office this morning. DeAndre was hit in the back of the head with a big hunk of wood."

"Do you have some time?" Lili asked. "Want to come over to my office and see what I've found so far about the Abbey's history?"

I looked at my watch. I needed to get back to my office and finish my application for the job at Friar Lake. But I could spare a half hour.

Lili took Rochester's leash. He was on his best behavior as we walked back to Fields Hall, past students dozing in the sun and a single maintenance worker trimming hedges, wearing a ball cap with a towel hung down the back to protect his neck from the sun.

Her office was on the ground floor of Granger Hall, the fine arts building. We waved hello to her secretary Matilda, and walked into Lili's glass-walled office. As she sat down at the computer, I pulled over the spindle-backed wood visitor's chair so I could look over her shoulder as she talked.

"My notes are a summary of what I've found online so far, starting with that French Benedictine monk, Dom Auguste Sanconnier." She had found a portrait of him online and pasted it into the document. He was a beak-nosed balding guy with rounded jowls, wearing a similar outfit to the one Brother Macarius and Brother Anselm had worn.

"I guess those guys never had to worry about changing fashions," I said, pointing. "Do you think their hemlines went up and down with new collections of monastic wear?"

"Doubtful," Lili said. "Dom Auguste came to the US and settled in Philadelphia. According to an account I found, in the early 1800s he met an Irish immigrant named Theodore Fitzpatrick who owned a coal mine outside Easton. Fitzpatrick was concerned about the spiritual health of his workmen, and he invited Dom Auguste to come up to Easton and celebrate Mass."

"So monks are kind of like priests?" I asked. "We didn't cover any of that in Sunday School or Hebrew School."

"I didn't study it in *shul* either. But I looked it up. As long as the monk is an ordained priest, too, he can celebrate the Mass."

Liliana Weinstock was the daughter of an Ashkenazi father with roots in Poland and a Sephardic mother whose family traced its lineage back to Spain. Her parents were both born in Cuba, met and married there, and Lili was born there, though she had grown up in various locations around the US. Her language was a mix of Yiddish, English, Spanish and Ladino, the Spanish dialect of her mother's ancestors. She was by far the most interesting woman I had ever met.

"In 1810, Fitzpatrick donated some land to the Benedictines, and funded the construction of the original chapel and a small dormitory," she continued. She had found an old etching of the abbey from the mid 1800s, when only those two buildings existed.

"Let's see what we can find out about Joseph Bonaparte," I suggested. "Was he even around when the abbey was there?"

"The student's best friend," Lili said, typing. "Wikipedia."

We both laughed. The online encyclopedia was generally a good resource—but as a starting point for academic research, not the end. She and I both found ourselves referring to Wikipedia whenever we needed a quick fact or two, though neither of us would ever cite it as a source in an academic paper.

Bonaparte's bio indicated that he had lived in New Jersey from 1817 to 1832, which jived with the early years of the abbey. At least part of that time was in Bordentown, which wasn't far away—on the other side of the Delaware, and a dozen or more miles downriver.

"He was French, and so was Dom Auguste," Lili said. "So it's logical they would have known each other."

"Look up St. Roch," I said, and I spelled it for her. She found his bio on a site indexing Catholic saints, and we read his story. His remains were allegedly carried to Venice in 1485, where, according to the site, they were still venerated at the church of San Rocco.

"There you are," I said. "St. Roch is in Venice. Not in Bucks County."

"You're so quick to jump to conclusions," Lili said. "Not so fast. There's nothing that says St. Roch's whole body is still in Venice. His thumb could be somewhere else."

"Hitch-hiking?"

She elbowed me. "Didn't you say that the monk said something to you about Joseph Bonaparte looting the crown jewels of Spain?"

"You think somebody stuck the saint's thumb in a crown? Gross."

"Don't play dumb, Steve. You know as well as I do that 'crown jewels' means more than just crowns. Haven't you been to the Tower of London?" She did some more typing. "See? The term means 'jewels or artifacts of the reigning royal family of their respective country.' So a reliquary holding some part of a saint's remains could easily be considered part of the crown jewels."

"All right. How can we tell if the Spanish crown jewels included a reliquary like the one Brother Anselm described?"

We did another search, which was less than helpful. There was no definitive listing of anything like the crown jewels of Spain, though we did find several sources that confirmed that Joseph Bonaparte had looted the Spanish treasure during his reign in Madrid, and that he had sold them in the United States. It wasn't a big leap to assume that he'd kept aside a few pieces, and that he had donated something—whether it contained the thumb of St. Roch or not—to the Abbey of our Lady of the Waters.

"So what do we have?" I asked Lili, as I pushed her visitor's chair back into place. "We know that the abbey was in existence when Joseph was in the area. We know he stole some fancy items from Spain, and brought them to the U.S. And we know that St. Roch was the patron saint of dogs."

"It's like a jigsaw puzzle with some pieces missing," Lili said. "We'll keep filling the pieces in as we find them."

I noticed the use of the word "we." It looked like the investigative team of Steve and Rochester had enlisted another member.

18 – A New Start

I left Lili at her office and walked Rochester back to Fields Hall. I spent another hour working on my online application for the Friar Lake job, and then finally was able to click the "submit" button. And because I knew how easy it was for a computer system to screw up, I sent an email to Elaine in HR confirming that I had completed my application, and that I looked forward to talking with her soon about the remainder of the process.

I wasn't sure that any of what Lili and I had found about the abbey's history had anything to do with DeAndre Dawson's death, but I typed a quick email to Tony Rinaldi about it. And since there was nothing illicit about what we'd done, I was able to use my college email address to send it to him.

My phone buzzed, and I thought perhaps it was Elaine – but it was Babson's secretary, and she told me he wanted to see me. "I'll be right down," I said.

It was late Friday afternoon by then, and most of Fields Hall had already shut down, But John Babson was still working the phones. I had to wait for him to finish his conversation.

"What's the latest about this body at Friar Lake?" he asked as soon as he hung up. "Were you able to find out the information the police needed?"

He motioned me to the chair across from him, and I told him about my trip to New York and what I'd discovered about DeAndre Dawson.

"That's just the kind of rumor we don't need to get started," Babson said. "Buried treasure. Far more likely that he was just using the property for some criminal activity. I want this wrapped up as soon as possible, Steve." He steepled his hands. "I may have misled you a bit about the Friar Lake project."

"Misled me?" Crap. What if he hadn't meant to promise me the job at all? Had I just been spinning my wheels all week?

"I have a lot of authority around here, as you know," Babson said. "But I do have a Board of Trustees to report to. I'm afraid that in my enthusiasm for the project I might have neglected to mention that the final approval has to come from the Board, at their next meeting. I have everything lined up properly – but if there's a scandal brewing about the property then my plans might be derailed."

And I might be out of a job, I thought. "I'll do my best to keep a lid on things," I said. "I've already been in contact with Ruta del Camion, and we're both agreed that the College shouldn't have any comment until we know more about who the dead man was and what he was doing out at Friar Lake."

"I'm not sure that will be enough," Babson said. "Let's talk again on Monday morning. If we can't get this resolved quickly I might have to postpone my presentation to the Board. And I don't want to do that unless I absolutely have to."

"Understood," I said. I walked back to my office through the empty halls. My head was swirling with ideas – worry about my job and that future I'd been imagining with Lili, topics for adult education seminars – and reasons why DeAndre Dawson might have been at Friar Lake.

Working on auto-pilot, I closed up my office, rounded up Rochester, and drove home. After I fed him dinner, while my own was in the microwave, I wrote down a list of questions I had. Seeing them all in black and white helped calm the turmoil in my head, even though I was no closer to answering any of them.

That evening, I took Rochester for a long walk down along the Delaware Canal. Our research into the 19th century reminded me of what an important role the canal had played in transporting coal from the mines of the Lehigh Valley down to the port of Philadelphia. And beyond that, it was a beautiful evening with a light breeze, and the canal was a great place to let Rochester loose to enjoy himself.

We walked out of River Bend, past the guard house, to Quarry Road, which led from an old long-unused stone quarry uphill, down to the river. We crossed the bridge over the canal, and then detoured into the park that ran along the old towpath. I let him off his leash and he romped ahead, while I took my time. The canal banks bloomed with daisies, black-eyed Susans, and the tiny pansies we called Johnny Jump-Ups. Birds twittered in the weeping willows and occasionally a fish splashed in the slow-moving water.

Rochester began barking. He was a few hundred feet ahead of me, his paws once more up against a tree. Another squirrel? I loped down the path toward him.

"If you found another body, Rochester, you're going to be in trouble," I called.

By the time I reached him, he was back down on the ground. A moment later, Mark Figueroa stepped out from behind the tree where Rochester had been barking.

"Busted," he said. "Your dog must be some kind of apprentice cop." There was a smudge of dirt on his right cheek, and his forehead was sweaty. He held a small plant with drooping purple flowers that looked like some kind of orchid. Bits of dirt dripped from his hands.

"What's that?" I asked.

"*Aquilegia Canadensis*," he said. "Wild columbine. I've been collecting them for a flowering bed at my house."

"Not exactly criminal activity," I said.

He shrugged. "It's state land. You could call this theft."

"Seeing as how I'm not a law enforcement officer, I'll let you go," I said. "Assuming Rochester agrees."

I scratched him under his neck, and he woofed. "See, you're in the clear."

"I found another one!"

We both turned at the sound of a voice, and saw Owen Keely emerging from the underbrush a few feet away. He had a similar plant in his hands, and he was smiling—the first time I'd seen him look happy.

"Oh," Owen said. "Good evening, sir."

Mark blushed, and I wondered if there was something more than an employee relationship between him and Owen. That wasn't my business, though, and I was glad that they both seemed happy.

"I'm afraid I recruited Owen to help with my nefarious deeds," Mark said. He turned to Owen. "That one looks great, Owen. Thanks." He handed a plastic grocery bag to Owen, and they both began wrapping the roots.

"We should get moving," I said. "I'll see you Tuesday at Friar Lake, right, Mark?"

"You bet."

I waved goodbye to both of them, hooked Rochester's leash, and led him back down the towpath. I liked Mark, and I knew from casual conversations that he'd had a rocky couple of relationships with guys who it seemed didn't treat him well. I worried if Owen, with his war-related trauma and his drug problems, was a drama waiting to happen.

Maybe it was because I'd found so much happiness with Lili that I wanted the same for my friends. But I was afraid that both Mark and Rick hadn't found the right match yet. Paula Madden was too high-strung, in my opinion. And I'd never gotten a gay vibe from Owen, though I knew of course there were plenty of straight-acting gay men.

I reminded myself once again, as Rochester and I turned back onto Sarajevo Court, that the love lives of others were not my concern. When we got home, I went back to *The Hunger Games*, and read for a couple of hours. I finished just before bedtime, but I was so intrigued with the story that I pulled out my Kindle and immediately bought the next book in the series.

Then I took Rochester for his last walk of the evening. "Don't go finding anyone hiding in the bushes," I said, as we walked outside. "No dead bodies, and no live ones, either. All right?"

He didn't pay me any attention, just scrambled forward in pursuit of an interesting smell.

The next morning I puttered around the house, trying to repair the damage caused when my over-exuberant golden retriever leapt up against the curtains in front of the sliding glass door in pursuit of some outdoor creature. My cell phone rang while I was up on the stepladder, and I had to jump down to grab it before the call was lost.

"Hey, Tony," I said. "You're working on a Saturday?"

"Shenetta Levy changed her schedule," he said. "I picked her and her son up this morning in Trenton, and we're up here at Friar Lake. But she won't talk to me. Everything I ask, I just get an 'I don't know' or a shrug."

"You think she'd talk to me?" I asked.

"Jamarcus keeps talking about your dog," Tony said.

I looked at my half-finished project, and my dog lying on the tile floor, watching me. "Tell you what. Bring them to the Cafette, and I'll meet you there with Rochester. I need a half-hour, though."

"Thanks, Steve. I appreciate it."

I scrambled into a pair of khaki shorts and a bright green polo shirt, and loaded Rochester into the BMW. When we got to the Cafette, we found Tony, Shenetta and Jamarcus just getting settled outside. Shenetta's blouse was the same bright blue as the beads in her hair, and she wore a khaki skirt and sneakers. Jamarcus wore little blue jeans and a yellow polo-type shirt.

Jamarcus and Rochester greeted each other like old friends. I said hi to Shenetta and Tony, then went inside for a lemonade and a dish of cold water for Rochester.

When I came back out Tony and Shenetta were sitting silently at a picnic table, watching Jamarcus tickle Rochester and laugh. The big goofy dog rolled on his back and waved his paws in the air.

"That means he wants you to rub his belly," I said to Jamarcus. He sat down on the slate next to the dog and did Rochester's bidding. As we all did.

"Is this your first time out here?" I asked Shenetta, sitting across from her.

She nodded.

"Does it look the way DeAndre described it?"

"Look, I keep telling this policeman, I don't know anything about what DeAndre was doing. I only came out here so Jamarcus could see what it's like in the country."

"I used to live in Manhattan," I said. "I went to graduate school at Columbia, and lived up there. Then a friend and I lived in this little walk-up on Delancey Street for a while. We used to climb up to the roof sometimes, just to feel like we were getting away from the city."

Shenetta nodded. "It gets so hot there, and Jamarcus wants to go out and play. But I don't like him out there without me to watch him."

Tony sat by quietly, sipping his iced coffee. I focused on getting Shenetta to talk. "How much longer til you finish nursing school?"

"I'll have my LPN at the end of the summer. I'm going to have to work for a while, though, before I can keep on going."

"You ever think about moving down here?" Tony asked. "My wife works for the college student health department," he said. "They use LPNs to take student medical histories, give shots and things like that. I could see if she knows of any jobs."

She turned to him. "Why would you do that? You don't know me or anything about me."

"I know Jamarcus lost his father," Tony said. "And that you cared about DeAndre, and that maybe both of you could use a new start." He pulled his cell phone out of his pocket. "Want me to make a call?"

She looked over at Jamarcus, now lying on his back on the grass with Rochester licking his face.

"Leighville's a good place," I said. "You could do a lot worse."

"Already have," she said. "Go on, make that call." She turned to me again. "You have something I could write on?"

Tony handed her a small spiral-topped pad from his pocket, and a pen, and she started writing. He stood up and walked in the opposite direction from Jamarcus to call his wife.

My admiration for Tony kept growing. I had seen him in cop mode and knew that he was smart and dedicated. But I hadn't realized what a genuinely nice guy he was until then.

While Tony spoke, and Jamarcus played, Shenetta wrote, then put the end of the pen in her mouth while she thought, then wrote some more.

Tony returned as she was writing. "Tanya will be over in a few minutes," he said. "You know, I have a boy about Jamarcus's age. She's going to bring him, too."

Shenetta smiled.

Tony and I sat there quietly while she did.

I'd never met Tony's wife or son, though I'd heard about them. As they approached across the lawn, I was surprised to see that she had skin the color of cinnamon, because I'd always assumed his wife was Italian, like he was. She had frizzy black hair tamed with a scrunchie, and wore black tights and a brightly patterned blouse. She leaned down and said something to the boy, who ran over to Jamarcus and joined in the Rochester Adoration Society.

"Tanya, meet Shenetta," Tony said. "And that's Frankie, over there."

"Pleased to meet you," Tanya said. Her New York accent shone through. "I'm a Puerto Rican from the Bronx, and if I can fit in down here you sure can, too. Come on, let's talk."

Shenetta handed the notebook back to Tony. "These are the friends of DeAndre's I met. There's another guy, a white guy, he hung out with some, but I never heard his name."

"Thanks, Shenetta." He took the notebook from her. "I'll get onto these on Monday."

Tanya and Shenetta moved to another picnic table to talk about nursing. "I hope Tanya can help her out," Tony said. He looked over to where his son and Jamarcus had jumped up and started chasing each other around. Frankie looked a lot like his dad, with skin a few shades lighter than his mom.

Rochester had rolled over and gone back to sleep. "Looks like Frankie and Jamarcus are getting along." He reached out to shake my hand. "Thanks, Steve. I appreciate the help."

I shook his hand, then collected Rochester. I waved goodbye to Shenetta and Jamarcus, and then called Lili. "Hey, the mutt and I are in Leighville. You busy?"

"Just playing around with Photoshop," she said. "Come on over. Though don't let Rochester hear you call him a mutt. I understand he's very proud of his pedigree."

I hung up and looked at my dog. "Have you been having private conversations with Lili, boy?"

He just looked at me, and kept his secrets.

19 – Consenting Adults

I had my Kindle with me, and so Lili and I spent the afternoon lying around together—her on a big easy chair with her feet curled underneath her, me stretched out on the sofa, both of us reading. Rochester was on the floor between us.

Lili finished the first book of *The Hunger Games* trilogy just before we had to get ready for dinner. Like me, she wanted to keep right on reading—but she was a traditionalist when it came to books. "I have to have the physical object," she said, when I suggested we could just share my Kindle. "I like to hold a book in my hands. If we get moving we can stop at the campus bookstore on our way to New Hope for dinner."

I didn't want to leave Rochester alone in Lili's apartment, so we had to leave early in order to drive down to Stewart's Crossing and feed and walk him. Before we left Leighville, though, we detoured past the college bookstore, which takes up half a block on Main Street, just below the wrought-iron entrance gates to the college.

It was just a few minutes before closing, and Rochester and I waited in the car while Lili darted in and bought the next two volumes in the series. Then we drove down to River Bend and saw to the bossy golden's every need. I ushered him into his crate, which he wasn't happy about—but I remembered that black glove he'd chewed up and I resisted the sad look on his doggy face. Then we drove back up river.

We met Rick and Paula outside Le Canal in New Hope, a French restaurant with big glass windows that looked out on the Delaware Canal. "You're wearing the palacios!" Paula exclaimed as soon as she saw Lili. "Don't you just love them?"

"I do," Lili said. Rick and I both looked down at her shoes, which looked like nothing special to me—dark brown leather over a cork sole. But the two of them chatted about the merits of the shoes while I held the door open and Rick spoke to the hostess.

I didn't see Lush, but I assumed the teacup Chihuahua was inside Paula's big shoulder bag. Once we were seated, though, he poked his little head out, sniffed the air, then went back inside, like a groundhog who expects a long winter.

Lili and Paula carried the conversation, talking about shoes and Paris and Paula's forthcoming buying trip to Buenos Aires. While Lili was giving Paula tips about the Recoleta neighborhood, near Eva Peron's tomb, I turned to Rick. "I met Tony Rinaldi's wife today, and his little boy."

"Tanya? She's a looker. Where'd you run into them?"

I told him about Tony's phone call, and how Rochester and I had met him and Shenetta at the Cafette. "You are such a yenta," Rick said.

"You aren't supposed to know words like that," I said. "You're not even Jewish."

"You don't to have to be Jewish to recognize somebody who can't help sticking his big nose into other people's lives," he said. "And I don't mean Rochester, though his nose is pretty big."

"If DeAndre's death becomes a big deal, and gets a lot of unwelcome attention for the college, then that could screw up my new job." I explained how Babson still had to get authorization from the Board of Trustees for the Friar Lake project.

"Well, that sucks," Rick said.

Paula wanted to know what was going on, so I gave her a quick recap. "But I don't understand how one more dead black guy could be a problem," she said, when I finished. "I mean, they kill each other all the time." She lowered her voice and said, "But that just shows you what kind of people they are."

I looked at Lili, and she raised her eyebrows. I said, "What do you..." and Lili cut me off before I could ask what kind of people she was talking about.

"I think it's wonderful that something good can come out of this whole situation," she said. "Paula, have I told you about the photographs I've been taking up at Friar Lake? I'm happy with the way some of them are turning out."

"You've been up there since we went the first time?" I asked. I hadn't realized that, and wondered if it was a secret Lili was keeping from me, or just a symptom of how little time we'd been spending together.

Lili nodded. "Just a couple of quick visits, trying to see the place in different light. I was up there for a while yesterday afternoon and saw Manuel from the maintenance department installing a new lock on the chapel door."

"You know the maintenance people by name?" Paula asked.

"Lili speaks fluent Spanish," I said. "You should hear her. I'm amazed."

"It's America," Paula said. "You shouldn't have to speak a foreign language just to live here. I can't tell you how many times people come into the store and they can barely speak English. We have to use hand gestures and hold up fingers."

I looked over at Rick. He was a pretty easy-going, liberal guy and I wondered how long he'd put up with Paula's attitudes before the sex stopped being worth it.

We kept chatting through the meal, and every now and then Lili and I would exchange glances at something Paula said, and we'd attempt to steer the conversation onto safer ground. Rick said nothing, but I could tell he was relieved not to have to manage the conversation.

Paula ordered a steak, and proceeded to feed most of it to Lush, in little tiny pieces that he nipped from her fingers. She was a real chatterbox, and by the time we left them in the parking lot, I was exhausted.

"How can he stand that woman!" I said to Lili as we drove back to Stewart's Crossing. "She's awful."

"No, she's not," Lili said. "I've run across a lot of awful people in this world, and as long as she's not killing small children with a machete, I'm willing to cut her some slack. She has some narrow opinions, but it's nothing she can't grow out of. Rick could be a good influence on her."

Every now and then Lili said something that reminded me of the life she'd had before coming to Eastern, and made me admire her even more. "If you say so. The first thing she needs to grow out of is needing to carry that little dog around with her everywhere, like he's some kind of child's teddy bear."

"You're one to talk. If you could fit Rochester into a shoulder bag you would." She jabbed me lightly in the shoulder.

"I only take him with me to work because he gets so upset when I leave him alone," I said defensively, though I knew she was right. "Like tonight—you watch, he'll go crazy when we get home."

"Only because you enable him. I'll bet he's sleeping peacefully right now."

I turned into the long access road to River Bend, I said, "All right, let's test out your hypothesis. We'll see if Rochester is sleeping or worrying."

I pulled into a guest parking space down the street from my townhouse. "If he's sleeping, and he hears the car pull up, he'll get up and start barking," I said. "If you're right and he's fine on his own, I don't want to disturb him."

We walked down Sarajevo Court and then quietly up the driveway. I didn't hear any barking. Lili and I stepped up together and peered over the courtyard gate.

He was lying on his side in the crate, asleep, his head toward the doors. "Busted!" I said, banging the gate. It was comical to watch him come to life, scrambling up and sticking his head against the metal. He began barking and yelping.

"You're mean," Lili said, laughing.

"Well, you were right," I said, unlocking the front door. "He was sleeping."

I let him out of the crate and he raced around the downstairs, skidding on the tile floor and barking non-stop. I grabbed him and hooked up his leash, and as we walked down the street, Lili got to observe first-hand his new trick of putting his paws up on tree trunks. "It's too bad the light is so low," she said. There was only a crescent moon, and low clouds blocked most of the stars. "He's just so adorable."

"He'll do it for you in daylight, too," I said. "If you want, we can take him over to the towpath tomorrow morning."

"I'd love that. I'll bet there are tons of flowers in bloom, too."

That reminded me of my encounter with Mark Figueroa and Owen Keely, and I described it to her. "It just got me wondering if they were doing something more back there than just looking for plants," I said.

"They're both consenting adults," she said. "Though if I were them I'd watch out for poison ivy."

She spent the night at my house. In addition to being a kind, compassionate person she was also lots of fun, and we laughed almost as much as we did other things.

The next morning I took the dog for his early walk while she made us scrambled eggs and bacon. When Rochester and I returned, he went wild at the smell of the fresh bacon frying, nearly tearing my arm off in his eagerness to get to the kitchen.

"Let me get your leash off, dog!" I said, stumbling behind him. He didn't stop until he was right next to Lili at the stove, where he planted his butt and looked up at her with those adoring puppy eyes.

"You can have the burnt piece," she said, dropping it into his open mouth. He chewed noisily, then followed us to the table, going back and forth from Lili to me hoping desperately for more bacon.

"I only have my little digital with me," she said. "I brought it to dinner in case I wanted to get a shot of the four of us. If Rochester's a good model, we'll have to schedule something else when I have all my cameras."

"So you thought about taking pictures last night, but you didn't," I said. "So does that mean you think Paula's not long for Rick?"

"Paula is very high-maintenance," she said. "And Rick is a low-maintenance kind of guy."

"They say opposites attract," I said, as I stood up to clear the table. I was still wearing my typical dog-walking clothes—a pair of nylon shorts, a T-shirt (in this case a relic from a long ago trip to Oxford, England, with a skyline of colleges and the legend 'the dreaming spires') and running shoes.

"Does that include you and me?" Lili asked, gathering the rest of the dishes and following me. "I think we're in sync most of the time."

"I think the differences between us are more low-lying," I said. "You have a sense of adventure and wanderlust, and I'm more a homebody. You look at the world as an artist and consider what you can make of it."

I began rinsing the dishes and stacking them in the dishwasher while Lili put away the butter, orange juice and so on. "I like to confront the world head-on and then find ways to sneak around and bend situations to my advantage."

"Have you been in therapy?" she asked. "You sure talk like you have."

"In prison. Mandatory counseling sessions. I talked a lot about Mary and why our marriage had failed, and how that was tied into my self-image."

"You said that your marriage was over after her second miscarriage," Lili said, stepping over Rochester in order to get back out to the breakfast nook.

"It was. The prison term was just icing on the cake. But the miscarriages weren't the underlying reason we broke up."

I closed the dishwasher and followed Lili out to the breakfast nook. "Mary thought my personality was something she could drill out of me by pushing me to dress better, to get a better job, and all that. Eventually we both realized that wasn't going to happen. If we'd had kids, we probably would have stuck it out for a while longer, but the end result would be the same.

"Well, I think your personality is just fine the way it is," she said, leaning over to kiss my cheek.

"And I'm very glad you do," I said.

Lili was barefoot, wearing a pair of my running shorts and another of my T-shirts. This one had a picture of a dog sitting up in a canoe, holding an oar in his paws. The legend underneath read "Dog Paddle."

"Let me put my shoes on and we can go out to the towpath," she said. "Remember, we have that College Connection welcome reception this afternoon."

I played ball toss with Rochester while Lili went upstairs. When she returned she was wearing those yellow shoes she'd bought from Paula Madden again. "Why do you think Rick's marriage broke up?" she asked, picking up her camera from the table.

"When he was serious and sober he said that Vanessa was an adrenaline junkie, that she loved driving fast and bungee jumping and stuff like that. That she got off on him being a cop because there was always a chance that he'd get killed on the job. Once he got promoted to detective she decided the thrill was gone, and she took up with a fire jumper and moved to Colorado."

"She does sound pretty awful," Lili said. "Did you ever meet her?"

I shook my head. "He and I weren't friends in high school— just knew each other because we had a couple of classes together. He got married while I was in New York, I think, and then divorced while I was in California. By the time I moved back here and met up with him again, and we got to be friends, Vanessa was long gone."

I hooked Rochester's leash and we walked outside. "Rick was pretty angry after Vanessa left," I said. "He used to bitch about her non-stop for the first couple of months I knew him. He used to say things like 'my ex-wife moved to Whoragon' and 'if a tree falls in a forest and kills your ex-wife, what do you do with the lumber.'"

Lili laughed, but said that she shouldn't. "Do you think he's over her?"

"I sure hope so. It's been nearly two years."

Rochester scrambled after a squirrel and I pulled him back. "My therapist back in prison would say that Rick is dating difficult women to avoid making a commitment to someone reasonable," I said. "What do you think?"

"I think you got more out of being in prison than you're willing to admit," she said. "It sounds like you came out of there knowing yourself a lot better than when you went in."

"I wouldn't argue with that," I said. "But all in all I'd rather have gone to some fancy rehab center like all the Hollywood stars."

We crossed the bridge over the canal and turned onto the towpath. "Keep an eye out for plant thieves," I said.

"It's Sunday morning," Lili said. "If Mark and this guy are having a relationship, they're in bed together right now. Not out scavenging for plants."

"We're out here."

"Yeah, but we've been together for months already. That initial surge of lust and desire has passed."

I opened my mouth in mock anger, then pulled her close for a long, deep kiss.

She finally pushed me away. "I want to take some pictures."

Rochester was a natural ham, looking up when I clicked my fingers so that his ears stood up. She followed him, snapping casual shots, even getting a good one of him paws-up on a weeping willow.

It was fun to watch her in her photographer mode, and I wondered if this was the way she'd been when she was a working photojournalist, traveling the world taking pictures to accompany news and feature stories. She looked happy and fully engaged, and I hoped she always maintained that sense of pride and pleasure in what she was doing.

Just before noon, she said, "We'd better get back to your house. I'll need to make a pit stop at my place before we go to the reception."

"Sure we can't just skip out?" I asked, as we turned and began walking home. "No one will miss us."

"Of course they will," she said. "And I want to get a look at these kids. Don't you?"

I held my hands out, palms up, as if I was weighing alternatives. "Spend the afternoon with you, or with a bunch of inner-city teens," I said. My hands went up and down. "I pick you."

"That's sweet, but we're still going." She leaned over and kissed my cheek.

20 – Ice-Breaker

On our way back to the townhouse, we passed Owen Keely watering his parents' yard. "So much for Sunday morning in bed," I whispered to Lili. We waved and said hello.

"Good morning, sir," he said, nodding. "Ma'am."

Lili and I smiled, but as soon as we were out of range she said, "I hate being called ma'am. It reminds me of old women in long skirts. And he's not that much younger than we are."

"I think it's a military thing," I said. "But you've got to admit it's nice to meet someone who's so polite."

Back at the house, we both read for a while, working our way through *Catching Fire*, the second book in the *Hunger Games* trilogy, and then I took a shower and changed into college-appropriate khakis and a polo shirt while Lili played with Rochester. When I walked halfway down the stairs, I stopped at the landing and looked below.

Lili was sitting Indian-style on the floor next to his crate. She had already tossed in a couple of chew toys and filled the water dish that clamped onto the side. Rochester was lying flat on the floor a few feet away from her, his head resting on one paw, looking at her. She had a bag of tiny training treats in her hand, and she was trying to coax him to crawl closer to her to retrieve each treat.

"That's a good boy," she said, dropping a treat on the tile just far enough from him that he had to scoot forward a few inches to retrieve it. I knew that her goal was to trick him into crawling into the crate on his own. He didn't like being stuck in there, even though all the dog-training manuals said he ought to feel safe and sheltered inside.

"It's not going to work," I said from the landing. "He's too smart."

"I agree that he's smart," she said, placing another treat on the floor. "He knows he's going in the crate eventually. I think he'll figure out he can go in willingly, with treats, or with you dragging him and no treats."

Rochester was a smart dog; I'd seen lots of evidence of that in the year and a half that I'd had him. But he didn't always have common sense; he continued to chase squirrels, for example, even though it was clear, at least to me, that he was never going to catch one—and wouldn't know what to do with it if he did.

Lili fed him another treat, and he inched closer. I stayed quietly where I was on the landing as she took the last treat and put it just inside the entrance to the crate. Rochester eyed it, then looked up at her. Then he hopped up and ran into the living room, where he curled up on the sofa.

I resisted the urge to laugh. I just went to the refrigerator and pulled out a package of Swiss cheese. At the sound of the door opening, he hopped back off the sofa and came into the kitchen, looking up at me with those big brown eyes.

I pulled off a piece of cheese and waved it in front of his nose. Then I tossed it into the crate, and as he scrambled in after it I shut the door behind him. He was still eating as Lili and I hurried out the front door.

On the way up to Leighville, we talked about how we were going to approach our seminar duties with the College Connection kids. Lili planned to take them out into the woods at the back of the campus, give them cameras, and ask them to take pictures of things that they might have seen in the book— trees, plants, water, animal tracks. Then she'd take them to the photography lab and help them put together their own collages.

"I'm thinking about communication," I said. "The way information is so restricted in Panem. I want to create some kind of a game for them to play, one that involves writing, sending messages and so on. Give them some exposure to college level writing, but make it fun."

"That would be cool," she said. "Since all three of the books center around the games."

"I've been reading this book about how game structure can be applied to academics," I said. "You need to provide a clearly defined goal, and steps that the kids can take to achieve it. Then you have to give them feedback so that they feel like they've accomplished something."

"It's an interesting idea," she said. "But you'd better get your act together fast. You do know you're teaching Tuesday and Thursday morning?"

"Is there a schedule already put together?"

She shook her head. "You really need to read your email. The kids are all staying in Birthday House, and they eat breakfast together every morning at Burgers Commons."

Like almost every college and university, Eastern named buildings after their donors. Howard M. Burgers, an alum who'd made a fortune in fast food, had funded the renovation of the main dining hall a few years before, and it had been named for him. The story behind Birthday House, the high-rise dorm where I had lived when I was at Eastern, was that the money for it had been donated by an alumnus named Hoare. There was no way Eastern was going to name a dorm Hoare House, though, so the donation was made on the man's birthday, giving rise to the name.

We stopped at Lili's so she could shower and change, and while she did I used her computer to access my college email account. Sure enough, there was an attachment I hadn't noticed which spelled out the week-long schedule for the CC kids. I'd been assigned a slot on Tuesday morning.

Lili and I arrived at the auditorium in Granger Hall to find a group of about fifty teenagers milling around in the lobby, looking at the student artwork that had been hung on the walls. "They don't seem too terrifying," I whispered to her.

Probably two-thirds of them were female; about fifty percent were African-American, another thirty percent Hispanic. A group of white girls clustered together, with a single white boy floating at the edge of their group. The rest were a mix of Asian, South Asian, and kids who probably had to check the "other" box on any official forms. They all wore lanyards around their neck with a plastic badge at the end giving their first name and the city they were from.

An awful lot of them had tattoos of one kind or another, and I couldn't help wondering if some of them might be gang-related. Almost every girl had something in the way of ear jewelry, from rows of studs to dangling rings to those big plugs called gauges.

Everyone began to file into the auditorium, and we followed. The program was mercifully short; President Babson welcomed everyone, and Dot Sneiss, the college registrar, gave them a brief overview of what to expect over the next week. Then she began introducing each of the faculty members. I was lucky that there were four of us representing the English department, and we all stood together. Lili was the only one representing fine arts.

After the program was over, we all walked back outside, to where aluminum folding tables had been set up with picnic foods. A group of Eastern students had been hired to act as mentors, and they organized the kids into groups to eat and play ice-breaker games. I noticed Yudame, one of my tech writing students, among the mentors. He was a light-skinned Puerto Rican kid with a dandelion puff of blondish-brown hair. He pronounced his name You-Dummy, which always amused me.

The CC kids had been divided into four smaller groups, each of about a dozen, and each assigned to one mentor. It looked like someone had been careful to compose the groups, as they each looked to be balanced between race and ethnicity.

Lili and I loaded up paper plates with hamburgers and fries, and walked over to where Yudame had staked out his section. "Hey, Prof, let me introduce you to my team," he said, standing up.

I scanned the group as he named them. Courtney was a skinny tough-looking white girl in a white wife-beater T-shirt that showed she had tattoos down both arms. Her blonde hair hung in dreads and she wore a ball cap backwards. Chinelle was twice her size, with a huge chest that nearly popped out of her low-cut blouse. She wore tight jeans and high heels, and her dark skin shone with some kind of makeup. The last to be introduced was Ka'Tar, and I remembered that was the name of DeAndre Dawson's half-brother. Could there be two kids with that same Klingon-influenced name?

He was a skinny kid with skin so dark it was almost black. I remembered Shenetta Levy had sad something about DeAndre's brother being handicapped in some way, but I couldn't remember how.

Yudame raved about what a good teacher I was and I had to jump in and say, "I already put in your grade for last term, Yudame. You don't have to suck up any more."

That got a laugh from the kids. We started to eat and talk to them, and I learned that they were mostly from New York and Philadelphia, as well as a few other urban cities in the northeast. They ranged from fourteen to seventeen. Two had just graduated from high school, but the rest were still enrolled.

"That's great that you're all still in school," Lili said.

"You gotta be in school to be in this program," a heavyset black girl named Ashanty said. "They won't let you in if you ain't." Her hair was pulled into cornrows so tight just looking at them gave me a headache.

"But you can be in any kind of school, right?" Yudame asked.

Ashanty nodded. "I'm in this program for teen mothers. I have a little boy and they have a day care right there at the school."

The other kids chimed in, and I was surprised at the range of educational opportunities available, from programs like Ashanty's to parochial schools, technical schools, work-study programs and pre-college academies.

When we finished eating, Yudame announced that the kids were going to play volleyball. As they stood up, I asked, "Ka'Tar, can I talk to you before you leave?"

He looked suspicious, like he had done something wrong but didn't realize it yet. He shuffled over to where Lili and I stood under the shade of a maple tree. "D'you have a half-brother named DeAndre?" I asked, deliberately trying to keep my tense vague in case I was right—and in case the boy didn't know that DeAndre was dead.

"True dat," he said, lowering his head and scuffing at the dirt with the toe of one shoe. "He the reason why I came here. He tole me about it." Then he looked up at me, suspicious. "How you know about DeAndre? He dead."

Up close, I saw that the fourth and fifth fingers of his right hand were fused together. I didn't think it was right to tell him that my dog had discovered his half-brother's body. "I never met him. But I know Shenetta. She was here in Leighville yesterday. Maybe she and Jamarcus are going to move down here."

"Shenetta good people," he said. "DeAndre always said so."

"Yeah, she is," I said. "Well, I don't want to keep you from volleyball."

"'S all right," he said. "They always pick me last, cause of my hand." He held it up. "DeAndre, he always saying he gonna get the money to get me fixed up."

My heart felt like it was going to break. I barely knew the kid, but I could see the hurt and disappointment playing on his face. He turned away from us and shuffled toward the volleyball net.

Lili put her hand on my upper arm. "You can't fix the world," she said.

"He's not the world. He's just one kid."

"I know. And I'm sure he's had a tough life. But at least he's here for the week, and maybe he can see something better in the future."

She took my hand and squeezed, and we walked back to where we had parked. "I should work on my program for the kids," she said, when we reached my car. "I can't believe I signed up to teach every day." She shook her head. "What was I thinking?"

"You were thinking that you wanted to do some good for these kids," I said.

I drove back to her apartment. "You'd better go home and get your class planned," she said, when I pulled up in front of the building. She leaned over and kissed me, and then hopped out of the car. "Now go take care of your dog," she said.

21 – A Need to be Educated

Back at River Bend, Rochester was sitting up in his crate watching the courtyard when I walked up, and began his pyrotechnics as soon as he saw me. I fed him and took him for a walk, then tried to focus on a game to help the CC kids learn about college.

I hadn't found any mention of higher education in the books so far, though I assumed that kids in the capital would have that opportunity. So I focused on the game itself in the first book. I thought I could assign them each a character, and then ask them to write a message to another character, providing some piece of important information.

Then the character who received the message would have to describe how he or she would use that information in the game. I fiddled around with the instructions for a while, then went back to reading. I'd only gotten through a chapter when Rick called.

"I need a beer," he said. "Hell of a day. You busy?"

"Not really. I picked up some Flying Dog the other day. Called Wildeman Farmhouse IPA. You want to give it a try?"

"Sounds like my day. Full of wildness. Let me pick up the Rascal and I'll be over."

I waited for Rick to show up before I opened the first bottle. I had one ready for him when I opened the door and Rascal charged in. "That's the kind of service I could get used to," Rick said.

"Get married again."

He shook his head. "Not to Paula Madden, that's for sure."

"Don't tell me you broke up already? Was it something we said last night?"

"It's not you, it's me," he said. "Isn't that a laugh? Actually, it wasn't you or me. It's Paula. She's crazy."

He took a long pull at his beer. "Another break-in last night at Crossing Estates. Turned out to be a friend of Paula's, and when I got there to talk to the homeowners, she was there. She wouldn't shut up—the poor people couldn't get a word in. Just kept criticizing me for not getting these burglaries solved. And that little dog. My god. Yapping right along with her. It was enough to give me a headache."

"What did you do?"

"I told her that if she couldn't keep her mouth shut long enough for me to talk to the people, then she needed to scoot her butt out of there. I thought I was making a joke – you know from the dancing. She didn't take it that way."

"What did she do?"

"She grabbed her bag so fast the dog nearly fell out. Had a few choice words for me—things I haven't heard since the last time I had to go down to the state prison in Chester. Then she stalked out and slammed the door behind her."

He shook his head. "The husband? He got up and followed her, opened the door and yelled after her that was his door she was slamming. Even the wife said she was glad Paula was gone, and what had I done to get her so riled up in the first place?"

"Sounds tough."

"Good riddance to her anyway," he said. "Her prejudices were really starting to get to me. You just got a little bit last night. A lot of people, if they've never had to deal with people of other races or other backgrounds, they're frightened, or just need to be educated. Paula was a whole other story. I can't imagine how she can travel around and buy shoes acting the way she does."

He took another long pull, and finished his beer. "Got another one of these?"

"Sure." By the time I got back with the beer, he had calmed down.

"Once she was gone, I finally got to talk to the people, and they didn't have a single lead to give me."

"How many burglaries so far?" I asked.

"Six. Whoever's behind it is very slick. Jimmy the lock on the sliding door, in and out fast."

"Where do they park?"

"You mean the victims?"

I shook my head. "No, I mean the crooks. You can't get out to Crossing Estates on foot—it's too far from anything. So they have to drive in, right?"

He nodded, then took another pull on his beer.

"And every house in the neighborhood has at least a two-car garage and a big driveway. So people don't park their own cars in the street."

"Your point is?"

"My point is that the crooks have to park somewhere. Probably not in the driveway of the house they're robbing, right? Too obvious. So they've got to park somewhere close by. And in a neighborhood like that, people notice when somebody's parked in front of their house."

"Houses are too far apart," Rick said. "You could park between them."

"Still. You could check with the neighbors and see if they noticed anybody parked who didn't belong."

"You have a good idea now and then, Frank Hardy," he said.

"Anything I can do to help, brother Joe," I said, tipping my bottle against his.

22 – Good People

Monday morning dawned bright and sunny. Rochester and I went for a good long walk around River Bend, meeting up with a couple of his doggy friends and giving him lots of chances to sniff and pee. After breakfast, I loaded him into the BMW and drove directly to Friar Lake. I had a nine o'clock meeting scheduled with Joe Capodilupo to pick up my own set of keys to the new locks. Then at ten I'd arranged to meet Mark Figueroa there and walk him around the property so he could get an idea of the scope of the work ahead of us, assuming that the project was a go.

Rochester was excited as I drove in the access road to Friar Lake—probably wanted to see if he could dig up any more dead bodies. But I kept him on a tight leash as we walked around. I spotted Joe standing in front of the chapel talking to a black guy in the khaki work uniform the Eastern maintenance staff wore.

The black guy's name was Ford, and he didn't like Rochester one bit. Every time we ran into him on campus he reminded me that dogs weren't supposed to be at Eastern unless they were guide dogs.

"Hey, Joe," I said, as we walked up to them. "Ford."

Ford glared at Rochester, and I had to pull his leash tight to keep him from jumping on the maintenance man.

"I'll get on those problems in the dorm, Mr. C," Ford said, and he turned and walked away—but not before casting one more baleful look at Rochester.

The bald spot on the top of Joe's bald head had been sunburned, and the white fringe that surrounded it reminded me once again of a monk's tonsure. "Have a good weekend?" I asked Joe, as he opened the door to the chapel.

"Went down the shore with the grandkids," he said. "Wildwood Crest. Crowds like you wouldn't believe."

I had grown up on Jersey shore summer vacations, or as we said, going down the shore. "I haven't been there since I was a kid," I said. "We used to go to Seaside for a week every summer."

"Looks the same," he said. "Acres of parked cars and hardly a piece of sand without somebody's umbrella already there."

Joe had a roll of plans under his arm, and as we walked around the chapel he pointed out all the work that had to be done. "I've got a contractor lined up for demolition as soon as Babson gives me the go-ahead," he said.

"You think this'll be a go?" I asked. Joe had been around Eastern a long time, and I wondered if he had any inside information.

"Whether the conference center project gets off the ground now, or a year from now, this building still needs to be renovated. We'll be knocking out unnecessary walls, removing the old plumbing and electrical wiring, and so on. That should take about a week. Once all the debris is gone we can start the rebuilding."

"I didn't realize how big a job it was," I said as we walked through a side door and out into the cloister, though I was thinking *a year from now? What would I do until then*?

"This is nothing. You should have been around for building Harrow Hall. Huge construction project right in the middle of the campus. Constantly moving barriers around so that we could bring in materials but not block student access to buildings. That was a nightmare."

It took us the full hour to walk through each building, making sure that the new locks had been installed and all the broken windows replaced. We were standing in front of the chapel when Mark Figueroa's white delivery van pulled up in the drive.

Mark hopped out of the driver's seat. It was almost comical to see him shake hands with Joe—the older man short and dumpy, while Mark was almost freakishly tall and skinny as a stick of beef jerky.

I was surprised to see that he'd brought Owen Keely with him. I'd thought Owen was just his delivery man.

Instead of romping over to say hello, as he did with almost everyone new, Rochester sat on his haunches by my side, watching Mark and Owen as if they were invaders ready to steal something.

I guessed Mark to be in his mid-thirties, seven or eight years younger than I was. Owen had to be in his late twenties, yet he looked as sullen as a teenager roped into accompanying his father on a boring excursion. While Mark wore creased khakis and a bright green polo shirt, Owen had on a black pocket T-shirt and faded jeans. If he hadn't been wearing a belt, I imagine the jeans might have sagged down his butt the way many a teenager's did.

After I made the introductions, Joe walked us around the chapel, pointing out the way the space would be broken up, and Mark took notes. I was glad to have Joe there, because he had answers to most of Mark's questions. "This is good material," Joe said, leaning down to rap his knuckles on the tongue and groove wooden floor in the chapel. "Once we're done, we'll sand it, polish it and put a layer of polyurethane over it."

"We'll need entry mats for the foyer, though," Mark said. "In case of rain and snow."

He pulled out a big tape measure, and he and Owen measured the doorways and the depth of the foyer. Owen always held the end of the tape, and Mark called out measurements to him, which Owen wrote down on a clipboard. Rochester sprawled on the wood floor, always watching them.

"Look at these," Mark said, pointing at a series of carvings along the side wall. "They're beautiful."

"The stations of the cross," Owen said. "We had them in St. Ignatius in Yardley." He walked up stand beside Mark in front of the first one. For a moment, I could see him as a wide-eyed kid in Catholic school, like Rick must have been. I wondered if Owen had played CYO basketball, too.

Mark nodded. "I think so, too. There are fourteen of them. This is the first one, where Jesus is condemned to death." He turned to Joe. "These are very valuable. If you're not going to preserve them, you need to find a safe way to cut them out of the walls."

Joe looked closely at the wall. "Can't take them out without destroying the wall," he said. "Probably why the Benedictines left them behind. I think we can put them behind glass eventually."

"That's good," Mark said. "Next up I want to measure the dormitories. How do we get there from here?"

"Over this way," Owen said, pointing toward a side door beside a row of three small rooms which I assumed had been used for confessions.

"You've been here before?" I asked.

"Catholic school trip," he said. I remembered Rick had mentioned the same kind of trip, but I wondered if Owen really would have remembered such a detail from so long before. Had he been up to Friar Lake since then? And if so, why?

We walked through the dormitory building, and Joe showed us how the building was going to be reconfigured into four-bedroom suites, each with a bathroom. The walls between the monastic cells would go, and the single antiquated rest room would be demolished.

"Gonna be a very different place when we're done," Joe said.

Maybe I was reading too much in, but a couple of times I noticed Owen checking the security of locks, pressing against windows and so on. The walk through with them took another hour and a half, and after they were gone Joe and I still had more checklist items to go over.

"I've got a trailer coming in as soon as I get the OK," Joe said. "Going to set it right over at the side of the driveway. There are three offices and a john inside. Once we started, you can have one of the offices."

"Who'll be in the others?"

"Construction superintendent for one. Probably use the other as a plan room or for meetings. I'll be coming out most days to check on things, but it would be good to have somebody from the college on-site all the time."

"Doesn't look like I'll have anything else to do," I said.

Rochester and I left Friar Lake around twelve-thirty, and I detoured past Crazy Chicken on my way back to the office. I ordered the three-piece meal at the drive-through, then parked and led Rochester over to a metal table outside the restaurant. As I ate, I fed him bits of chicken and biscuit, then went back to the office.

He slumped contentedly in the corner while I scrambled to put together my program for the College Connection kids the next morning. I created a series of challenges for the kids that would improve their communication skills while showing them what college level work was all about. I figured I should have a PowerPoint presentation to introduce them to what I wanted, and I began searching for and embedding movie clips.

That's when Santiago Santos walked in.

I felt an immediate surge of panic – would he quibble with what I was doing? Suppose he wanted to make sure I wasn't illegally downloading movies? Then I took a deep breath and said, "Good afternoon."

"Afternoon," he said, sliding into the visitor's chair beside my desk. He peered over at my computer. "Watching movies?"

Rochester looked up at him, then rolled over and went back to sleep. I gave him a quick rundown of the College Connection and what I was putting together. "But you must have come over here for some reason," I said. "Since we just met last week. What's up?"

"Spoke to Rick Stemper at the gym," he said. "You're snooping around a police investigation again?"

"You make it sound like a crime," I said. "Tony Rinaldi from the Leighville Police asked me for some help. It's connected with my job here, and I got permission from the college president. Why is that your problem?"

"My problem," he said, emphasizing the word, "is that I am in charge of keeping you on the straight and narrow. Every time you step off the path you're supposed to be on, there's a chance you can revert back to your old habits."

I crossed my arms over my chest and stared at him.

"No good cop is going to want you to do anything illegal, Steve. And if you dig around online where you're not supposed to, you'll only get yourself and this other cop in trouble."

My first instinct was to justify myself – but I knew I'd only end up digging myself deeper into trouble. So I held my temper down and said, "You don't have anything to worry about."

"Keep it that way," he said. He pushed his chair back and stood up. Rochester looked up at him again.

"I deal with a lot of addicts in my job," Santos said. "And you've got all the traits I see in them, except for the runny nose and the bloodshot eyes. I may only be in charge of you for the next couple of months, but trust me, I will be watching you."

Then he turned and strode out. I grabbed my cell phone, ready to call Rick and ream him one for ratting me out to Santos. What business did he have anyway, talking about me behind my back? That wasn't something a friend would do.

Was he really my friend, though? Or was he just using me, my dog, and my abilities when it suited him? My anger boiled up, and suddenly Rochester jumped up and put his paws on my thighs, leaning forward to lick my face.

"Go away, dog," I said, pushing him back. But he wouldn't give up, and he kept nosing me, then frolicking around on the floor, chasing his tail. I started to laugh and then gave in, playing with him for a couple of minutes until my anger had dissipated. Rick probably hadn't seen what he did as ratting me out – more like protecting me from my own bad impulses. And that was something a friend would do, right?

I went back to my presentation and finished embedding the movie clips. By the time I was done I was really looking forward to meeting with the kids the next morning.

Tony Rinaldi called me late in the afternoon. "Thanks for your help on Saturday with Shenetta," he said. "I wouldn't have gotten her to open up if you hadn't come over."

"I bet you would have. She seemed to get along with Tanya."

"Yup, looks like Tanya might be able to help her out. She has an LPN going on maternity leave in August—just after Shenetta finishes her class work."

"That's good. Any of the leads she give you pan out?"

"Still working on them. I've been trying to track down the half-brother, but he and his mom left the place they were living on short notice and didn't leave a forwarding address. Shenetta said she'll let me know if the kid calls her. Called his school, too, but they only had that address, and since he's not registered for summer school they said the only thing they can do is wait for him to show up in the fall."

"I know where he is," I said. "Right here in Leighville."

I explained about the College Connection, and that I'd met Ka'Tar the day before.

"Why didn't you call me as soon as you met him?"

"When he told me that he knew DeAndre was dead, I figured you'd spoken to him already."

"You know where I can find him?"

"The kids are staying in Birthday House and eating at Burgers Commons." I looked at my watch. "You could probably catch up with him over there in about half an hour. Look for a tall skinny kid with a big bush of brown hair. That's Yudame, and he's the sort of camp counselor in charge of Ka'Tar's group."

We said good bye and he hung up. I really wanted to join Tony for his talk with Ka'Tar—but he had said he didn't need me, and I had to honor that. A short while later, I hooked up Rochester's leash and we headed for my car.

A group of the CC kids were hanging around outside Fields Hall, with no adults or counselors in sight. A couple of them were smoking, and I thought I recognized the scent of marijuana in the air. That wouldn't be the first time I'd smelled it at Eastern, though, and it could have been coming from some college kid in the area.

I looked around for Ka'Tar but didn't see him. I hurried Rochester along before we ran into Tony and he accused me of meddling in his case.

I talked to Lili while I was fixing dinner, and then spent the rest of the evening reading. It was such an unexpected pleasure, to be able to fall into a good book, and yet to be able to feel virtuous about it, too. I loved to read, and during my year of incarceration I had gone through book after book from the prison library. The one time Mary visited me I asked her to bring me a box of books from my bookcase—all the ones from the unread shelf. She hadn't paid much attention, tossing books in willy-nilly, so I'd found myself re-reading Jane Austen and William Gibson—a back-to-back effort that took me from the distant past to the near future, without a stop in reality—which was just fine with me at that time.

I finished the second book in the *Hunger Games* trilogy just before it was time to take Rochester for his walk, and loaded the last book onto my Kindle with a sense of sadness, realizing I had only that book left before I would be stepping away from Katniss's world.

The next morning was not so sunny, with clouds threatening to put a damper on our walk, so Rochester and I stayed close to home. When we arrived at Eastern, he settled down with a rawhide chew and I answered some emails.

I left him dozing and walked to the computer classroom in Blair Hall. Though I was a few minutes early, Yudame and his crew were already waiting for me. "Morning, my prof," he said. "I gots a real good group for you here."

I smiled at them as I slipped the card key into the slot, opening the classroom door. As they filed in, I noticed Courtney, the tough white girl with the blonde dreads. She reminded me of Katniss, and I considered how I could use that information in my presentation.

I began with a list of the main characters in the first *Hunger Games* book. Then I began assigning parts. Courtney became Katniss, and Ka'Tar volunteered to be Peeta, her partner in the game. Once everyone had a part, I went on to talk and show them bits about communication in Panem.

"Information is very tightly controlled," I said. "Can anybody give me an example?"

No one raised a hand. So, these kids were like my college-level students in that regard. "How much do Katniss and Peeta know about the Hunger Games before they begin them?" I asked. I looked down at my roster. "Rohanna Bhatt?"

"You can call me Ro." She was one of two Pakistani girls who sat next to each other. Ro had sleek black hair and olive skin; she wore a T-shirt and jeans. Zazeem wore a Muslim headscarf that covered her forehead and her hair. Her skin was lighter than Ro's but she was badly in need of acne treatment.

"They watched it on the TV every year," Ro said. "So they knew the kind of challenges."

"But the game changes from year to year," Courtney said. "So they didn't really know shit."

The class tittered. "You're both right," I said. "They knew the general outline of the games, but they didn't know what they were going to encounter. Kind of like you guys coming out here to Leighville, right? You must have had a general idea of what to expect, but you didn't know the details."

A couple of the kids nodded in agreement. "That's because the information about the games—and information about what was going on in the other districts—was very carefully controlled." We talked about information for a while, and then I gave them a writing assignment. The session wasn't as much fun as I had hoped it would be, but they had some good ideas, and I wrote a couple of their sentences up on the board and critiqued them, pointing out some of the basics of grammar, and then our time was up.

I pulled Ka'Tar aside as the kids were filing out. "How's it going?" I asked.

"You the one that sent the po-po to talk to me?" he asked.

It took me a second or two to figure out what po-po meant. "Yeah. I thought he could tell you more about what happened to DeAndre."

"DeAndre dead. Ain't much more to know about."

I closed the classroom door behind me. "Come on, I'll walk over to lunch with you," I said.

23 – Interesting Findings

"DeAndre sounds like he was a good brother," I said to Ka'Tar as we walked under the shade of an overarching maple tree. Light filtered through the leaves and dappled the flagstone path.

"We got the same pops," he said. "But we didn't even know each other til a couple years ago."

"Really? How'd you meet up?"

"DeAndre come looking for me. Said the po-po was looking for our pops, come talk to him, and they say he got a brother. He really into *Star Trek*, just like my moms. We used to do the salute thing, you know?" He held up his damaged hand. "He was like, bro, you got a head start on bein' Vulcan. We used to talk about bein' long-lost cousins of Tuvok – you know, the black dude."

"He talked to you about coming down here?" I asked as we approached the glassy front of Burgers Commons.

"Yeah, how pretty and shit it was. Told me to come to this program."

We got to the front door, and Chinelle came up to us. "Hey, Tar," she said shyly.

"How you doin', beauty?" he asked. He put his arm around her shoulder and opened the door for her, and I left the two of them to their romance.

I stayed with the CC kids through lunch. I sat between a shy light-skinned black boy named Steehle Mills and a Chinese girl named Wong Wei, though I wasn't sure if her first name was Wong or Wei. We talked more about *The Hunger Games*, and then I walked back to my office with a pocket full of food for Rochester. I took him out for a walk, thinking about the coincidence of DeAndre's brother showing up so soon after his body was discovered. Had Ka'Tar been involved in whatever DeAndre was doing? Or was he in Leighville just because DeAndre liked the town and the college and told him about the program?

Lili came over as I was getting ready to leave for the day. "I found something interesting," she said. "I want to show you."

She came over to my desk, and I got up and let her sit down at my computer. "What did you find?"

"I was looking for photos of the abbey," she said. "I got onto Pinterest, and found that one of the monks who used to live at Friar Lake set up a board for the abbey. I found a couple of old ones I can incorporate, as long as I get the monk's permission. And then I saw this one, which looks pretty recent."

She turned the monitor so I could see. "Do you think that's DeAndre there?"

The picture was of three men standing in front of the chapel. The elderly man on the left wore the plain brown robe and rope belt I had seen at the drop in center.

"Holy crap," I said. "That's Brother Anselm, for sure. And the white guy on the right? That's Owen Keely, who's living with his parents down the street from me, and who's working for Mark Figueroa."

I stood up and started pacing around. "So Owen Keely has been out to Friar Lake before. I knew it. Yesterday morning I asked him if he'd been to Friar Lake before, and he said back when he was a kid. Why didn't he mention this trip?"

"Because he was there with DeAndre, and DeAndre's dead," Lili suggested.

"That implies that he knew DeAndre was dead—which would mean he had something to do with it." I sat down in the spindle-backed chair by the desk. "Do me a favor? Open up my jump drive. I saved a booking photo of DeAndre there. We can compare it."

She turned to face me. "How did you get hold of his booking photo?"

"It's all good," I said. "I guess booking shots are public domain, and there's a company that posts them online. If you want them to remove it, you have to pay them. I just copied the picture from there."

She opened the folder on my jump drive and we compared pictures. "That's him," I said. "Wow. That adds a whole different dimension. Tony Rinaldi ought to talk to Owen." I dug my cell phone out of my pocket and dialed Tony. I got his voice mail. But the message was too complicated to leave, so I just left my name and said, "I'm emailing you. Call me when you get the message."

Lili got up and I returned to the computer. "I've got to get back to Harrow Hall," she said. "Tomorrow morning the CC kids start working with the pictures they took. I want to get some things set up for them."

"Dinner?" I asked, as my email program opened.

"No, I'll just grab something on my way home." She leaned down and kissed my cheek. "Talk to you tomorrow."

I typed out a message for Tony Rinaldi, and copied Rick Stemper on the email too, since Owen lived in Stewart's Crossing and I thought he'd want to know. Then I hit send.

I was on my way home with Rochester riding shotgun when Rick called my cell.

"I got your email about Owen Keely," he said. "Coincidence, since I'm looking for him myself."

"Why?"

"Mark Figueroa called me this morning. Some stuff is missing from his shop, and when he tried to reach Owen at home, Mrs. Keely said that he had gone away for a while."

"I knew there was something shifty about him," I said. "Poor Mark. Did Owen steal a lot?"

"Hold on, Hardy Boy. Don't go accusing anyone of theft until all the facts are in. Mark's missing a few hundred bucks in cash and a couple of small pieces of jewelry he said could add up to a couple of grand, depending on whether they're pawned or sold for gold."

"Come on, Rick. Owen goes missing at the same time as Mark's stuff. Not a big leap."

"Hey, you're the one with the imagination," Rick said. "I'm sure you could spin a half-dozen stories without Owen Keely as the bad guy."

"I feel bad for Mark. I thought he looked really happy when Owen was around. And the only time I actually saw the guy smile was when he was with Mark." I told him about finding them looking for plants along the canal. "And his parents are probably going to be broken up, too. I know they put a lot into getting him off drugs."

"Once an addict, always an addict," Rick said, and for a brief second I thought he was talking about me and my hacking addiction. "Hey, you want to meet up at the Drunken Hessian later? Seven o'clock?"

"Sure. " He hung up, and I decided to detour past Mark's antique shop on the way home. "You're going to have to stay in the car, boy," I said to Rochester, lowering the windows as I pulled up in the narrow driveway next to the antique store.

He woofed, but then settled down on the seat, his head resting across the gear shift box. The lowering clouds that had been around all day were still overhead, but it didn't look like it was going to rain.

I walked up the short steps onto the porch of the gingerbread Victorian, and then opened the door. The little bell rang, and Mark came out from the back. "Sorry about Owen," I said.

"It's my own fault," Mark said. "I always pick the wrong guys."

"Hey, you were doing his mother a favor by hiring him," I said. "Not your fault."

"Oh. I thought you knew—when you saw us down by the towpath the other day."

The tumblers clicked. "So you were a couple, too?"

"I wouldn't call it that. We never went out anywhere on a date or anything. Now I'm thinking he was just stringing me along."

He looked pretty miserable. "You shouldn't let it get you down," I said. "At least you got rid of him quickly, and cheaply. I was stuck with my ex-wife for years, and it cost me a whole lot more to get rid of her."

He smiled. "I suppose I could look at it that way."

"Hey, I'm meeting Rick for dinner at the Drunken Hessian at seven. Why don't you join us?"

"I wouldn't be good company."

"You'll be better than Rick. Come on."

"I could use a beer or two," he admitted.

"Cool. See you then."

I drove Rochester home, fed him dinner, and took him for a long walk. Then I sat down on a kitchen chair. "You think I can trust you outside the crate this time?" I asked him. "No chewing on gloves, or anything else?"

He slumped on the floor in front of me. "How about if we compromise?" I stood up and walked over to the entrance hall closet. I had a folding gate there I had used when Rochester was very young, to keep him on whatever floor I was on. "I'll put up the gate, and you can have the whole first floor to yourself. But if you misbehave..."

He rolled on his side and waved his front paws in the air.

I put up the gate, made sure he had water, and locked the door behind me. As I walked out through the courtyard, I looked back and saw him with his nose pressed against the sliding glass door.

Mark Figueroa was walking toward me as I pulled into the Drunken Hessian's parking lot. "Do you live above the antique store?" I asked, as I met him halfway.

"Cuts down on the commuting time," he said. "Hard to get away from work, though. I'm always thinking of something I need to do and then going downstairs."

"And Owen?"

Mark looked sheepish. "He didn't like to stay overnight—said that his mother would worry about him. So last night I didn't think anything of it when he walked out. Must have been some time after eleven. "

"That's the last time you saw him?"

"Yup. He was supposed to come in at ten this morning—that's when I open. But he didn't, and I waited an hour to call his cell. No answer. So I called Marie to ask about him. She said she was worried, because he'd never come home last night."

He pulled the door to the Drunken Hessian open and ushered me in ahead of him. "I was worried about him—what if he'd gotten into an accident on his bike somewhere after he left me. But I had a couple of deliveries that needed to be made, and he wasn't there, so I closed the shop up and took the van out."

The hostess was a tough-looking older woman who'd been working at the Hessian for as long as I could remember. "Table for two?" she asked.

"Three," I said. As she was pulling out the menus, Rick walked in and joined us.

We slid into the booth, and Mark said, "I was just telling Steve what happened. I made my deliveries, and got back to the store around one. Had a customer waiting, wanted to buy this porcelain statue she'd had her eye on for a while. When I pulled it out for her I noticed that there were a couple of pieces missing from the shelf. She paid in cash, and when I went to make her change I realized the petty cash was gone."

The waitress came over, and we ordered a pitcher of beer and a platter of nachos.

"After my customer left I took a good look around. That's when I realized I'd been robbed. I called Rick and he came right over."

Rick picked up the narrative. "We made a list of everything missing, and Mark signed the complaint. I drove over to Owen's parents' house. Didn't realize they lived just down the block from you. I recognized Mrs. Keely from seeing her on that three-wheeled bike of hers."

"I've known Marie for a couple of years," Mark said. "I've been in and out of her house a dozen times. Used to see the pictures of her kids and I always thought Owen was a real stud. Then when he came home from rehab and was staying with them, I met him one day, and he was a hundred times sexier than he was in the pictures."

The waitress delivered the pitcher and three tall pilsner glasses. I poured as Mark continued, "I don't usually lust after straight guys, but there was something about Owen that really floated my boat. The next day he showed up at my shop and he... well..."

Mark's face reddened.

"When I was in prison, there wasn't anything like gay or straight," I said. "I never fooled around with anyone, but I saw guys have sex with each other just for the human touch, or for the power."

"I tried to get Owen to talk about his past—had he been with other guys, that kind of thing. He'd never say anything. I guess he wasn't really gay at all – just having sex with me so he could take advantage of me." He turned to Rick. "What did Marie say when you talked to her?"

"We had a long talk about Owen and all his problems. He had nightmares, and it was tough for him to adjust to being home." He looked over at Mark. "You knew about the drugs, right?"

Mark shrugged. "He admitted he'd had some problems with drugs in the past. But he swore he was clean."

"That's what his mother said, but he wouldn't be the first kid to hide something like that from his parents."

"And he isn't a kid," I said. "How old is he?"

"Twenty-eight," Mark said. He picked up his beer glass and took a long drink.

Rick nodded. "I looked through his room. He didn't have much there, but his parents said he hadn't come home with much, either. Some clothes in the closet and the dresser. Nothing personal, though."

"Didn't he have some friend who came to help him with moving furniture?" I asked. "You think he could be staying with him?"

"Striker. I suppose."

"You have this Striker's real name and address?" Rick asked, pulling out his pad and pen.

Mark shook his head. "I know I shouldn't have, but I paid the guy in cash. He was kind of paranoid, wouldn't even tell me his last name. But Owen vouched for him, and it was easier that way. No paperwork."

I turned to Rick. "Was Owen's bicycle at his parents' house?" I asked

Rick shook his head. "Nope. I spoke to the guard. No video surveillance at the gate, and the night guard didn't notice Owen come back in."

The nachos arrived and as he reached for a chip, I noticed that Mark was wearing a nice gold signet ring, and asked, "He didn't take any of your personal stuff, did he? No jewelry or anything?"

He shook his head. "No. But that reminds me—I found an earring in the van this afternoon, when I was cleaning it out after my deliveries. Wasn't from my stock."

He dug in his pants pocket and brought out a gold earring with a thumbnail-sized red stone hanging from it. "That's a genuine ruby," he said. "I checked. Must be worth something to someone."

Rick took it from him. "This looks like one from a pair that was taken from the Orlandos," he said. "The house that was burgled Sunday night. The wife described something like this to me."

"You think Owen was using my van for burglaries?" Mark asked.

"Remember, we saw Owen driving the van around Crossing Estates when we were there last week," I said to Rick.

"That's right, you called me, Rick," Mark said. "But it wasn't strange that he'd be out then. We have to deliver when the customer is home to accept the merchandise, and sometimes that's in the evening. And we had to coordinate when Owen's friend could come down and help."

He thought for a minute. "And you know, a couple of times he asked if he could borrow the van—wanted to go somewhere he couldn't get to on his bike." He frowned. "Shit. You think those times he borrowed the van he was using it to rob people? Holy Bible in a purse!"

We both looked at him. "Sorry, that's an old family expression. When my brother and I were teenagers we weren't allowed to say things like holy shit. My mom had this purse with a bible built into it—the holy bible in a purse, they called it. My brother and I used to say that as a curse."

"Sounds like something Robin would say to Batman," I said. I picked up a tortilla chip and scraped some cheese and meat onto it. "Rochester's usually the friendliest dog, but he never liked Owen."

"Next time I think about going on a date, I'm going to borrow Rochester," Mark said. "Maybe I'll have better luck that way."

24 – Good to Go

We went through the pitcher, and the nachos, and then the waitress delivered us a round of burgers and another pitcher. Mark was rambling, talking about some pictures he'd taken of Owen, and how maybe they would help Rick find him.

"That reminds me," I said. "Lili found a picture online of Owen up at Friar Lake, with DeAndre and one of the monks."

Both Rick and Owen said, "DeAndre?" at the same time.

"DeAndre Dawson," I said to Mark. "The guy whose body we found up at Friar Lake."

"I read about that in the Boat-Gazette," he said. "It was someone Owen knew?"

I nodded. "When Lili and I went out to Friar Lake last week, right after I got assigned to manage the place, we took Rochester with us. He was running around the property, and I noticed he was digging something up by the lake. When I got over there I realized it was a human hand."

Mark looked green, though it was hard to tell in the dim bar light. "That part didn't make the paper."

"Step back," Rick said. "Tell me about this picture Lili found."

I felt the beer getting to me, and I made a conscious effort to clear my head. I took a long drink of water, then said, "Lili is putting together a photo book about the Friar Lake property, and she was looking for old pictures online. She stumbled on this photo on a Pinterest board of Owen with DeAndre and this old monk named Brother Anselm. I doubt either Owen or DeAndre knew the Benedictines even used Pinterest."

"Any idea when it was taken?" Rick asked.

"I'll have to check with Brother Anselm. But he said he was out at Friar Lake in the early spring, and there's a dogwood with new blossoms in the background."

Mark looked from me to Rick. "You don't think Owen killed this guy, do you?"

"Don't know what to think," Rick said. "Right now I just know I want to talk to Owen. And not just about what he might have stolen from Mark."

By the time the evening was winding down I was still a bit shaky, but I'd drunk a lot of water and eaten a lot, and I thought I was good to drive. I could tell Mark Figueroa was completely wasted, though.

Rick and I walked him over to the antique shop and made sure he got inside all right. Then we walked back to the parking lot. When we got to his truck, Rick opened the passenger side and pulled a gadget out of the glove compartment. As he turned it on, I said, "What's that?"

"Breathalyzer. Want to make sure we're both good to drive." It beeped, and he said, "Watch me." He blew into it for a couple of seconds, then held it away from him.

The parking lot light above us buzzed, and a car passed down Ferry Street, heading toward the river. "You think Owen Keely ran away?" I asked Rick.

"As opposed to?"

"As opposed to somebody killing him," I said. "Like DeAndre Dawson."

"Don't know yet." He looked at the device. "I'm good. You try."

He held it up to me, and said, "Blow out long and steady, all right?"

I followed his instructions, only stopping when he took the device away from my face. "Do you think Owen killed DeAndre?"

"Like I said, I don't know yet." He held the device up to me. "Can't drive in Pennsylvania over .08. You're at .04. You feel okay?"

I nodded. "Yeah. I'll take it easy going home."

"All right. Talk to you tomorrow."

It was almost eleven o'clock, and I only passed two other cars on my way back to River Bend, but I still drove with exaggerated care, and felt relieved when I pulled into my driveway. As I opened the front door, I remembered I'd left Rochester uncrated, and braced myself for damage.

All I saw, though, was the dog eagerly greeting me, and it looked like he'd been good. I hooked up his leash and we went for a quick walk, and after some more water and a couple of aspirin I fell into a deep and dreamless sleep.

Wednesday morning, I walked Rochester down Sarajevo Court past the Keelys' house. I hoped that Phil would be out working in the yard, or Marie riding on her tricycle, but Phil's SUV, usually parked in the driveway, was gone, and the garage was closed. Had they gone after Owen? Or were they just out running errands or off to see a doctor?

Not my business, I reminded myself. If Rick asked, I'd be happy to help him. But I wasn't a cop and it wasn't up to me to investigate anything.

The rash of break-ins at Crossing Estates finally made the *Bucks County Courier-Times* that morning. It was in only a small article in the second section, but I knew it had to be causing trouble for Rick Stemper. I wondered about the earring that Mark had found in his van, and if that clue had helped Rick show he was making progress.

I'd only been in my office for a few minutes when Elaine from HR called. "Good news, Steve. Your application has everything we need, and President Babson has authorized me to close the search."

"Does that mean I have the job?"

"There are still a few more hoops, but this is a good step forward. The hiring site is down right now – something to do with that crappy Freezer Burn software, I think. I'll be glad when they finally get that removed from every computer. Once it comes back up I have to finish the formal job description and schedule an interview with you where we discuss the job. Assuming he gets the approval he needs from the Board of Trustees, then I prepare an offer letter for you and get Babson to sign it."

After I hung up I sat back in my chair. I felt better—but not completely. I wouldn't be satisfied until I knew that the Board had signed off on Friar Lake, and I had the counter-signed offer letter—maybe not even until I'd been established in the job for a while.

Joe Capodilupo called me about eleven, as I was packing more boxes to send to Ruta del Camion in the press office. "I'm up at Friar Lake," he said. "Looks like there was a break-in here."

"A break-in? Was it vandalism?" I asked. "There wasn't much there to steal."

"A broken window in the anteroom at the back of the chapel. Then a big mess in the chapel itself." He turned away from the phone to call a workman over. "Remember that hole under the altar? Whoever broke in made it a lot bigger, and dragged a bunch of crap out from underneath the altar."

"Looking for something," I said. I remembered the reliquary that DeAndre had been searching for. It seemed to be at the center of everything. Had DeAndre found it and been killed for it? If so, then why was someone still searching the abbey?

Or what if Owen had been working with DeAndre, and then for some reason Owen had killed him before they found the reliquary. And then, after leaving Mark Figueroa's, Owen gone back up to the abbey and found it — and that's why he'd left town?

"Don't know what they'd be looking for under there," Joe said.

I didn't share my suspicion with him. Instead I said, "I'm going to call the Leighville cops. Don't touch anything that looks like it was disturbed—maybe they can get fingerprints or something."

"I want to get that window fixed by dark," Joe said.

"I'll get on it right now. I'll let you know what I hear."

"Better call John Babson too. He'll want to know."

Great. I just loved taking bad news to the president. What if he used this information as a reason to hold off on talking to the Board of Trustees? Where would that leave me?

First, though, I hung up and dialed Tony Rinaldi. "There was a break-in last night at Friar Lake," I said. "I think it might be connected to DeAndre's death. Can you get one of your crime scene techs up there to take fingerprints?"

"Connected how?" Tony asked.

"Rick told you about the photo Lili and I found, that linked Brother Anselm, DeAndre and Owen, didn't he? I think Owen knew about the reliquary, too, and he broke into the chapel to look for it."

"You think the thing really exists?" Tony asked.

"Doesn't matter what I think right now," I said. "Seems to me like DeAndre believed in it, and Owen, too."

"I'll get a guy up there," Tony said. "Owen Keely was in the Army so I'm sure there are prints on file somewhere."

After I hung up, I walked down the hall to President Babson's office. "Is he in?" I asked his secretary.

She looked down at the phone console on her desk. "He's on a call with one of the trustees," she said. "You want to wait?"

I didn't see that I had much choice. I sat in one of the spindle-backed chairs and thought about the suspicions I had. I realized I'd only been taking Brother Anselm's word about the existence of the reliquary. Sure, Lili and I had seen a grainy photograph of something that might have been the reliquary. But was it? If it existed, surely someone else must have know about it. I pulled out my cell phone while I waited and began searching for information on Saint Roch. The connection was painfully slow and my screen way too small to read much, but I found the same things that Brother Anselm had told me, about his sainthood and his connection to dogs.

"He's off the phone," Babson's secretary said.

I hopped up and knocked on his door, then pushed it open. "Have a moment?" I asked. When he nodded, I said, "I wanted to let you know that there was a break-in last night at Friar Lake."

"What?"

I stepped farther into the room and told him what Joe Capodilupo had told me.

Babson shook his head. "First a dead body, now a break-in." He looked thoughtful. "Have a seat, Steve."

I sat, worried about what he was going to say. What would I do if the job fell through? I'd already been told I was being phased out of the fund-raising campaign. Could I go back to adjuncting? Freelance writing?

"Do you think maybe this project is too far from campus? Too hard for us to keep a handle on?"

As it often did in my conversations with President Babson, my heart rate zoomed. Was he asking me if I thought the whole idea was a bad one? I sure wasn't going to agree to that, when my job depended on it. I thought very carefully before speaking.

"You know I have my master's from Columbia," I said. "They have all kinds of additional centers. The Lamont-Doherty observatory, Arden House in the Catskiils." I warmed to my topic, knowing just which strings to play. "Every good college has them. Middlebury College has the Bread Loaf Center, up in the mountains."

Babson nodded. "You're right. If Eastern is going to keep its reputation as a very good small college, we need to match the resources our competitors have. But I need you to keep a lid on these problems before the Board of Trustees gets cold feet. Have the police wrapped up their investigation of that body yet?"

"I'm in touch with the detective regularly," I said. "I'll let you know once there's news."

"Good. I have the paperwork from Elaine about your job right here. As soon as I get things firmed up with the Board, I'll sign it." His secretary buzzed to let him know he had a call, and I stood up and walked out, feeling like I had just dodged one bullet. I just worried how many more there would be before the job was really mine.

Back in my office, I continued searching online for information about St. Roch. After a few minutes, Rochester got up from his place on the floor and nosed at my legs. Looking from him to the screen I had a bit of a eureka moment. 'Roch' was the first syllable in 'Rochester.' What a wild coincidence. My dog was named after his patron saint.

Of course I'd had nothing to do with that. Caroline Kelly had named him after the romantic hero of Jane Eyre, and if she'd known of the saintly connection, she'd never mentioned it to me.

Did he know that I was looking for information on his namesake? Or did he just want to go out for a walk? I opted for the second choice, and hooked up his leash.

I was distracted as we walked, still thinking about the reliquary. I picked up a sandwich from one of the lunch trucks and took it back to my office, where I ate while I continued searching. At long last, I discovered a church in Philadelphia that had an archive of old photos of all the churches and other religious buildings in the diocese there.

I called and spoke to Esther Washington, who told me she was in charge of the archive. "Do you have any material there on the Abbey of Our Lady of the Waters, in Leighville?" I asked.

"I can't be sure," she said. "We have an awful lot of material that hasn't been catalogued yet. But you're welcome to come down and take a look, if you'd like."

I established how late she'd be there, and then hung up. I dialed Lili's office and told her what I'd discovered. "Do you have time this afternoon to go down there with me?" I asked. "You might find some other pictures there."

"Give me a half hour to finish up for the day," she said.

Rochester and I finished eating. "You ready for an adventure, boy?" I asked. "Even if it's just into Philadelphia?"

He woofed in agreement.

25 – St. Mary Martyr

We met Lili by my car in the parking lot. Seeing her, Rochester immediately clambered into the back seat. I lowered all the windows and we headed south.

As we drove down River Road I told her about the break-in at the abbey chapel.

"You think it was Owen Keely?" she asked.

"He's the logical suspect. I'm sure that Brother Anselm told him about the reliquary, too. Maybe he found it after he left Mark's, and that's why he took off—to sell it somewhere."

"Do you think he killed DeAndre, too?"

"I don't know. Hell, I don't even know if I believe this reliquary thing is real. We only have Brother Anselm's word that it ever existed. There could be some other explanation for DeAndre's death and Owen's disappearance."

"Maybe there will be something more about it in these archives," she said. The church's address was on Germantown Avenue in North Philly, and she used her cell phone to pull up driving directions. "It says we should go down US 1," Lili said. "Isn't that a long way?"

I shrugged. "When I was a kid that used to be the way we went into Philly. It's a lot of traffic lights, but I think it puts us closer to North Philly than taking 95." We hopped onto I-95 at the Scudder Falls Bridge, just north of Yardley, and then took it a few miles south to where it met up with US1 – or "useless 1," as my dad used to call it.

"Sometimes I forget how lucky we are to live out in the country," Lili said, as we drove through Bristol, the original terminus for the Delaware Canal. The divided highway was lined with warehouses, motels, used car lots and superstores with huge parking lots. "You can hardly see a piece of grass around here except for that cemetery over there."

"The city keeps spreading," I said. "I remember coming down this way to visit friends of my dad's, or to go to some special store. It was pretty built up even then."

As we continued into the heart of the city, the suburban sprawl was replaced by rows of brick apartment buildings and strip shopping centers that had long ago lost their parking lots to road expansion. In Germantown, the street was lined with two-story row houses with street-level storefronts—hair salons and dry cleaners and consignment stores, cheap-looking Chinese, Mexican and burger restaurants.

A group of teenage boys played a pickup game of basketball in a park across from an Acme grocery. On the side streets we saw more row houses, these a bit more modern, with jutting second-floor projecting bays.

There were trees here and there, but the sidewalks were damaged and some of the windows on Germantown Avenue were broken. We began to see exterior bars on windows and roll-up gates on storefronts.

"The College Connection kids come from places like this," Lili said.

"So did DeAndre. I can see why he fell in love with Leighville and encouraged his half-brother to go into the program."

The church of St. Mary Martyr was a vaguely gothic stone building, with a couple of arched windows and a square tower over the entrance to the sanctuary. A long sloping concrete walkway, built to meet ADA requirements, I was sure, snaked along one side of the old building. I could see traces of old graffiti on the stone, and the grass outside was parched from lack of water or care.

An electric trolley car rattled past as we pulled into the parking lot behind the church. When I got out of the car, Rochester hopped out behind me, and immediately peed against a lamppost. "They probably won't let you bring him inside," Lili said.

"I'm not leaving him in the car in this neighborhood. If we have to, he and I will wait in the lobby while you look through the pictures."

Esther Washington was a black woman in her late sixties who worked in the church office. "My goodness, what a beautiful dog!" she said when we walked in.

Rochester went right up to her and sat down on his haunches. She reached over and petted him. "My, my. I had a dog just like you, sweetheart. A long time ago."

She looked up. "You must be the gentleman who called earlier."

"I'm Steve, and this is Lili," I said. "And that's Rochester."

"What a handsome name," Esther said. I assumed she meant Rochester. She stood up. "I'm afraid what we have isn't in any kind of order. But I can take you into the social hall and you can look through the boxes."

I helped Esther carry two big boxes of pictures to a table in the warm, drafty social hall. Lili opened her messenger bag and pulled out her iPad and a portable scanner. She slid the iPad into the scanner's dock, and then ran a photo through to test it. I was impressed at the quality of the picture that showed up on the iPad's screen.

"Very cool gadget," I said.

We each took a box and began looking through the photos, which had been haphazardly tossed together. "This is a big project," I grumbled. "Most of these pictures aren't even labeled."

"We both know what Friar Lake looks like. Let's just see if we can find anything that matches what we've seen."

We spent nearly an hour before Lili found a picture that she thought looked like the abbey at Friar Lake. She pulled up a recent picture on her iPad and we compared it. "Yeah, that's a match," I said. "See the tracery around the stained glass window? It's the same in both photos."

I looked over to see Rochester nosing into one box. "Rochester! Come away from there!"

He didn't respond, so I jumped up and crossed the room to the box he was sniffing. "Is there something in here, boy?" I asked.

I carried the box over to the table where Lili and I sat, and lifted out a frayed white robe embroidered with gold thread. Underneath was a small waxed-paper sleeve of round cookies. "False alarm," I said. "He found some cookies."

I shook my head at him. "These are so old they're stale," I said. "You can't have one."

"They aren't cookies," Lili said. "They must be communion wafers."

"Oh. That makes sense." Under another robe, though, we found a cache of black and white pictures of Our Lady of the Waters from the 1950s. "Good boy, Rochester," I said, scratching beneath his chin. "You did find something after all. You'll get a treat when we get home."

Rochester recognized the word treat, and he lifted his big head up and nodded a couple of times. When he realized there was no treat coming, though, he lowered his head and slumped back to the floor.

Lili and I looked through the pictures. Monks in traditional robes stood outside the chapel, the dormitory and the kitchen. Someone had written the date and the monks' names on the back of each photo, in a spidery, faded handwriting.

There were some indoor shots, too—a monk in his room, another in the kitchen. The last set were taken in the chapel. Maybe it was just the age of the photos, but the place looked pretty worn. Monks stood by the windows, next to the baptismal font, and at the foot of the altar. In one close-up shot of the altar various ceremonial objects had been laid out on an embroidered runner.

Lili went to get Esther while I ran the pictures through the scanner. "We're hoping you can tell us what some of these things are," Lili said as they walked back in. "Neither of us are that familiar with Catholic objects."

"What a lovely picture," Esther said, when we showed her the altar close-up. "Look at the detail on that altar cloth. You don't see work like that anymore."

She began moving down the line of objects. "That's the paten," she said, pointing at a flat plate with the letters IHS inscribed in the center. "You put the Eucharistic bread on it. And that's the Christogram there—the first three letters of Christ's name in Greek." It was a simple round plate, and the goblet next to it was very plain as well. "The chalice, for the wine."

There were several crucifixes laid out on the altar cloth, and the positioning of Jesus's body was slightly different in each. One even had a skull and crossbones beneath his feet.

"That's a symbol of Calvary, where Jesus was buried," Esther said. "In Hebrew they call it Golgotha, which is supposed to mean the place of the skull. Some traditions say that Jesus was buried directly on top of Adam and Eve, and the skull and bones represents that."

It was creepy—but then, the whole idea of displaying a dead or dying man creeped me out. I had been in a speech and debate club in high school, and our team often competed in meets at Catholic schools, where the crucifix was as ever-present as the American flag in our classes. I had become desensitized to them—but when I looked closely at these I was struck by the horror and the pain.

The last item on the altar cloth was a rectangular box about six inches long. "What's that for?" I asked Esther, pointing.

She shook her head. "I don't know." We all looked more closely at the box. Unlike the plain paten and goblet, the box was inscribed with ornamental curlicues, and inlaid with stones. In the center there was a tiny etching, and Lili had to enlarge the photo several times before we could make it out.

"Why, it's a man with a dog," Esther said. "How sweet."

"Oh, wow!" I said. "That's Saint Roch, the patron saint of dogs."

Lili and I shared a glance and I could tell she was as excited as I was. We'd finally found something that substantiated Brother Anselm's story about the reliquary. We couldn't tell from the picture, of course, if there was a saint's thumb bone inside, or even if the jewels on the box were real. But the details matched.

Esther looked at me. "Now, how did you know that?"

"Because there are a lot of people looking for a box like this," I said.

Lili finished scanning the last couple of pictures, and then we packed up our gear. "Thank you so much for your help," Lili said. "Would you like me to send you copies of the pictures I scanned?"

"That would be lovely," Esther said. She handed Lili a flyer about the church. "Our email address is right there on the bottom."

Rochester stopped to pee on the same light post before he got back in the car, and then we headed back toward the suburbs. The sun had gone in and the skies were gray, and I was glad to be leaving the inner city behind.

"So it's real," Lili said, sitting back in her seat. "The reliquary."

"You bet. When you zoomed in on that picture, my heart skipped a couple of beats. Now we know that the monks had it as late as the 1950s. The question is where it's been since then, and who has it now."

"Not to mention," Lili said, staring out the windows as the grim urban landscape fled past, "who might have killed DeAndre to get it."

26 – Runaways

Lili had work to do before her class the next morning, so I drove her up to her apartment in Leighville. "I'll email you the pictures I scanned," she said. "I'll try and zoom in on the box and get as good a print as I can."

As I drove back downriver toward Stewart's Crossing, I realized it was already dinner time and I didn't feel like cooking, so I called Rick. I kind of wanted to show off to him, about what we'd discovered about the reliquary. "You want to split a pizza?" I asked. "I'll pick up from Giovanni's?"

"Works for me," he said. "Although I know you're only offering so you can squirm your way farther into these investigations."

"As long as we're clear," I said. I hung up and ordered the pizza. Giovanni's was in a small strip shopping center in the middle of Stewart's Crossing, perpendicular to Main Street. It was sandwiched between a Laundromat and a State Store, the government-run outlet for liquor, along with a greeting card store, a dry cleaner's, and a karate donjon.

I left Rochester in the car with the windows down while I went into the pizza parlor. There was a line for takeout, and I had to force myself to be patient until it was my turn. By the time the cashier had pulled the large sausage-and-mushroom pie from its warming spot on top of the pizza oven my mouth was watering and my stomach was grumbling.

Carrying the hot-bottomed box by its edges, I shouldered open the restaurant door and walked to the trunk of the BMW. I was surprised that Rochester wasn't hanging out the window salivating. I slid the box into the trunk and then opened the driver's side door.

Rochester was gone.

I scanned the parking lot. "Rochester! Where are you, boy?"

I couldn't see him anywhere. Had someone stolen my dog? Or had he run away? There were a dozen or more cars in the lot, but he was too big to hide under anything smaller than an SUV.

A father exited the donjon with two little boys in white robes, and a matronly woman was crossing the parking lot toward the State Store. There was no one else around to ask if they'd seen a big golden retriever.

When I was a kid, I explored every corner of Stewart's Crossing on foot or on my bike, alone or with friends. I knew there was a creek behind the shopping center that fed into the mill pond down the street. Could Rochester have gone back there? Or had he run toward Main Street? He was a smart dog, but impulsive, and I worried that he'd run in front of a car.

I tried to shut down my fear and focus. Should I go toward the street, or the creek? If Rochester had jumped out the car window on his own, which way would he have gone?

I went with my gut instinct and took off at a run for the creek, calling his name. "Rochester! Rochester! Where are you, boy?"

The two boys in karate robes looked at me open-mouthed as I ran past them. I rounded the corner of the shopping center and skidded to a stop. Rochester was knee-deep in creek water, his front paws up on the trunk of a sloping weeping willow.

"Rochester! Come here right now!"

He looked over at the sound of my voice, but then turned back to the tree and barked once.

My heart was pumping and I was panting for breath. I guess I hadn't sprinted like that since high school.

"I am going to kill you," I said, stalking through the underbrush to the creek. Just before I reached him I banged my shin on something. "Ow!" I looked down and realized it was the handlebar of a bicycle. "This is not a dump! What kind of a jerk throws a bike back here?"

Maybe it was the two words, jerk and bike, together in one sentence, that made me think of Owen Keely. "Crap," I said. I pulled my cell phone out of my pocket and dialed Rick's number.

"You know what kind of bike Owen Keely rode?" I asked.

"I thought you were bringing pizza."

"We had a bit of a diversion. The bike?"

"Hold on. Let me check. I don't have all this information at the tip of my tongue, you know."

"I know," I grumbled. Rochester kept trying to climb the tree, and I saw a squirrel in a branch high above us, chittering down at him.

Rick came back on the line after a minute. "His mother doesn't know the brand. But it has a blue body and cream-colored fenders."

"I think Rochester found it," I said.

"Where are you?"

I told him, and he said he'd meet me there. There was no guarantee it was Owen's bicycle, though it looked pretty new, not the kind of bike you'd just throw in the trash.

Rochester was still sniffing around the tree, though the squirrel above had long since hopped away. I had forgotten to bring his leash with me so I had to grab him by his collar.

"You are a very bad dog. Don't you ever run away from me again!"

He splashed in the creek and the water sprayed my pants legs. He tried to reach up and lick my hand but I pulled him forward. Holding the ring on the end of his choke-chain collar, I led him to the car and he jumped in the front seat. "Sit!" I said.

He plopped his butt down, but by the time I had gone around to the trunk he had jumped to the back seat and was sniffing toward me, leaving muddy paw prints everywhere.

I had to remind myself that even though he was two years old, he was still a puppy in many ways, and that it was my own fault for leaving the windows in the car open enough so that he could jump out. I wouldn't make that mistake again.

My hands were still shaking as I opened the trunk and pulled out a slice of pizza. No reason to let the pie get cold while I waited for Rick, I thought. I fed some crust to Rochester through the back window and wished I had a beer with me.

I forced myself to take some deep, calming breaths, as Rochester sniffed and scratched at the back seat. I felt worn out—not just from the run, but from the fear that I might have lost my dog for good.

I was calmer by the time Rick pulled up in his truck. I closed the trunk and put Rochester's leash on as Rick got out. "Where's the bike?"

"I'll show you." With Rochester pulling forward, we went back to the creek, and I told him how Rochester had run away. "It freaked me out," I said. "And it reminded me he's still a big puppy. I need to be more careful about him. I just kept imagining him running in front of a car, or him galloping away and me never seeing him again."

"I know how you feel. I had Rascal at the dog park a couple of weeks ago and when this ditzy blonde opened the gate, he ran right out and took off down the street. Had to chase him for three blocks until he got distracted by a squirrel."

I led him a couple of feet into the thicket, and pointed at the bike, half-hidden under the brush. "I guess you need a crime scene tech here," I said.

"What's the crime?" Rick asked. "Illegal dumping?"

"But doesn't this mean..." I began.

"All it means is that somebody dumped a bike back here that might be Owen Keely's. Back the dog away so I can drag it out."

It was hot and muggy back there by the creek, and Rick's cargo shorts and T-shirt were sweaty and dirt-stained by the time he had the bike out of the muck and thrown into the back of his truck.

"You get the pizza?" he asked, wiping his hands on a rag.

"Yeah. Probably cold by now."

"That's what microwaves are for."

I followed him back to his house. Before I got out of the car, I clipped Rochester's leash onto his collar, and then I held it tightly as I navigated removing the pizza box from the trunk and opening the gate to Rick's yard.

Rascal came tearing toward us. The combined force of the two big dogs nearly knocked me over, and Rick had to jump forward and grab the pizza box.

He put a couple of slices of pizza into the microwave as I opened his fridge and removed a bottle of beer. I sat at the table and he brought out plates and paper towels.

"Lili and I drove into Philly today," I said. "And guess what we found?"

"It can't be a bicycle," he said dryly. "Already dealt with that."

"How about a photograph of this reliquary Brother Anselm talked about," I said. As we ate, I explained about calling the church on Germantown Avenue, and then going through all the pictures. "There was a lineup of stuff on the altar—probably all their valuable pieces. We saw this one box that looked like the reliquary."

"How could you tell?" he asked, feeding a piece of crust to each dog.

"Let me see if Lili sent me the picture and I'll show you." I opened my phone and checked my email. I clicked on Lili's latest message, and a close-up of the picture appeared. "We think this is it," I said, showing the phone to Rick. "See that guy with the dog? That could be St. Roch, the patron saint of dogs. And even in black and white you can see that those look like jewels around the edges."

"You send this to Tony?"

I checked the message, and saw that Lili had copied him. "Yup."

I sat back in my chair. "Lili's working on a pictorial history of the property. I'm supposed to be helping with the text."

"And how's that?" Rick asked. "Working with her?"

"So far it's okay. I can remember times I had to help Mary with her projects, and we use to squabble about every little detail. Lili and I don't seem to work that way."

Mary was smart and tough and good at communication and convincing people. She had built a career in corporate marketing, and we had moved from New York to Silicon Valley so she could take a big job with one of the computer companies. She was often up til the early hours of the morning, reading, answering emails and working on presentations.

Sometimes, though, the technical aspects of what she was working on would overwhelm her, and she'd ask for my help. I had built up the ability to communicate technical information clearly, and I'd try to untangle her sentences to clarify and focus.

But that always led to arguments. "It needs to read that way," she'd say.

"But it's not clear."

Our voices would climb, and we'd end up yelling at each other over some stupid point like the storage capacity of a jump drive, and then one of us would get fed up and stalk away, slamming doors and nursing hurt feelings.

It wasn't like that with Lili—at least not yet. So far we'd been getting along just fine. I struggled to remember the first years with Mary, double-dating in New York with Tor and Sherry, but it was all a blur.

"When you were first married, did you get along with Vanessa?" I asked.

"What kind of a question is that? I wouldn't have married her otherwise."

"Yeah, but even when Mary and I were first going out, we used to argue about little things—like where we'd go to dinner, and what the best way was to get somewhere on the subway. I think that set a pattern for our whole relationship."

"And it's not like that with Lili?"

"No, so far we get along well."

Rick sat back in his chair with his bottle of Sam Adams in his hand. "Vanessa and I were all about sex," he said. "We were both so hot for each other we didn't pay attention to anything else. Yeah, if I look back on it now, I see we liked totally different things. She was a girly girl, into her clothes and her makeup and her shoes."

He leaned forward and put the beer bottle down on the table hard. "Shoes."

"As in Paula Madden," I said.

"Shit. What do I keep doing with these women?"

I had an idea but I wasn't going to say. I thought I'd broken my pattern with Lili, but maybe it was too early to say.

"That's it," Rick said. "My new year's resolution. No more dating women like Vanessa."

"It's July," I said. "Kind of late for a New Year's resolutions."

"Better late than never, right? But I thought you came over here because you wanted information."

"Well, yeah. You have any to share?"

"Went back out to Crossing Estates this afternoon. Paula's friend identified the earring that Mark found in his van. One of a pair her husband gave her for their twentieth anniversary."

"So that connects Owen to the robberies," I said.

"Circumstantially. Couldn't lift any fingerprints from the earring—it was too tiny. Because we only have Mark's word that Owen had the van, an attorney could certainly raise reasonable doubt. I'd need a lot more evidence to connect Owen to those burglaries. The only thing I can connect him to right now is the theft from Mark's place—and even for that, we only have Mark's word."

"Assuming that's Owen's bike, what do you think it was doing back by the creek?" I asked.

"No idea. I looked around in the woods around the Yardley railroad station and couldn't find any sign that the bike had been ditched," he said. "Checked with drivers on the bus route through town, too, and none of them remember him getting on with the bike."

"Suppose he met someone at the shopping center," I said. "It's set back from Main Street so Owen could hang around there, say if he was waiting for someone to pick him up."

"Why ditch the bike?"

"Maybe he didn't ditch it – maybe he just hid it there because he couldn't take it with him, wherever he was going. Or somebody killed him over the relic, and ditched the bike."

"Both are hypotheses," Rick said. "So far no evidence to support either one."

"He must have had a cell phone," I said. "Have you checked it?"

"Right now all I have him on is a suspected robbery from Mark's place. It's not enough to convince a judge to give me an order for Owen's phone records."

He looked at me. "And don't you go trying to hack into those records either," he said. "Because you know that's not only illegal, but can violate your parole."

"You don't have to hack for that," I said. "All you need is the carrier name, the phone number, and a good password-breaking program."

"Which I'm sure you don't have," Rick said. "Right?"

"I have no intention of trying to hack his phone records," I said.

I didn't even have to cross my fingers behind my back. I had a better idea.

27 – Password Problems

On my way home from Rick's, I called Mark Figueroa. "Did Owen have an email account?" I asked.

"Yeah, we sent some messages back and forth. Why?"

"Just curious. Can you give me the address?"

"I already tried emailing him. He's not answering. But feel free to try yourself, if you want. It's owenvet at mymail.com."

"Thanks, Mark. Do you know if Owen had any friends in the area—guys with cars who might have given him a ride after he left your place?" I told him about finding a bike that looked like Owen's behind the shopping center.

"No, he didn't have many friends. Just Striker, as far as I knew."

Rochester squirmed around on the car seat next to me and rested his head on my lap as I drove. I stroked his golden fur. "You were a bad boy today, Rochester. Don't you ever try and run away from me again, all right?"

He didn't answer, but he did drool on my leg.

When I got home, I climbed up to the attic and retrieved Caroline's laptop. While it warmed up, I searched through my software for a good random password generator tool. I'd been able to hack into the MyMail servers a few months before, and was pretty confident I could do it again, but I didn't know Owen well enough to begin to guess what his password might be.

I plugged a bunch of data into the generator before I set it loose. His full name, his parents' address on Sarajevo Court and the one in Crossing Estates where he'd grown up. Then I threw in anything else I could think of – Afghanistan, the bases where he'd been stationed, and so on.

The MyMail servers had been upgraded since the last time I visited, and they had installed a program that kicked you out after too many password attempts. After the first two times the connection was cut, I got up and started making myself some cappuccino. I wasn't going to let any crappy email system get the better of me.

I had to keep breaking in over and over again and went through a big mug of café mocha. Then I started to worry that they might be tracking my IP address, and that any minute I'd be getting a knock on my door from Santiago Santos. I wasn't sure if I was sweating because of the hot coffee or the worry, but I pushed forward.

Finally the password generator scored a hit on a random set of numbers and letters. "Hello, Owen," I said, rubbing my hands together. At least he was smart enough not to use something common, I thought. But I was smarter.

Yeah, cockier, too. I knew that. I forced myself to slow down, to take every precaution I could, even though I knew that the longer I stayed online and illegally connected to Owen's account, the greater the chance that I could get caught.

I downloaded everything from Owen's account to a zipped file on Caroline's laptop, then I broke the connection to the MyMail server.

Owen Keely wasn't a big emailer, just as he didn't talk much. There were only a couple of dozen messages there—a few from Mark Figueroa, some junk, and then a couple from another MyMail address—Striker23.

That had to be the friend of Owen's that I'd met. I opened the first of the messages, but all I read was a date and a time a couple of months before. Not very helpful.

The next few messages were similar. It looked like Owen and Striker had been meeting every couple of weeks, beginning in early March. Always on a Saturday morning.

I sat back in my chair. That made sense; if they were meeting to go searching for something at Friar Lake, morning was a good time to start. Perhaps Striker had a day job, and was only free on Saturdays.

There was only one email that had anything different. It was a link to a website, and beneath it the letters PW, followed by a colon and a combination of letters and numbers.

After I clicked the link, a window popped up asking me for an ID and password. I had the password, but what was the user ID? I tried Striker, and got kicked out.

It was already after eleven, and I was tired and cranky, and Rochester was nuzzling my knee, ready for his late-night walk. I gave up and shut down the laptop. I climbed back up the stepladder and returned it to its place in the attic. I'd try that site again the next day, when I was fresher.

I walked Rochester down past the Keelys', just on the off chance that I'd see something—but the house was shut up and dark.

In the morning, the story was still the same—no activity. That was strange, because in the past there had always been someone outside—Phil, trimming trees or weeding the flower bed; Marie, on her tricycle; or Owen, sitting on the grass smoking. Usually the garage door was open, and often I could hear music floating out of the house.

On our way back, I passed Bob Freehl, dragging his garbage can out to the curb. He loved Rochester, and we stopped so he could pet the dog and tell him what a good boy he was. "Haven't seen the Keelys lately," I said.

"On vacation," Bob said. "Took one of those paddle-wheelers up the Mississippi. Don't know where Owen is—he's supposed to be watching the house for them." He shook his head. "Just between you and me, there's something not right about that boy."

"He does strike me as odd," I said.

"I think it's the drugs," Bob said. "Phil said they've had a world of trouble with that boy. He got hooked on something over there in Afghanistan, and he's been through rehab a couple of times."

He reached down and scratched under Rochester's chin. "No worry about having that kind of trouble with a dog, is there?" Bob said. "Sometimes I wonder why any of us have kids at all."

I knew that Bob had a couple of grown daughters, and at least one of them was married with kids of her own. But I didn't know what kind of trouble they'd caused him and his wife.

As I drove upriver to Eastern, I wondered if all the Keelys had been in on whatever Owen was up to. It was hard to imagine Phil, the retired Marine, breaking into the chapel at Friar Lake. Or Marie crawling under the altar in search of lost treasure. Maybe they'd gone off on this "vacation" just to avoid the trouble. It did seem awfully convenient.

I dropped Rochester at my office and walked down the hill into Leighville. The college was running short of administrative space, so several departments, including human resources and the news bureau, had been moved into a sixties-era building just off campus with a Wawa grocery on the ground level.

I climbed the stairs to the second floor to the glass door that read "News Bureau." When I was an undergraduate, I had a work-study job there for year, though back then it was housed in a long-gone building that had been replaced by Harrow Hall.

As a college student, I was under the influence of Ernest Hemingway, and I wanted to be a foreign correspondent like Papa, traveling the world, romancing beautiful foreigners and narrowly escaping danger. It was ironic that instead of becoming that guy, I'd fallen for a woman who had done just that.

To get my press credentials going, I'd signed up for the college newspaper and taken the job with the News Bureau. As a cub reporter on the *Eastern Daily Sun*, I wrote brief articles about the most mundane events on campus—rehearsals for a student musical, the arrival of new recycling bins, and so on. I was painfully shy back then, and I hated having to go up to people, introduce myself, and ask for information.

The job at the News Bureau was similarly unsatisfying. Instead of writing press releases and attending college parties, I worked in the file room, made photocopies and ran errands. My enthusiasm for journalism waned quickly.

I opened the door to a large room with file cabinets along one wall with half-glass walls at the back revealing two small offices. Ruta was an olive-skinned girl with long brown hair with gold highlights, and if I hadn't already met her I'd have thought she was a work-study kid like I'd been. She sat at a big desk in the center of the room. It was littered with magazines and newspapers.

She was sitting sideways to me, typing at her computer, her iPod headphones in her ears. It didn't look like she'd heard me come in, and I stood there for minute, uncertain what to do. Then I walked around in front of her.

Still no response. I leaned down, and waved my hands in front of her. She looked up, startled. "Oh, hi Steve," she said, when she pulled her headphones out. She motioned around the office. "Sorry for the mess, but I'm the only one here right now. It's been kind of crazy."

"Really? When I was a work-study here there was a whole staff."

"Welcome to the world of downsizing. My boss, the manager, quit three months ago and still hasn't been replaced, and even though I don't have the experience for the job, I'm handling it and everything else around here. But between you and me, if I don't get a raise soon, I'm out of here. I'm twenty-four years old and I should at least be making my age in salary."

I was surprised. I had been making nearly double that when I was working on press relations for the fund-raising campaign, with a lot less responsibility.

I sat down across from Ruta and went over the couple of projects I had in the works. "I don't think I'll be too busy at Friar Lake for a while, so I'm happy to help you out, if I can," I said. "I could keep working on those alumni profiles for you."

"That would be terrific," she said. "You think I could convince you to write the press release for Friar Lake, too? I need something to send out to the local papers, and I was hoping to get a feature together for the alumni magazine."

"I can do that," I said. I explained that I was working with Lili on the coffee table book about the history of the Abbey of Our Lady of the Waters, and I could pull together something from that research.

"That would be terrific!" Her phone rang, and she answered. I could tell from the conversation that it was going to be a long one, so I motioned that I'd call her, and walked out.

I stopped at the Wawa and got a cup of coffee and a doggy treat for Rochester. As I climbed back up the hill, I thought about the circumstances that had kept me at Eastern. Lucas Roosevelt had been kind enough to give me a couple of adjunct gigs when I had no other means of support. Then Mike MacCormac had taken me under his wing and gotten me the full-time job.

None of that would have happened without the support of President Babson, though. Though my felony conviction might not have come up when I was hired as an adjunct, I was sure Babson had learned about it before I was offered the full-time job with Mike's office. Had he been looking out for me all this time? Why? Just because I was an alumnus? Or had he seen something worth saving in me?

I finished my coffee as I reached Fields Hall. I gave Rochester his treat, then went over to Blair Hall for my second class with the College Connection kids. I was pleased to see that when Ka'Tar filed in, he was laughing and joking with the other kids.

I got them up and moving around, acting out the messages they were going to send to the other characters from *The Hunger Games*, and then had them take an online quiz about the book and the movie. Then we talked about the proper structure of a paragraph, with a topic sentence and supporting details, I had them each write a paragraph about their experiences so far at Eastern.

I put a couple of the paragraphs up on the screen and walked them through how a professor would approach reading and responding to their writing. By the time our hour and a half was over, I felt that I'd given them a pretty good introduction to college-level writing.

Once again, I accompanied them to lunch after class. On our way to Burgers Commons, I walked next to Ka'Tar. "Are you having a good time here?" I asked.

"Oh, yeah. Only thing I ain't seen yet is that place DeAndre talked about, the one with the monks."

"Friar Lake?" I asked. He nodded.

"What did he tell you about it?"

"How pretty it was—the old church and the lake and the woods and all. He'd never seen any place like it."

"Did he ever tell you how he got out there?" I asked. "It's hard to get to without a car."

"He knew this skinny white dude from the drop-in center, guy by the name of Striker," Tar said. "DeAndre used to take the train down to some place in Jersey where Striker live, and they drive together."

Striker? The same friend Owen had been talking to and emailing? "His friend Owen there too?" I asked.

"Owen? The crazy dude from Afghanistan? DeAndre talked about him sometimes. He was some kind of meth head."

"I thought he was over all that," I said.

"You don't never get over something like that," Ka'Tar said. "DeAndre never did nothing more than smoke dope, and he told me to stay clean, too. He said when that Owen dude was high he was scary."

I could see that, I thought, as I held the door to Burgers Commons open for Ka'Tar, and then a couple of his classmates. The couple of times I'd seen him, he'd been pleasant enough, though I had always sensed some kind of edge beneath his surface. I wondered if Owen had been high around Mark, and Mark hadn't noticed.

What had Rick avoided seeing about Paula until their confrontation out at Crossing Estates? Was there something I wasn't seeing about Lili? How could any of us really know the object of our affection?

28 – Anonymous

Thursday afternoon Lili was busy trying to put together all the photos that the College Connection kids had been taking and working with, so once again I was on my own with Rochester. I spent the afternoon with her research materials on Friar Lake, beginning to write the narrative that would accompany her photographs.

I was so engaged in the work that I didn't notice the time passing, until Rochester got restless and started thrashing around one of his toys, a hard plastic starfish with blue-and-white ropes radiating from it. He grabbed one of the ropes in his teeth and started shaking his head back and forth.

That's when I looked up and noticed it was after five. "No wonder you're antsy," I said. I stood up and stretched, then closed down the computer and got his leash. We took a quick walk around the campus for him to sniff and pee, then drove back home. I boiled up some pasta and microwaved a frozen container of sauce I'd prepared a bucket of a few months back, and while the dinner cooked I climbed upstairs and retrieved Caroline's laptop.

Once I was finished eating, I opened the laptop and once more opened the link to the protected website Striker had emailed Owen. I tried "owen" as the user ID to go along with the password Striker had emailed him. The password window evaporated, and the website opened beneath it.

"Duh," I said out loud. "I must have been dense last night."

Rochester didn't say anything, just lay sprawled on the kitchen floor behind my chair. It looked as if I was visiting some kind of eBay clone: there was a line-up of products, each with one or more photos and a brief description. But there was no heading on the page, and no indication of how to bid on or buy any of the items. There were several dozen items on the page, too, and it took me a couple of minutes to realize that they were all religious artifacts of some kind.

The first item was a silver spice box of the kind used at the havdalah services on Saturday evening, at the conclusion of the Jewish Sabbath. A six-sided box sat on an embossed pedestal, with a silver spire atop it, surmounted by a pennant with a Star of David on it. I'd seen pictures of similar items, but since I had grown up as a Reformed Jew, mostly attending only the High Holy Day services, I'd never seen one in use.

This box, though, was more special than the ordinary ones I might have seen. According to the description, it was from the seventeenth century and had been used in the main synagogue in Warsaw for several centuries.

The items in the collection weren't limited to Judaica, though. There were gold patens and chalices from various Catholic churches, a Greek Orthodox censer, and a Persian Quran, ornately decorated with ink, watercolor, lapis lazuli, and gold, which was said to have been rescued by an American soldier. The same soldier was said to have also listed several other items of non-religious significance from the same area; details upon request.

The last item on the list was a reliquary said to contain the thumb of St. Roch, patron saint of dogs. I zoomed in on the picture. It was a lot clearer than the one we had seen at St. Mary Martyr, and in color. Someone had placed a ruler in the shot to show the scale of the box. "This item, long in the possession of a Benedictine abbey in Pennsylvania, has recently come onto the market," the description read. "Made of Spanish silver in approximately the early 17th century, it was part of the royal treasures of the Spanish crown, looted by Joseph Napoleon and presented to the abbey during his residency in New Jersey. The box is locked, and there is no key, so its contents remain a mystery. Does it include the saint's thumb? If you buy this item you can determine for yourself!"

Somebody had done his homework, I thought. Or at least embellished the story told by Brother Anselm.

There were a few more descriptive details, and photos of the reliquary from several different angles—front, side, back, top and bottom.

But that was it—no indication of who to contact to purchase the item, or how much it would cost.

There was no domain name for the website as part of the URL, only an IP address-- a 32-bit numeric address written as four numbers separated by periods. This one was a dynamic URL—one that was created in response to a query to a database. That meant in addition to the IP address there was a question mark at the end followed by a series of numbers and digits.

The IP address in this case was 10.140.205.60. I opened a new window for whois.com to see if I could find where the site was registered. Only a post office box was listed, though, which I copied down, and there was no administrative contact.

Then I sat back and tried to work out a time line. DeAndre hung around the drop-in center and spoke to Brother Anselm, who thought that the reliquary might be hidden at the abbey. Ka'Tar had told me that DeAndre knew Striker through the drop-in center, and Striker had been in Afghanistan with Owen Keely. I'd seen the Pinterest picture showing Brother Anselm, DeAndre and Owen at Friar Lake.

Once the monks had left for western Pennsylvania, DeAndre, Owen and Striker could have searched the property without fear of being discovered. Something happened, though, and DeAndre ended up dead. Had Striker or Owen killed him?

At some point the reliquary had been found. I guessed that it had finally come to light during the most recent break-in; otherwise, why keep looking? Then someone had photographed the reliquary, written the description, and posted it online. Presumably there was a clientele out there for discreet purchases of religious objects without concern for provenance.

Striker had emailed that website address to Owen. Striker had been a soldier in Afghanistan, and so I was willing to make the leap that he was the soldier who had supplied the Persian Quran and the other artifacts – or at least, that he knew that soldier.

I called Rick Stemper. "You home? I want to come over."

"Sure. But I'm out of beer."

"Don't worry, I have a six-pack in my fridge I can bring over."

I typed up the IP address, the user name and the password, and then printed it out. I found a rubber glove in the kitchen and used it to pull the paper out of the printer and fold it up. Then I slipped it into a plastic bag. Then I returned Caroline's laptop to the attic.

I grabbed the beer and put a leash on Rochester, then piled him into the BMW. It was almost nine o'clock, late for an excursion, but I wanted to pass this information on as soon as I could.

"What's up?" Rick asked when he opened his front door to me and Rochester. The dog bowled right past us and began chasing Rascal around the living room.

"Can you check out a website?" I asked.

"Sure, but the computer's in the spare bedroom."

I left the beer on the kitchen table and followed him.

"What's there?" he asked.

"The reliquary from Friar Lake."

"How did you find that?"

"Inquisitive fingers."

"In other words I don't want to know."

"Exactly."

He crossed his arms over his chest. "Steve. If you got this information illegally then I can't use it because that would make me an accessory to whatever crime you committed to get it. Oh, and by the way, if you're still hacking, then you've violated your parole, and as an officer of the law I'm required to report that information to Santiago Santos."

"When did you become such a boy scout?" I asked. "You've been willing to use information I found for you in the past."

"And I was wrong. I admit that. I see what's happening to you, Steve. You keep giving in to whatever addiction you've got to this hacking business. As your friend, and as a cop, I can't keep ignoring that."

"I haven't killed anybody. I haven't stolen a 17th century religious artifact and put it up for sale on a website along with a whole lot of other stolen goods. So I broke in to Owen's email account. Big deal. You're not interested in this? No problem. I'll find a way to get it to Tony Rinaldi so he won't be able to connect it with me. And since he isn't my friend he shouldn't have a problem with it."

I turned to walk out but Rick said, "Steve. Wait."

"What?" I looked back at him.

He sat down at his desktop computer, on a wooden door placed on two short file cabinets. "Where do I go?"

I opened the plastic bag and dumped the paper out next to him, then put the bag back in my pocket.

"Even if your fingerprints aren't on this paper, I still know it came from you."

"Your word against mine," I said.

He sighed, then unfolded the paper and typed in the address. When the log-in window appeared, he entered the ID and "owen" as the password.

The list of items popped up, and he said, "Shit. You weren't kidding."

"Check out the last item on the bottom line," I said, pointing.

He scanned through the site and then looked at me. "This is big, Steve. Way bigger than Stewart's Crossing or Leighville."

"That's what I figured."

We were staring at the screen when a chat window popped up.

"Shit," Rick said. "Are we busted?"

u looking at something the message read.

I leaned over Rick's shoulder and typed, *yeah, showing customer.*

"Steve..." Rick said.

b careful im watching, our mystery fence replied.

I typed, *ok signing off,* and then closed the window and the website.

"I can't just sit on this," Rick said. He turned away from the computer. I sat on the edge of his spare bed, across from him. "I've got to notify somebody. But how am I supposed to say I got this information?"

"Didn't you say you searched Owen Keely's room?"

"Yeah. But I didn't find anything."

I kept my mouth shut—I know, something new and different for me.

"Steve. I can't manufacture evidence." He stood up. "I need a beer."

We went back out to the kitchen and we each opened a beer. The dogs were lying next to each other on the living room floor.

"You know you could go back to prison for this," he said.

"But I'm not, unless you – or somebody else – finds evidence that I did something to violate my parole. You're not going to find that."

"You can't keep doing this, Steve. I'm telling you this as your friend. One of these days you're going to screw up and get caught. And the consequences aren't going to be pretty."

I finished my beer. "I know. Believe me, I do. I wish I could just stop. I keep telling myself I have to. But I can't."

"Yeah, I know," he said. "I hear those kind of excuses from every criminal I pull in."

The criminal tag stung, but that's because it was true. Was I any better than Owen Keely, DeAndre Dawson or the mysterious Striker?

Well, yeah, because I hadn't killed anybody or stolen anything that didn't belong to me.

I stood up. "Rochester, let's go."

He scrambled up and rushed over to me.

"Talk to you later," I said to Rick. "Don't worry, I can let myself out."

29 – Catch You Later

As I drove back home from Rick's, I kept coming back to what he'd said—that he heard the same kind of justifications I spouted from every criminal he arrested.

"Am I a bad person, Rochester?" I asked, reaching over to stroke the soft fur on the top of his head. "I don't think so. I'm trying to do good things."

He didn't answer. But then, there wasn't anything else to say, was there?

We went for a long walk, and Rochester sniffed a lot of trees and bushes. He peed and chased a squirrel. Business as usual for him.

I had a lot of trouble falling asleep. I kept squirming around in bed, my brain full of conflicting thoughts. How could I justify continuing to hack into websites and email servers when it was against the law? But didn't I have a moral obligation to do whatever I could to bring a criminal to justice?

Who was I, though, to make those decisions? I wasn't a cop. I wasn't a private eye or an insurance investigator or anything like that. How could I justify my actions when I was just an ordinary guy? And how could I stop when I got such a high from doing what I did?

There were no answers to those big questions, and I finally drifted off to sleep in the middle of the night, only to be woken at seven by a big dog sniffing and licking my face.

I yawned and struggled out of bed. I was still troubled by my conversation with Rick the night before. What if he called Santiago Santos and reported his suspicions? I could wipe out the hard drive on Caroline's laptop, then take it apart and discard the pieces in a dozen different trash cans. Without evidence, Santos couldn't send me back to prison.

The laptop wasn't the problem. If I had to, I could walk into any computer store and pay cash for a new machine, then go on line and reload all the tools I needed. But that would be a final acknowledgement that I couldn't stop hacking. I was scared to see where that path would lead me.

I'd rather take my chances with Santos. The worst he could do would be to crack down on me, forcing me to report in more frequently, subjecting me to an endless series of lectures about my behavior. Maybe even make me go to some kind of addiction counseling.

Did I need that? It wasn't like I was pulling out my secret laptop every night and hacking random websites, or even doing the kind of thing that had gotten me in trouble in the first place, breaking into credit bureaus and changing records. I could not name a single innocent person harmed by anything I'd done. Except myself – and I wasn't innocent.

Rochester was not interested in philosophical discussions. He just wanted to go out for his walk like usual, poop and pee and sniff and socialize, then come back home for his breakfast.

We were halfway down Sarajevo Court when my cell phone rang.

"I'm not lying for you," Rick said. "Even if what you did helps catch whoever killed DeAndre Dawson, it was still wrong."

"Good morning to you, too."

"Don't get smart with me, asshole. I was up half the night trying to figure out what to do. Hell, the murder isn't even my case. All I'm supposed to be doing is looking for Owen Keely to ask about the stuff he stole from Mark Figueroa."

I took a deep breath. "Look, I'm sorry if I put you in a bad position. But I stand by what I did. Whoever killed DeAndre needs to be caught, and punished. We owe that to Shenetta and Jamarcus and Ka'Tar."

"Save me the moralizing. You provided some valuable information, and I need to deal with that. After this is over, you and I are going to have a long talk and come up with an action plan."

I wanted to tease him about appropriating corporate double-speak—but for once I kept my mouth shut.

"For now," he said, "I know a guy with the FBI in Philly, Hank Quillian. I worked on a case with him once. I'm going to give him a call and pass on this website information. See what he has to say."

"Why don't you just call Tony Rinaldi? The murder is his case."

"And he'll know just where the information came from. Hank, on the other hand, has never heard of you or your itchy fingers. I'll let him know that the website is connected to DeAndre's murder and he can contact Tony himself."

Rochester spotted a squirrel and took off, dragging me along behind him. "Sounds good," I said.

"I want you to do something before I do, though. Go see Mark and show him the website, and see if anything that was stolen from him shows up there."

"Why me?"

"I don't know. I'm flying with my gut here, and I want to know everything I can before I call Hank. But I don't think I want it on the record that I spoke to Mark before I passed the info to the FBI."

"All right. I'll go over there on my way to work."

When I got back home, I called Mark. "Hey, it's Steve Levitan. Can I come over and show you a website?"

"Something good or something bad?" he asked.

"Let's call it neutral for now," I said.

He said he'd be home until he opened the store at eleven. "There's an outside stair behind the store, that leads right up to my apartment," he said. "Come around that way. I've got a fenced yard back there, if you want to bring your dog."

"Cool. See you in an hour or so."

I cut up some fresh strawberries into a container of Greek yogurt and wolfed it down while I scanned the morning paper. There was an article about the spate of robberies in Crossing Estates, and I knew that wasn't good for Rick. But the reporter hadn't connected them to the ones in Leighville, or to Owen Keely.

After a quick shower, I got dressed and loaded Rochester into the car. I drove down Main Street, passing Bethea, our local crazy lady, on the way. She had a habit of crossing the street very slowly, over and over again, tying up traffic. Most people just accepted her as local color—unless they were in a hurry.

I wasn't.

I turned down Ferry Street and parked in the driveway beside Mark's store, behind his van. I opened the gate that led into the fenced yard behind the building, and then let Rochester off his leash to run around.

Mark had the second-floor door open as I climbed the stairs. "Is this about Owen?"

"Yeah. You heard anything from him lately?"

He shook his head, and stepped back to let me into his kitchen. He had his laptop open on the table. "The things that you think Owen stole from your store," I said, as I sat down. "Any of them have any religious significance?"

He thought as I opened a web browser and typed in the IP address for the list of stolen items. "Just one," he said. "A Russian icon—a painting on wood, about the size of a three by five card. A saint in a red cloak, with a halo over his head."

"I found this website online, with a whole list of religious artifacts for sale. The reliquary from Friar Lake is there. And I think I saw that icon there, too."

When the ID and password window popped up, I entered the information I had used before.

The small window disappeared—but instead of seeing the list of items I got a message that the password I had entered was invalid. "Crap," I said.

"What's wrong?"

"Striker must have figured out someone else had Owen's password, and he changed it."

Mark was confused, and as I started to explain to him, I called Rick. "Better get your FBI guy on that site right away," I said. "Striker changed the password."

"Can't you find the new one?"

"Excuse me?"

"If I'm going to tell Hank anything I have to give him the right information."

I looked over at Mark. I didn't want to say anything too explicit. "You know what you're asking me, don't you?" I said to Rick. "I'm sure the FBI can do what I can do. And they'll do it legally."

"But if they can't see the website, they won't have enough to get a warrant to investigate further." He took a deep breath. "Where are you now?"

"At Mark's."

"I'll meet you at your house in fifteen minutes."

"No, Rick. I'll get you what you want. But you don't have to get your hands dirty."

"That's not the way I roll, pal." He hung up.

"What's going on?" Mark asked.

"I'll have to fill you in later," I said. "Trust me, you don't want to know anything right now."

I hurried down the outside staircase, and Rochester came bounding over to me. We got back in the car and drove back home. Rick's truck was already parked there.

"I've been turning my back on you and your little adventures for long enough," Rick said as I walked up to him. "I want to see what you do first-hand."

"Can you turn on the espresso machine?" I asked, unlocking the front door. "I'll be right back down, but we're going to need some coffee."

Rochester followed Rick into the kitchen as I went upstairs to retrieve Caroline's laptop. By the time I got back downstairs the machine was beginning its brew cycle.

"You have a special computer?" Rick asked, as I set it up on the kitchen table in the breakfast nook.

"Used to be Caroline's," I said. "Santos doesn't know I have it."

He just shook his head.

The machine started to whistle, and Rick got up to make the coffee while I set up the password generating software. I left it running and joined him in the kitchen. "You want a mocha?" I asked.

"I'll stick to the cappuccino." He foamed the milk while I got out the chocolate syrup for myself. We made our drinks in silence and then walked back to the breakfast nook. The password software was busy running through combinations and permutations.

"What's happening?" Rick asked.

I explained what I was doing, and he nodded along. "Where'd you get the software?"

"Found a guy on a bulletin board who had it for sale. It's way out of date by now, but it still works."

We sat there in silence for a long while, drinking our coffee and watching the software work. "This could take a couple of hours," I said. "You don't have to stick around."

"I do. How long did it take you last time?"

"Last time I had the password from an email I intercepted. All I had to figure out was the user ID and that was easy. Now? I have no idea. Let's hope Striker gave Owen a simple password—not something randomly generated that could take hours to crack."

I had a sudden wave of panic. "What if he didn't give Owen a new password at all," I said. "Maybe he just removed his access."

"Can you tell that?" Rick asked.

I shook my head. "We'll have to hope that isn't the case. But I want to try something else."

I minimized the windows and opened a new one. This time I entered the password that had worked before, but instead of *owen* as the user id, I entered *striker23*.

Like magic, the window evaporated and the website opened. I paged to the bottom and pointed to the item next to the reliquary. I right-clicked on it and saved the picture of the Russian icon, then closed the window.

I went back to the first set of windows and closed them, too.

"What just happened?" Rick asked.

I explained everything I'd done. "I'm going to email this picture to Mark right now," I said, as I opened my mail program. I remembered his address; I had found several messages from him when I hacked Owen's account, and it's hard to forget an address like gaylover33 at mymail.com.

As soon as the message was sent, I called Mark. "Can you check your email?"

"Already there," he said. "I just saw a message from you."

"Is that the icon that you think Owen stole from your store?"

"Yeah, that's it."

I thanked him, and hung up. "I think you'd better call your FBI guy ASAP," I said. "We don't know how long the striker23 ID and password are going to be active."

Rick stood up. "I'm heading to the station right now." He nodded toward the laptop. "Better put that back where you got it from."

"Will do."

He walked to the front door, then stopped and turned back. "I see why you do it," he said. "You get this look on your face and you seem – I don't know – more alive somehow." He paused. "Thanks for the coffee. Catch you later."

I knew it was just a phrase—but as he walked out and closed the door behind him I kept hearing *catch you* over and over again.

30 — Gone Missing

It was almost eleven o'clock on Friday morning by then. I called Lili to check in with her, but got her voice mail. I figured she was probably tied up with the College Connection kids, probably showing off the collage of their photos she had been working on.

There was no reason for me to drive up all the way up to Eastern. All I had on my plate was working on the text for the book with Lili, and I could do that just as easily from home. I didn't even have a boss I had to clear it with.

I was able to retrieve the files I'd been working with, and I sat down with another café mocha and my laptop to get to work. Rochester got hold of one of his toys and spent some time shaking it and chewing it, then settled down for a nap behind my chair.

As usual, I got lost in the work, without the distractions of an office. It was close to two o'clock when my cell phone rang and I saw from the display it was Rick.

"Tony Rinaldi's here at the station," he said. "Can you join us?"

"I guess the only appropriate answer is yes," I said.

"You'd be guessing right."

"Give me ten minutes."

I hung up, got dressed and set the gate up preventing Rochester from getting to the second floor. "I'm trusting you, big guy," I said. I took him out front for a quick pee, then led him back into the townhouse.

He was watching me through the sliding glass doors as I left the house and got into the car. As I backed down the driveway, I wondered what would happen to him if I was arrested, and sent back to prison. Would Lili take him? Rick? How would he feel about being abandoned again?

For the first time, I realized that there was someone who could be very hurt by my hacking – Rochester. Did I owe it to him to stop?

I drove to the police station and parked in the back lot. Around the front, I introduced myself to the desk sergeant, and he called Rick.

Rick appeared behind him a minute or two later. "We're in the conference room," he said.

I followed him down the hall, past the interview rooms and into a small room with a circular table and four rolling armchairs. There was an American flag on a pole in one corner, the Pennsylvania state flag on a similar pole in another. A couple of old photos of Stewart's Crossing had been enlarged and framed and hung on the walls.

Two of the chairs were occupied. I knew Tony, of course. "This is Agent Quillian," Rick said, as we walked into the room.

My heart began hammering in my chest. Had Rick brought me there to turn me over to the FBI?

The FBI agent was in his early thirties, with the kind of weathered, wary look I'd come to associate with ex-military guys. I shook his hand and said hello to Tony Rinaldi. Between his crisply pressed shirt and pants, the G-man's dark suit, blue tie and white shirt, and Rick's button-down shirt and khakis, I felt under-dressed.

"Interesting website you found," Agent Quillian said. "Want to tell me how you got there?"

I'll say one thing for being an English teacher. You learn the value of considering what it is you say and write, and how you can cover your tracks with a careful use of language. "I followed an email trail," I said. "Mark and Owen had been communicating via email before Owen disappeared. The link was in one of Owen's emails."

I avoided making eye contact with Rick. If Quillian wanted to assume that the link had been in a message from Owen to Mark, which Mark had passed on to me, I wasn't going to contradict him. But I was sure I'd fail any lie detector test at that point; my pulse was racing and my palms were sweaty.

Quillian nodded. "You recognized this item you believe was stolen from the abbey?"

It looked like I'd passed that test, and I took a couple of deep breaths. I explained about going through the photo archives at St. Mary Martyr, and how the picture of the reliquary on the website seemed to match the one Lili and I had found.

"Mark Figueroa identified the icon he said was stolen from him as well," Rick put in.

"I was able to match a couple of other stolen items to that site," Quillian said. "I've got a guy tracking down the site registration right now."

My heart began to return to its normal rhythm. I wiped my sweaty palms on my pants and nodded along. "Have you been able to find out Striker's real name? He and Owen served together in Afghanistan," I said. "Maybe someone from the same platoon would recognize the nickname."

"Already done that. James Striker. Served in the same platoon. Anything else you know?"

"Nothing that I haven't already told Rick or Tony."

"Thanks for coming in."

I looked from Rick to Tony. Neither of them said anything, so I stood up. "Good luck," I said.

I was driving back to River Bend when Lili called my cell. "Have you seen Ka'Tar Winston today?" she asked.

"No. I haven't been up to campus at all."

"He was supposed to be at the final assembly but he didn't show up, and none of the kids have seen him. Dot Sneiss is freaking out."

"He told me yesterday that he wanted to see Friar Lake," I said. "That DeAndre had talked a lot about it. Maybe he went up there."

"How could he get there?" Lili asked. "He didn't have a car."

"Could have called a taxi, I guess. Or hitch-hiked."

"I'm going up there to look for him. Can you meet me there?"

"Sure. But I'm in Stewart's Crossing. It'll take me a half hour."

"Call me when you get close," she said, and hung up.

I had just turned onto Quarry Road from Main Street. I could have bypassed the entrance to River Bend, and gone straight on down to the Delaware to pick up River Road.

But if we were going to look for a missing kid, I thought Rochester's nose and instincts could be important assets. I drove quickly to the townhouse, where I grabbed Rochester's leash as he danced around me.

I loaded him into the car and then headed up north, rocketing down River Road as fast as the curving, narrow road would allow. When I had to stop for a light in Washington's Crossing I put a Springsteen CD in for additional motivation. By the time I turned down the entrance road to Friar Lake, I was singing along with the Boss and "Born in the USA" was blasting through the open windows.

When I pulled to a stop next to Lili's Mini Cooper, Rochester tried to jump out the window, but I grabbed his collar and told him, "No more exiting the vehicle on your own!"

Lili stepped out of the chapel, and Rochester and I met her there. "I haven't found him anywhere," she said. "But I know he has to be here."

"Have you been down to the lake yet?"

She shook her head. "I assumed he'd follow the road up here."

"Well, let's go down there and look." We took a narrow path through the woods behind the chapel, down to the lake and the small house where the mendicant friars had lived. It was cool and dim in there, the trees and underbrush crowding in against us. Long fiddlehead ferns stroked my legs as I ducked under a low-hanging maple.

About halfway down, Rochester began pulling, and I nearly lost my footing. I had to grab the trunk of a slim birch to steady myself. He romped back up toward me, and I reached down and unhooked his leash. "Don't get lost, boy," I said. "And don't dig up any more bodies!"

He scampered downhill. Lili and I followed more slowly as the dirt path snaked around between massive old oaks. The sunlight filtered down to us with a greenish tint, and the air was moist and heavy.

"You're going to have to do something about this path," Lili said, as some dirt skittered from under her feet, and she grabbed my arm. "Either close it off or pave it. Otherwise it's just an accident waiting to happen."

"Fred Searcy from the biology department knows his botany," I said. "Maybe I can get him to come up with some signs identifying the trees and flowers. Then we can make this a kind of nature walk."

Branches of a skinny maple swayed as a squirrel scampered somewhere inside the thicket of leaves. We reached the bottom of the hill and stepped back out into the sunlight. We were at the edge of the meadow next to the house, the one where Rochester had found DeAndre's body.

Up ahead of us we saw an open trench that looked to be where the body had been. Ka'Tar sat Indian-style beside it, and Rochester was on his belly beside him. As we approached, Ka'Tar reached out and stroked Rochester's shimmering flank.

Lili hung back, and I heard the shutter of her camera begin to click in rapid succession. I remembered that she'd once told me, "When there' s something I don't want to see, I let the camera see it for me."

I thought that the photos of the dark-skinned boy, the golden dog and the open grave would be very poignant, though I doubted they'd make it into our coffee-table book on the history of the abbey.

"Hey, Ka'Tar," I said, as I got close to him. "You had us worried."

"This is where he was buried, isn't it?" His right hand rested on Rochester, and the sun glinted on the fused fourth and fifth fingers, the ones DeAndre had hoped to have repaired.

"Yup." I sat down catty-cornered to him. Rochester didn't move.

"Do they know who kilt him?"

I shook my head. "Not yet. But I know the police are working on it."

Tar looked up at me and held out his hand. "When the kids teased me about my hand, DeAndre say I was just perfect to him. That God made me this way for a reason."

"I believe that," I said. "I think God cares about every one of us, even when we do things that aren't right."

I thought about the hacking I'd done. Would God, in all his mercy, have approved? I thought so—but maybe that was just my hubris.

"He was right. It's real pretty out here." Ka'Tar looked out toward the lake. "You think they could bury him out here for real? They's that cemetery up on the hill."

Lili joined us, holding her camera loosely in her right hand. "Hi, Ka'Tar," she said.

"I don't know," I said. "But Shenetta and Jamarcus are going to move down here, so maybe we can find DeAndre a spot in a real cemetery, out here in the country."

Ka'Tar nodded. "I like this place a lot. And Mrs. Dot say if I keep my grades up this year I can apply to be a real student."

I stood up. "Mrs. Dot's worried about you," I said. "Why don't you let us drive you back up to the college?"

Ka'Tar nodded, and stood up. "You want to ride with me and Rochester?" I asked. "Or with Professor Weinstock?"

"I like Rochester," he said, and the dog nuzzled his hand. "He like me, too."

"He's a good boy," I said.

31 – Tennis Ball

Once we were on our way back to Eastern, I called Dot's office to let her know that we had found Ka'Tar. Lili walked him over to Harrow Hall to rejoin the rest of the CC kids, and I tracked down Joe Capodilupo to talk to him about how we could make the path that connected the abbey to the lake safer.

I called Rick on my way back to Fields Hall, but went right to voice mail. "Call me when you can," I said.

It was nearly six o'clock on Friday evening. Dot had arranged a big graduation dinner at Burgers Commons to celebrate the conclusion of the College Connection program. I couldn't take Rochester there, so I left him in my nearly empty office with a rawhide and a bowl of chow.

I was pleased to see the kids I'd had in class; they all looked so much more comfortable and confident than they had when they'd gotten off the bus on Sunday. Babson was there, glad-handing and beaming.

"Looks like this program was pretty successful," I said to Lili, as we stood in line for turkey breast, stuffing, mashed sweet potatoes and cranberry sauce.

"They're great kids," Lili said. "A couple of them have some real artistic talent. After we eat I'll show you the collage I put together. I promised Aquamarisha and Zazeem that I'd help them keep taking pictures, and point them to some websites where they can post them."

"You're really working from A to Z," I said.

She laughed and shook her head. We got our food and joined a group of kids at a long table. We ate and talked with them, and then President Babson came over to us. "I'm glad you're here, Steve," he said. "I had a phone conference call with the Board of Trustees this morning, and they gave me the okay to go ahead with the Friar Lake project. I signed your offer letter and sent it to Elaine. You should get your copy on Monday."

He reached out, and we shook hands. "I have every confidence you'll do a great job," he said.

"Thank you, sir. I won't disappoint you."

He left us then, walking over to Dot Sneiss, and Lili and I hugged and kissed. "Congratulations!" she said. "I'm thrilled the project is going to go through. Even though that means I'll have to get back to work on the book about the abbey. I need to get that done before the fall term starts."

"I'll make sure to keep you on schedule," I said. I took her and and we walked back to her office in Harrow Hall to look at the collage. Then we kissed for a while, celebrating again, until I realized that I'd left Rochester alone in my office for an awful long time.

"I'll talk to you tomorrow morning," she said. "Maybe we'll go to the flea market."

"Sounds like a plan." I kissed her again, and then picked up the plate of leftover turkey breast for Rochester.

I fed him pieces as we drove back to Stewart's Crossing. It was about nine in the evening by then, and the sky was darkening. As we drove down Sarajevo Court, I noticed a shadowy figure in the Keelys' front yard.

I slowed down and tried to see if it was Owen Keely, but his back was to me, and I couldn't just stop there. There was no car parked in front of the house and the lights were dark.

I continued on down the street to my own driveway, and as I did I fumbled for my cell phone and called Rick.

"There's somebody outside the Keelys' townhouse," I said. "I couldn't get a good enough look to see if it was Owen or not."

"I'll get a uniform right over there," he said. "And I'll come over, too. In the meantime see if you can keep an eye on him."

I turned the car off and hooked up Rochester's leash. "Come on, boy, let's go for a walk," I said. I grabbed the emergency tennis ball I kept in the glove compartment, in case I needed to create a distraction, and stuffed it into my pants pocket.

We began walking back down the street toward the Keelys' house. Rochester seemed to know what we were doing; instead of sniffing every bush and tree trunk, or going after squirrels, he was focused on heading down the street.

"Slow down," I said to him. I didn't want to confront Owen Keely, if that's who it was. I just wanted to keep an eye on him for Rick.

I reined Rochester in as we got closer to the Keelys. When I wanted him to dawdle, he refused. "Sniff something!" I whispered to him.

The shadowy figure was leaning up against the side of the Keelys' garage, smoking a cigarette. I couldn't tell if it was Owen or not.

I began a steady chatter to Rochester. "Come on, boy, time to go pee-pee," I said. "Doesn't this place smell good? Please? Go peepee for Papa?"

As we got closer, I noticed that the guy standing by the garage had an artificial leg. Well, that meant he wasn't Owen.

Rochester strained to go over to him, but I pulled him back. A light popped on in an upstairs room, and I wondered if that was Owen, looking for something. If so, then was this guy in the yard Striker?

A couple of things came together all at once. When I was at the Brotherhood Center, I'd been introduced to a guy with tattoo-filled arms and an artificial leg who said he knew DeAndre, though only to say hello to. His name was Jimmy, I remembered. Jimmy, short for James. And James was Striker's first name.

I stole another glance at the guy by the garage. He wore a T-shirt, but I could see lots of tattoos on his arms. I knew it was an assumption, but my brain was telling me that this had to be the elusive Striker. I'd never gotten a look at him when he was helping Owen move furniture, or I could have been sure.

So where was the uniform Rick had promised to send? Where was he?

I checked the display on my cell phone. I'd only called him seven minutes before, though it seemed a lot longer. I took a deep breath and moved a few feet farther down the street with Rochester.

We were directly across from the townhouse by then, in front of one on my side of the street that was currently unoccupied. I nudged Rochester into the driveway and he took the hint, tugging me up toward the gate that led into the house's courtyard. My heart began hammering as I walked up and opened the gate, trying to appear nonchalant.

I didn't look back until I was already inside the darkened courtyard. Striker was still standing by the house, though as I watched he dropped his cigarette butt to the ground and crushed it under the heel of his good leg.

Rochester sat on his butt next to me as I pulled my cell phone out again and called Rick. "I'm in the courtyard of the townhouse across from the Keelys," I said, keeping my voice low. "It looks like Owen's in the house, upstairs. I think maybe the guy outside is Striker."

"I couldn't get a uniform to respond," Rick said. "There's a problem at the Drunken Hessian and the two guys on patrol in this area are both there. The other two are out in the country somewhere on a DUI."

"Where are you?"

"On my way. Should be at Quarry Road in about five."

"I'll keep an eye on them."

"Don't do anything stupid, Steve," Rick said.

"The name's Joe Hardy, remember?"

He snorted and hung up. When I looked at the house again, the light in the upstairs window winked out.

Rochester sprawled on the ground next to me. I stood just behind the courtyard gate in the shadows. It seemed like every second took at least a minute to pass. The front door across the street opened, and in the glow of the motion-sensored outside light, I recognized Owen Keely. He had an Army-style duffle bag over his shoulder.

He walked quickly across the lawn and out of range of the light. It shut off as Striker joined him at the curbside. The two of them began walking up Sarajevo Court toward my house.

As quietly as I could, I opened the courtyard gate of the empty house. Rochester scrambled up to his feet and joined me as we walked back toward home.

"We ought to go out and party," Owen said. "After all the shit we've been through."

"No party," Striker said. "We're just going to lie low until we sell that shit from the church. Then we'll celebrate."

"You are such a pussy," Owen said, and he punched Striker in the arm. Striker just kept walking.

The mailboxes for our chunk of River Bend were located at the far end of the street, and there were a half-dozen guest parking spaces there. I assumed that's where Striker had left his car. If I could stay behind him and Owen until they reached there, at least I could give Rick the license plate and a description of the car.

All the townhouses along Sarajevo Court have outside lights, though many homeowners keep them off to save on electricity. Some, like the Keelys, have motion detectors so the lights wink on when a person or a car passes. Staying in the shadows myself, I was able to keep an eye on Owen and Striker as they moved quickly down the street.

I couldn't hear what Owen said, but he punched Striker in the arm again. This time, Striker whirled on him and I heard him say, "Did you do a bump while you were in the house?"

"Just to take the edge off," Owen whined.

"Dude, I told you you can't do that shit. Not if you're going to stay with me."

Rochester knows our house, and usually as we approach he pulls to turn in at the driveway, ready to get inside, drink some water, and sprawl on the tile floor with one of his toys. But that night he continued straight ahead, as if he knew we were following the two men, not just out for a late-night walk.

"You better be good to me, dude," Owen said, accenting the last word. "I know what you did to DeAndre."

Sarajevo Court makes a left turn just before the small grassy island that holds the mailboxes. The dogleg allows for the placement of one row of guest parking spots. But, as I'd noted many times when walking Rochester, the configuration of the houses, and the fact that there was no streetlight near the mailboxes, left a patch of darkness at the end of the street.

I often pushed Rochester to walk quickly through that area. On nights like this one, when there was no moonlight, I couldn't see whatever it was he stopped to sniff, and I didn't want him to get hold of something not allowed, like a candy bar wrapper or a discarded paper towel. I worried myself about stepping in something.

My cell phone buzzed. "I'm coming in the gate now," Rick said. "Where are you?"

"Following them toward guest parking at the end of Sarajevo Court.

"I'm almost there."

Owen and Striker entered the dark space and I lost them. There's a small park just behind the mailboxes, and a row of guest spots behind that. I worried that they might be able to get to a car, and get away, before I could cross the park.

Rochester strained forward, and I let him have his head, hurrying behind with but still holding tight to his leash. He turned for the mailboxes but instead of stopping to sniff around the stanchions, as he usually did, he went right for the park area behind them.

I heard them before I saw them. I reined Rochester in as the two men came in sight. They were both on the ground, and watching them was like seeing a mixed martial arts fight on a TV with bad reception. One got hold of the other around the neck; there was punching, kicking, and wriggling.

I edged closer, trying to hear what the two men were saying to each other. What had provoked this fight when they were so close to escape? Was it the cocaine?

"You're not cutting me out of this, asshole," Owen said, panting, as he squirmed around in Striker's embrace. "This was my deal."

"Fuck that," Striker said, his voice equally labored. "You just lucked into this from that dimwit DeAndre. And you didn't give a damn when I knocked him out of the picture."

"He was my friend," Owen said. "I couldn't leave him there on the ground."

"So you buried him. Big fucking deal. You're soft, Keely. Always have been. You're just a damn junkie."

"And you're not?" Owen said. "You turned me on to the shit in the first place."

"Yeah, but I kicked it." Striker reared back and aimed a roundhouse kick at Owen's midsection. Owen flew backwards and I heard his body hit the pavement with a sickening thud. Striker jumped onto him and grabbed his head.

Headlights approached from behind us, illuminating Striker straddling Owen, banging his head against the pavement. Even though I thought Owen Keely was a colossal asshole, I couldn't stand there and watch him get killed. "Get off him!" I yelled.

Rochester and I began to run toward Owen and Striker. Blood streamed from Owen's head. Striker looked up at me and there was something in his eyes that reminded me of a wild animal.

He leapt off Owen and took off toward the parked cars. Rick roared his truck to a stop and jumped out. "Police!" he yelled. "Hold it right there!"

Striker ignored him. Rochester strained at his leash, trying to get away from me and take down the bad guy, but I held tight. I wasn't letting him get anywhere near Striker, not with that crazy look in his eyes.

Rochester tried to fake me out, darting to the right, but I held on tight. He was so strong, though, that he pulled me along behind him. I couldn't plant my feet enough to stop him, and I didn't want to try and grab more of the leash for fear I might lose my grip.

Striker jumped into a beat-up old sedan and turned on the ignition. As it roared to life, Rick got close to him and pulled out his gun. Striker put the car in reverse and hit the gas, rocketing backwards from the parking space. I dove into the flowerbed on the other side of the street from the mailboxes, pulling Rochester with me, as the car roared toward us.

Rick fired his gun in what sounded like a series of small explosions. When I looked up I saw the Chevy veering crazily as the two driver's side tires went flat. I sat up, still holding tight to Rochester's leash. Striker leapt out of the car and took off at a run away from Rick.

He was going to run right past me. I didn't think; I just ran on instinct, and I hoped that Rochester would, too. I pulled the tennis ball from my pocket, and threw it directly in Striker's path.

As it bounced once, Rochester took off. I jumped up, holding tight to his leash, and the ball flew across Striker's path. Rochester had forgotten about the bad guy in his eagerness to get the ball, and he raced right past.

Striker saw the taut leash blocking his path, but it was too late for him to stop. He tripped over it and went flying to the pavement.

Rochester's leash flew out of my hand as he rushed ahead and retrieved the tennis ball. Rick ran up to Striker and slapped a pair of handcuffs on him as he was still on the ground. I caught up to Rochester and scratched below his chin. "Good doggie," I said.

32 – Hardly Boys

I dialed 911 and requested an ambulance for Owen as Rick called in for backup. I told Rochester to sit, and knelt beside Owen, who was moaning in pain. "Ambulance is on its way," I said. "Just hold on for a few minutes." The blood was pouring out of his head, and I took off my shirt and created a makeshift bandage, applying pressure to the wound.

A couple of neighbors came out to see what was going on, including a slim blonde named Kelly Vincent who had a schnauzer Rochester liked to play with. She was some kind of doctor, and as soon as she saw Owen she ran back into her house and returned a moment later with a medical kit. She took over from me, and I stood up, feeling dizzy.

Rochester came over to me, sniffing at my blood-covered hands. A state police car arrived a few minutes later in response to Rick's call for backup, and then the two cops who'd been busy at The Drunken Hessian showed up, along with an ambulance for Owen.

Striker had hit his head on the pavement too, which I thought was a kind of poetic justice, though his wound wasn't nearly as severe as Owen's. Once the uniforms had taken Striker into custody, Rick came over to me. "You look like shit," he said.

I was shirtless, and there was blood on my hands and my chest—either Owen's, or my own, from a multitude of cuts and scrapes.

"Another triumph for the Hardy Boys, huh?" I said, as we watched the patrol car drive away, its lights strobing the darkness.

"We're hardly boys," he said. "And you're not even a cop. How do you keep getting yourself into these situations?"

"Blame it on the dog," I said. "He's the one who found DeAndre's body in the first place."

I related to Rick the conversation I'd overheard between Owen and Striker. "If Owen hadn't done that bump of cocaine, he probably wouldn't have lashed out at Striker, and they could have made a clean getaway."

"I have to track down the Keelys and tell them about Owen," Rick said.

"I hope this is the wakeup call he needs to turn his life around," I said.

"Awake or asleep, he's going to prison."

I wondered how long that word, prison, would create such a visceral reaction for me. "I ought to get cleaned up," I said. "Come on, Rochester. You deserve a treat."

Back home, I took a long hot shower, dressed my cuts and scrapes. After a couple of pain pills I was able to get to sleep.

It was about noon on Saturday when Rick called me. "Turned Striker over to the Feds as part of their investigation into the thefts of those religious objects," he said. "Tony Rinaldi will have to work out with them how to charge him for DeAndre's murder. I have a few charges to place against him myself, but they'll have to wait." He paused. "I'm at The Chocolate Ear. You want to come down here?"

"I can be there in ten." I took Rochester out for a quick pee, then loaded him in the car for the trip downtown.

Rick was sitting at a square table on the sidewalk when Rochester and I walked up. He looked like he hadn't been to bed yet—his brown hair was tousled, and there were puffy places under his eyes. I felt guilty for getting a good night's sleep—but then, as he had pointed out, he was the cop, not me.

Gail came outside and I ordered a café mocha and a Napoleon. I thought the pastry was particularly appropriate given the case's connections to Bonaparte.

"Put it on my tab, Gail," Rick said.

She agreed and said she'd bring the pastry out with the coffee when it was ready.

I sat down across from Rick. "In all the confusion yesterday, I didn't tell you. The project at Friar Lake is a go, and I still have a job."

"That's good news," he said. He raised his hand to wave, and when I turned around I saw Lili approaching us. She looked New York-chic in her black capri pants and black tank top. The only bright spot in her outfit came from her hot pink ballet flats, with a matching pink ribbon pulling her hair back into a curly ponytail.

I got back up and kissed her hello. "What brings you down here?" I asked.

"Rick called me."

I looked over at him, but he was ignoring me, focusing on some paperwork in front of him.

Gail came out with my coffee and pastry, and Lili ordered an iced tea and a croissant. As Gail walked back inside, I expected to hear more from Lili, but she just sat down and put her hand on Rochester's head. "How's my good boy?" she asked him and I felt a momentary pang of jealousy.

He looked up and snuffled her hand. I looked from Lili to Rick, but neither of them said anything. "What's going on?" I asked.

The café door opened, and Gail returned with Lili's order. When she had gone back inside, Rick said, "It's called an intervention." His face was grim, his lips tight.

I looked from him to Lili. She looked more sad than anything else. "Rick and I have been talking," she said. "You've got to stop the computer hacking, Steve. It's too dangerous, and I want to be sure you're going to be around for a long time."

"But," I began.

"Save it," Rick said. "I've heard it all before. It's not a problem. You can control it. And you're not hurting anybody."

I took a deep breath, and let it out. Rick was right; those were the things I would have said. I figured I had two choices at that point. I could listen to that little devil perched on my shoulder who kept telling me that I could control my computer use. That would mean getting up and walking away from The Chocolate Ear, sacrificing my friendship with Rick and my budding relationship with Lili.

Or I could listen to these two people, who had cared enough about me to take drastic measures.

They both were quiet. The only noise was the low hum of some French pop music from inside the cafe, and the traffic along Main Street.

I broke off a piece of Lili's croissant and handed it to Rochester. Then I looked up at my two friends. "How do I get started?" I asked.

Made in the USA
San Bernardino, CA
11 November 2017